SNUGG
HASHISH

Brian Stableford's scholarly work includes *New Atlantis: A Narrative History of Scientific Romance* (Wildside Press, 2016), *The Plurality of Imaginary Worlds: The Evolution of French roman scientifique* (Black Coat Press, 2017) and *Tales of Enchantment and Disenchantment: A History of Faerie* (Black Coat Press, 2019). In support of the latter projects he has translated more than a hundred volumes of *roman scientifique* and more than twenty volumes of *contes de fées* into English. He has edited *Decadence and Symbolism: A Showcase Anthology* (Snuggly Books, 2018), and is busy translating more Symbolist and Decadent fiction.

His recent fiction, in the genre of metaphysical fantasy, includes a trilogy of novels set in West Wales, consisting of *Spirits of the Vasty Deep* (2018), *The Insubstantial Pageant* (2018) and *The Truths of Darkness* (2019), published by Snuggly Books, and a trilogy set in Paris and the south of France, consisting of *The Painter of Spirits*, *The Quiet Dead* and *Living with the Dead*, all published by Black Coat Press in 2019.

SNUGGLY BOOKS

SNUGGLY TALES OF HASHISH AND OPIUM

EDITED, INTRODUCED AND TRANSLATED BY
BRIAN STABLEFORD

THIS IS A SNUGGLY BOOK

ISBN: 978-1-64525-040-1

CONTENTS

INTRODUCTION

POPULAR wisdom frequently asserts that all legends have some foundation, however remote, in fact. Like most popular wisdom, that is probably an exaggeration, but it might contain a seed of truth. In any case, the more interesting observation is that much of what is mistaken for history—and not necessarily remote history—is really founded in fiction. For instance, countless contemporary works of supposed non-fiction will assure you that there was a "Club of Hashishins" in Paris in 1845, which included in its membership numerous writers associated with the French Romantic Movement, including Théophile Gautier, Charles Baudelaire, Gérard de Nerval and Victor Hugo, who were fed with hashish by a physician and proto-psychologist, Joseph Moreau (1804-1884), who preferred to style himself "Moreau de Tours."

There is a seed of truth in the legend; Moreau was real, and he published a book, *Du haschisch et de l'alienation mentale* (1845; tr. as *Hashish and Mental Illness*), in which he suggested that hashish and other psychotropic substances might have considerable therapeutic value in the treatment of "mental alienation" as well as various physical ailments. Like many of his contemporaries he also believed that there was a kinship between literary genius and madness; he was undoubtedly familiar with *Du demon de Socrate* (1836) by Louis-François Lélut, a pioneering work of "retrospective pychoanalysis" studying the supposed mental aberrations of dead writers, and also with Thomas De Quincey's *Confessions of an English Opium-Eater* (1821), which offered an account of the effects of the author's laudanum addiction on his literary creativity and his life. He would have been aware that De Quincey was not the only English Romantic addicted to laudanum, and would have been familiar with the story put about by Samuel Taylor Coleridge that "Kubla Khan" had been dictated to him during an opium dream, but suddenly cut off when his recapitulation of the dream was interrupted.

The writers of the French Romantic Movement were also familiar with that anecdote, with De Quincey's *Confessions*, and also with the suggestion—again put about by the author—that their favorite German Romantic writer of hallucinatory fantasies, E. T. A. Hoffmann, was a drunkard who obtained his inspiration in taverns. They were probably aware of other anecdotes of a similar stripe, such as the story that while studying the properties of nitrous oxide at Bristol's Peneumatic Institute, Humphry Davy—who was an aspiring Romantic poet before he became a great experimental scientist and inventor—had supplied the gas in question to experimentally-inclined writers of his acquaintance, including Coleridge. One French Romantic who certainly took an interest in such anecdotes was Théophile Gautier, who published an early story entitled "Le Pipe d'opium" as a "feuilleton" in *La Presse* in 1938.

La Presse was the first "popular" newspaper in France, launched in 1836 by Émile de Girardin, a publisher closely associated with the Romantic Movement, who hired members of the Movement to edit his publications, including S. Henry Berthoud and Jules Janin, who trawled Romantic cenacles and salons for copy and published much of Gautier's early work. Girardin was the inventor, in *La Presse*, of the "feuilleton," a line drawn across the front page (and, at the outset, page two) in order to isolate a section at the foot. In the mid-1840s that space became the venue for long-running serial novels such as Alexandre Dumas' *Les Trois mousquetaires* and Eugène Sue's *Les Mystères de Paris*, which became an important marketing tool for many papers, but in the beginning it simply separated items that were not, strictly speaking, "news," from the paper's routine reportage and advertisements; longer items were sometimes serialized there but in the beginning the space mostly played host to articles of social comment, although short stories like "Le Pipe d'opium" were sometimes inserted, and occasionally extended over more than one issue of the paper.

"Le Pipe d'opium" is a mock-anecdotal story supposedly describing a dream that Gautier has after smoking opium with another young journalist associated with the Movement, Alphonse Karr, in the course of which he "evokes" a third, Alphonse Esquiros. In the anecdote, Gautier reports that he cut short the smoking session with Karr because he had to write a feuilleton. Filling that section of a daily newspaper was always a challenge for the editors, who often commissioned their contributors to supply material on a quasi-regular basis, although few could keep up the required pace of production for long.

In spite of the fact that it is narrated in the first person and features real individuals, it is highly improbable that anyone mistook "Le Pipe d'opium" for an item of reportage, although readers might well have been prepared to believe that Gautier and Karr did smoke opium occasionally. When Gautier repeated the narrative strategy, however, in "Le Club des haschischins" in 1845, the circumstances were different. The story appeared in the *Revue des Deux Mondes*, a staid monthly periodical with no feuilleton. In keeping with the periodical's policy, the title simply appeared in the contents page, alongside the titles of the articles that were the periodical's principal stock-in-trade, with nothing to indicate that it was a *conte*, the only clue being that it was a matter of editorial policy to include one item of fiction per issue, and it was the only item that could be so identified. It is, in fact, very obviously a work of fiction, which borrows extensively from Hoffmann, and presents within the context of a hallucination a brief tribute to the history of the extravagant fringe of the French literary and visual imagination. The possibility was nevertheless there for any reader devoid of intellectual subtlety to misconstrue it as an item of autobiography, and some did.

The rest is history—or, more accurately, legend.

When Gautier eventually reprinted "Le Club des haschischins" it was in the collection *Romans et contes* (1868), explicitly advertised as a *conte*, but by that time, the legend was established, largely due to the efforts of Charles Baudelaire, who had treated the story as if it were reportage, and claimed to have been a member of the club of hashishins himself, in his mock-philosophical comparative study of psychotropic substances *Les Paradis artificiels* (1860), which draws very heavily on De Quincey's *Confessions*, parts of which are translated in the text. It was Baudelaire's apparent endorsement rather than the lack of identifying markers in the *Revue des Deux Mondes* that cemented the misrepresentation of Gautier's work of fiction as reportage. In the mock-autobiographical section of *Les Paradis artificiels*, however, Baudelaire reported—surely tongue-in-cheek—that he and Gautier had both given up attempting to use artificial stimulants as aids to creativity because they were poor suppliers by comparison with the power of a writer's unaided imagination.

Baudelaire was, of course, also the principal French translator of the works of Edgar Poe, a notorious practitioner of literary hoaxes, who had been posthumously represented by his arch-enemy Rufus Griswold, who claimed (fraudulently) to be Poe's literary executor in order to blacken his name by branding him a madman and a drunkard. That Baudelaire used laudanum himself, as well as producing literary celebrations of its hallucinatory effects, is indubitable, but whether he was an addict, and the precise extent to which his literary creativity was opium-inspired, remains a rich topic for speculative debate, in the arena of literary criticism—which is essentially a genre of speculative fiction, like biography. (Autobiography is somewhat different, consisting entirely of self-serving lies strategically built around a kernel of fact; whereas most biography is merely misinformation, most autobiography is disinformation.)

It is not impossible, of course, that Joseph Moreau actually did supply hashish to writers of his acquaintance in an experimental spirit, although the idea that there was a "club" like the one described in Gautier's story is surely fanciful, however esthetically attractive the notion might be. What is beyond doubt, however, is that numerous writers experimented themselves, tentatively or, in some cases, obsessively, with psychotropic substances as a potential source of inspiration. Almost all of them found the substances wanting in that regard, and most of them gave it up swiftly—but they were not always honest about that in their "confessional" writings. The French writers most vocal in that regard include Théo Varlet, Gabriel de Lautrec and Maurice Magre, all of whom are represented in this sampler, alongside writers who might well have had some experience in the use of such substances but were careful not to make any such confession, and writers who probably did not, but were sufficiently fascinated by the possibility to consider it hypothetically.

It is, of course, quite impossible to determine where the borders between small kernels of truth and the abundant pulp of imagination lie, and representing such intersections as planes is probably an atrocity of conceptual geometry, but some interesting comparisons can be made within the work and lives of the writers who represented themselves most boldly as users of psychotropic substances. Théo Varlet wrote an elaborate confessional account of his experiments in *Aux paradis du Hachcich, suite à Baudelaire* (1930), but records that the trials in question only lasted six years, some time before his career as a writer took on real substance, and its legacy, in his poetry and prose alike, is both slight and evidently artificial. Lautrec's experiments with hashish produced one volume of *Poems en prose* (1898; tr. divided between *The Vengeance of the Oval Portrait* and *The Sacred Fire*), but the quasi-autobiographical account of their production in *Le Feu sacré* (1904) acknowledges the difficulties of that manufacture and the fragmentary nature of its results, and Lautrec developed a career thereafter as a casual humorist. Magre was often quoted by journalists as having described himself as an opium addict, but his autobiographical essays admit frankly that his experiments were very short-lived and that he soon gave them up, long before he began using opium as a literary device. It is notable that his representation of the use of the drug in his early feuilleton serial, *La Tendre camarade* (1918; tr. in *The Call of the Beast*) is quite different from that in the novella reproduced here, which was probably commissioned by its publisher as a commercial exercise, and the more elaborately earnest but conscientiously artificial employment in the phantasmagorical novel *Le Mystère du tigre* (1927; tr. in *The Mystery of the Tiger*).

The confessional strategy adopted by Varlet, Lautrec and Magre was at least partly a deliberate cultivation

13

of notoriety, a matter of image-building or a species of exhibitionism. Varlet was also a committed nudist, while Lautrec also dabbled in fashionable occultism, decorating his lodgings in a quasi-Satanic style also favored by such flamboyant *fin-de-siècle* dandies as Jean Lorrain, whose own stimulant of brief choice was ether. Lorrain's lifestyle fantasies are mercilessly parodied by Jean de La Vaudère is *Les Androgynes*, (1903; tr. in *The Demi-Sexes and The Androgynes*) although photographs of the internal décor of her own lodgings depict a similar, albeit more conscientiously antiquarian, exoticism. Lorrain was a great admirer of Oscar Wilde, as were Louis Latourrette, author of *Coeur immolé* (1898) and Frédéric Boutet, author of *Contes dans la nuit* (1898), two of the young writers who befriended Wilde in Paris during his tragic last years, both of whom flirted with *fin-de-siècle* lifestyle fantasy in the same fashion as Lorrain, echoed in their early literary works, before they moved on to more commercial work—a move reflected in the stories translated herein, penned when they had left decadence behind.

The writer who provided the most abundant literary advertisement for opium and its effects, "Claude Farrère" (Charles Bargone), whose collection *Fumée d'Opium* (1904; tr. as *Black Opium*) achieved a minor *succès de scandale*, also followed a similar career trajectory, ending up sufficiently respectable to be elected to the Académie Française. (*Fumée d'opium* is not sampled herein because Bargone did not die until 1957, and his work is not yet in the public domain.) The pattern of desertion followed by disapproval is commonplace among writers, and probably represents, at least to some degree, a process of natural selection, history always being written—which is to say, invented—by the survivors, and many of the would-be writers who committed themselves most heavily to artificial aids were not among that number.

The particular trajectory followed by Lautrec and Boutet, from hallucinatory dabbling to humorist writing, is not uncommon, and can be detected in many of the early contributors to the Romantic Movement—many of whom, including Gautier and Baudelaire, took themselves less seriously than some of their commentators. "X. B. Saintine" (Joseph Xavier Boniface) wrote intensely earnest melodramatic novels, but showed a much lighter touch in his short fiction and made a living writing vaudevilles, while also keeping a journal of his dreams, the literary spinoff of which he collected late in life as *La Second Vie*. His serious work was never taken entirely seriously because of his vaudevilles, and the same was true of Adrien-Charles Basset, who signed his work "Adrien Robert" or "Charles Newill", diplomatically avoiding his own surname because it was employed by his father, a prominent newspaper editor. Basset's affiliation to the Romantic Movement went largely unnoticed, save for a complimentary essay on his work by Barbey d'Aurevilly, but his light-hearted response to "Le Club des haschischins," included herein for the sake of context, like Saintine's contribution, demonstrates a real insight into the sociology of psychotropic fashionability.

Another commonplace of popular wisdom is that history always repeats—the French dictum *"plus ça change, plus c'est la meme chose"* was apparently coined by Alphonse Karr, Gautier's alleged smoking-companion—although it is sometimes modified with the observation that it is only those who fail to learn from history who are doomed to repeat it, usually credited to the Romantic philosopher George Santayana; "first as tragedy, then as farce," a further addendum asserts, credited to Karl Marx, reflecting on an earlier observation by G. W. F. Hegel. Modern history, or legend, certainly supports those allegations with regard to the literary response to and reportage of the twentieth-century popularization of LSD: an episode on which we can now look back with a certain amused nostalgia, although it cannot seem as quaint to modern eyes as nineteenth-century dealings with hashish and opium.

The history and legendry of LSD is not yet complete, of course, any more than that of cannabinoids and opiates, but literary responses have been greatly refined along with the substances themselves, and it is no longer possible to regard cannabis and heroin through the same Romantic lenses that were available on prescription to the likes of Théophile Gautier, Théo Varlet and Gabriel de Lautrec. Precisely for that reason, however, their pioneering endeavors retain a certain relevance as well as a certain fascination. Although this sampler is, inevitably, a collage rather than a sequential story, the ensemble does add up to an interesting work of *art pour l'art*, of which Théophile Gautier, the great popularizer of that esthetic philosophy, would surely have approved.

—Brian Stableford

SNUGGLY TALES OF HASHISH AND OPIUM

THE CLUB OF HASHISHINS

by Théophile Gautier

I
The Hôtel Pimodan

ONE December evening, obedient to a mysterious invitation drafted in enigmatic terms understood by affiliates but unintelligible for others, I arrived in a distant quarter, a kind of solitary oasis in the middle of Paris, which the river, surrounding it with its two arms, seemed to be defending against the encroachments of civilization; for it was in an old house on the Île Saint-Louis, the Hôtel Pimodan, built by Lauzun, that the bizarre club I had just joined held its weekly meetings, in which I was going to take part for the first time.[1]

---

1 The Hôtel Lauzun is the actual house to which the story refers. Many sources allege that it was actually called the Hôtel Pimodan in 1845, but that is probably an aspect of the story's contribution to modern folklore. Some sources allege that Gautier and Baudelaire were resident in the house—by then broken up into apartments—at the time, others that Gautier consumed hashish there in the home of the painter Fernand Boissard (1813-1866), while others credit the physician Joseph Moreau, alias Moreau de

Although it was scarcely six o'clock, the night was black.

A fog, rendered even thicker by the proximity of the Seine, was blurring all objects with its ragged cotton wool, perforated at intervals by the ruddy aureoles of lanterns and threads of light escaping from luminous windows.

The pavement, inundated by rain, was shining under the street-lights like a lake reflecting illuminations. A bitter wind, charged with icy particles, whipped your face and its guttural whistling composed the higher register of a symphony whose swelling waves breaking against the arches of the bridges formed the bass; that evening lacked nothing of the rude poetry of winter.

It was difficult, along the deserted quay, in that mass of somber buildings, to distinguish the house I sought, but my coachman, standing up on his seat, succeeded in reading on a marble plaque the half-obscured name of the old house, the meeting-place of the initiates.

I lifted the sculpted knocker, the use of bells with copper buttons not having penetrated this remote land as yet, and I heard the cordon grate several times without success. Finally, yielding to a more vigorous traction, the rusty old bolt opened and the massive wooden door was able to turn on its hinges.

Behind a window pane of yellowed transparency, the head of an aged porter, sketched by the tremor of a candle, appeared as I went in: a ready-made painting

---

Tours, with organizing such parties. The assertions cannot all be true, but might all be false.

by Skalken.[1] The face made a singular grimace, and a thin finger, extending outside the lodge, indicated the direction I should take.

As far as I could make out, by the pale light that always falls, even from the darkest sky, the courtyard I was traversing was surrounded by buildings of ancient architecture, with sharp gables; I felt my feet getting wet, as if I were walking through a meadow, for the interstices between the paving stones were full of grass.

The high narrow-paned windows of the stairway, flamboyant on the somber façade, served to guide me and did not permit me to go astray.

Having crossed the perron I found myself at the bottom of one of those immense staircases of the kind constructed in the time of Louis XIV, on which a modern house could easily dance. On a pedestal, an Egyptian chimera in the style of Lebrun,[2] ridden by an amour, stretched out its paws, holding a candle in its claws, cupped to form a sconce.

The slope of the steps was gentle; the well-disposed pauses and landings attested to the genius of the old architect and the grandiose life of centuries gone by; as I climbed that admirable stairway, clad in my thin black frock-coat, I felt that I was making a stain on the ensemble and usurping a right that was not mine; the service stairs would have been good enough for me.

---

1 Presumably Gottfried Schalcken (1643-1706), whose work made much of the play of artificial light inside dwellings.
2 Presumably Charles Le Brun (1619-1690), Louis XIV's court painter.

Paintings, the majority devoid of frames, copies of masterpieces of the Italian school and the Spanish school, decorated the walls, and at the top, in the shadow, a grandiose mythological ceiling was vaguely designed, painted in fresco.

I arrived at the designated floor.

A tambour of Utrecht velvet, crushed and shiny, the yellow braid and round-headed nails of which testified to long service, enabled me to recognize the door.

I rang. It was opened to me with the usual precautions, and I found myself in a large room illuminated at its extremity by a few lamps. On entering it, one made a backward step of two centuries. Time, which passes so quickly, seemed not to have flowed over that house, and, like a clock that one has forgotten to wind, its hands always marked the same date.

The walls, paneled with white-painted wood, were partly covered by darkened canvases bearing the stamp of the epoch; on the gigantic stove stood a statue that one might have thought stolen from the arbors of Versailles. Over the ceiling, rounded in a cupola, snaked a negligent allegory in the style of Lemoine,[1] which might have been his.

I advanced toward the luminous part of the room, where several human forms were agitating around a table, and as soon as the light, as it reached me, en-

---

1 Presumably François Lemoyne or Le Moine (1668-1737), Le Brun's successor as Louis XIV's court painter, who decorated ceilings at Versailles and in the church of Saint-Sulpice, rather than any of the other painters of note with the same surname.

abled me to be recognized, a vigorous hurrah shook the sonorous depths of the old edifice.

"It's him! It's him!" cried several voices at the same time. "Give him his share!"[1]

The doctor was standing next to a sideboard on which there was a tray laden with little Japanese porcelain saucers. He took a lump of greenish jam or paste, about the size of a thumb, from a crystal jar, by means of a spatula, and placed it on each saucer next to a silver spoon.

The doctor's face was radiant with enthusiasm; his eyes were gleaming, his cheeks blushing crimson, the veins of his temples bulging; his dilated nostrils were inhaling forcefully.

"This will be embezzled from your portion of paradise," he said to me, as he handed me my dose.

Everyone having eaten his dose, coffee was served in the Arab manner—which is to say, with brandy and without sugar.

Then we sat down at the table.

That reversal of culinary habitude doubtless surprises the reader; in fact, it is scarcely customary to take coffee before the soup, and it is usually only at dessert that jam is consumed. The thing surely merits explanation.

---

1 The original version of the story in the *Revue des Deux Mondes* has a chapter-break here, the brief text that follows being titled "Mustard Before Dinner," but that break is eliminated from the version of the story in the 1866 collection *Romans et contes*, and the numbering of the subsequent chapters adjusted accordingly.

II
Parenthesis

There once existed in the Orient a redoubtable order of sectarians commanded by a sheik who adopted the title of the Old Man of the Mountain, or the Prince of Assassins.

That Old Man of the Mountain was obeyed without question; the Assassins, his subjects, marched with an absolute devotion to the execution of his orders, whatever they were; no danger stopped them, even the most certain death. At a sign from their chief, they would hurl themselves from the top of a tower, or go to stab a sovereign in his palace in the midst of his guards.

By means of what artifice did the Old Man of the Mountain obtain such a complete abnegation?

By means of a marvelous drug of which he possessed the recipe, and which has the property of procuring dazzling hallucinations.

On awakening from their intoxication, those who had taken it found real life so sad and discolored that they sacrificed it gladly in order to reenter the paradise of their dreams; for every man killed while accomplishing the orders of the sheik went to Heaven by right, or, if he escaped, was admitted again to enjoy the felicities of the mysterious composition.[1]

---

1 This modern myth was probably discovered by Gautier in Joseph Moreau's account of hashish, but Moreau acknowledges having found it in a speculative article by the Egyptologist Antoine Isaac, Baron Silvestre de Sacy (1758-1838), "Mémoire sur la dynastie des assassins et l'origine de leur nom" (1809).

Now, the green paste that the doctor had just distributed to us was exactly the same one that the Old Man of the Mountain once had his fanatics ingest without them perceiving it, making them believe that he had at his disposal the Heaven of Mohammed and houris of three shades—which is to say, *hashish*, from which comes *hashishin*, or hashish-eater, the root of the word *assassin*, the ferocious meaning of which is perfectly explained by the sanguinary customs of the affiliates of the Old Man of the Mountain.

Assuredly, the people who had seen me leave home at the hour when simple mortals take their nourishment did not suspect that I was going to the Île Saint-Louis, a virtuous and patriarchal place if ever there was one, to consume a strange foodstuff that an impostor sheik had used, several centuries before, as a means of excitation to impel illuminates to murder. Nothing in my perfectly bourgeois attire would have enabled me to be suspected of that excess of Orientalism; I looked more like a nephew going to dinner with his old aunt than a believer on the point of savoring the delights of the Heaven of Mohammed in company with a dozen Arabs who could not have been more French.

Before that revelation, if you had been told that there existed in Paris in 1845, in that epoch of railways and speculation in shares, an order of hashishins of which Monsieur de Hammer has not written the history,[1] you

1 The reference is to *Die Geschichte der Assassinen aus morgenländischen Quellen* (1818; tr, into English as *The History of the Assassins*, 1835) by the self-styled Baron Joseph Freiherr von

would not have believed it, and yet nothing is truer—as is usual with unbelievable things.

III
Agape

The meal was served in a bizarre manner and in all sorts of extravagant and picturesque vessels.

Large Venetian bowls traversed by milky spirals, German tankards decorated with blazons and legends, Flemish ewers in enameled stoneware, and flasks with slender necks, still surrounded by their rush matting, replaced glasses, bottles and carafes.

The opaque porcelain of Louis Leboeuf[1] and floral English faience ornamenting bourgeois tables were conspicuous by their absence; no two plates were similar, but each had its particular merit; China, Japan and Saxe counted specimens of their most beautiful pottery and their richest colors, all slightly cracked and chipped, but in exquisite taste.

Hammer-Purgstall (1774-1856), who had simply been baptized Josef Hammer, a minor Austrian diplomat who had once been attached to the Austrian embassy in Istanbul and subsequently became a prolific writer of travelers' tales and "translations" of Arabic, Persian and Turkish authors, which were severely criticized by German scholars for inaccuracy and blatant invention, but who was taken much more seriously in France and England, where his supposed expertise went largely unchallenged.
1 Louis-Martin Leboeuf (1792-1854), co-founder in 1841 of Leboeuf, Millet et Cie of Montereau, prolific manufacturers of cheap porcelain.

The dishes, for the most part, where enamels by Bernard de Palissy[1] or Limoges faience; sometimes, the slicer's knife encountered, beneath the real foodstuffs, a reptile, frog or bird in relief. The edible eel mingled its coils with those of the molded snake.

An honest philistine would have experienced some alarm at the sight of those hairy guests, bearded and moustached or shaven in a singular fashion, brandishing sixteenth-century daggers, Malay krises or navajas, hunched over nourishments to which the reflection of vacillating lamps lent suspect appearances.

As the dinner came to an end some of the most fervent adepts were already feeling the effects of the green paste; for my part, I had experienced a complete transposition of the sense of taste. The water I was drinking seemed to me to have the flavor of the most exquisite wine, the meat was changed in my mouth to strawberries, and vice versa. I could not have told the difference between a cutlet and a peach.

My neighbors were beginning to seem somewhat eccentric to me; they opened large owlish eyes; their noses were elongated into probosces; their mouths were stretched into the orifices of bells; their faces were tinted with supernatural hues.

---

1 Bernard Palissy (c1510-1590) was a potter and engineer who tried hard to imitate Chinese porcelain but became best-known for rather garish "rusticware" that often featured small animals molded in relief, and was widely imitated for several centuries, although its inventor, who was a Huguenot, fell victim to persecution in spite of protection by Catherine de' Medici and died in the Bastille before he could be executed.

One of them, a pale face in a black beard, was laughing in bursts at an invisible spectacle; another was making incredible efforts to lift his glass to his lips, and his contortions in order to achieve that result excited deafening jeers.

One, agitated by nervous spasms, was twiddling his thumbs with an incredible agility; another, slumped against the back of his chair, his eyes vague and his arms dead, was allowing himself to ooze voluptuously into the bottomless sea of unconsciousness.

With my elbows on the table I considered all that by the light of a residue of reason, which went away and came back at intervals like a night-light about to go out. Muted pulses of heat ran through my limbs, and madness, like a wave breaking on a rock and returning in order to launch forth again, attained and quit my brain, which it ended up invading entirely.

Hallucination, that strange guest, had installed itself within me.

"To the drawing room, to the drawing room!" cried one of the guests. "Can't you hear the celestial choirs? The musicians have been at the lectern for a long time."

In fact, a delightful harmony reached us in gusts through the tumult of the conversation.

IV
A Monsieur Who was Not Invited

The drawing room is an enormous room with sculpted and gilded paneling, a painted ceiling, with friezes ornamented with satyrs pursuing nymphs through reeds, a vast colored marble fireplace, and ample brocatelle curtains, in which the luxury of times gone by respires.

Tapestried furniture, settees, armchairs and wing-chairs, broad enough to permit the skirts of duchesses and marquises to be spread out at ease, received the hashishins in their soft and ever-open arms.

A fireside chair at the corner of the mantelpiece made advances to me; I established myself there and abandoned myself without resistance to the effects of the fantastic drug.

After a few minutes, my companions disappeared, one after another, each leaving no other vestige but his shadow on the wall, which soon absorbed it, as the brown patches left by water on sand vanish as they dry out. And as I no longer had any consciousness of what they were doing after that, it will be necessary for you to content yourselves this time with the story of my own personal impressions.

Solitude reigned in the drawing room, only starred by a few dubious gleams. Then, suddenly, a red flash passed behind my eyelids; an innumerable quantity of candles lit up of their own accord, and I felt bathed by a warm blonde light. The place where I found myself was still the same, but with the difference between a sketch and a painting; everything was magnified, richer and more splendid. Reality only served as a point of departure for the magnificences of hallucination.

I still could not see anyone, but I divined the presence of a multitude.

I heard the rustle of fabrics, the creaking of sloe-leather, whispering voices, a lisping and stuttering su-

surrus, stifled bursts of laughter and the sound of table- and chair-legs. Porcelains clinked, doors were opened and closed; something unusual was happening.

An enigmatic individual suddenly appeared to me.

By what means had he come in? I don't know; but his appearance did not cause me any alarm. He had a nose curved like a bird's beak; green eyes surrounded by three brown circles, which he wiped frequently with an immense handkerchief; a heavy white cravat, through the knot of which a visiting card was passed, on which was written: *Daucus-Carota of the Pot of Gold,*[1] was stran- gling his thin collars and causing the skin of his jowls to overflow in red creases; a black frock-coat with square tails, from which clusters of amulets hung down, im- prisoned his body, swollen like the breast of a chicken. As for his legs, I must confess that they were made of a mandrake root, bifurcated, black and rugged, full of knots and warts, which appeared to have been freshly uprooted, for particles of soil were still clinging to the filaments. Those legs were quivering and writhing with an extraordinary activity, and when the little torso that

---

1 *Daucus carota* is a flowering plant of the same family that pro- duced the comestible carrot, which bears some resemblance to poisonous hemlock, contact with which can cause skin rashes; it was long used medicinally as a contraceptive and abortifacient. The latter part of the inscription refers to a classic phantasma- gorical and quasi-allegorical novella by E. T. A, Hoffmann, "Der goldne Topf" (1814; tr. into English as "The Golden Pot"), al- though Daucus Carota is one of several names attributed to the gnome Corduanspitz, the would-be tyrant of the vegetable king- dom in a different Hoffmann novella, "Die Königsbraut" (1821; tr. into English as *The King's Bride*).

they were sustaining was exactly facing me the strange individual burst into sobs, and, wiping his eyes with his arms by turns, said to me in the most plaintive voice: "It's today that it is necessary to die of laughter!"

And tears as large as peas rolled down the sides of his nose.

"Laughter . . . laughter . . ." repeated a chorus of discordant and nasal voices, like an echo.

V
Fantasia

I looked at the ceiling then, and perceived a host of disembodied heads, like those of cherubim, which had expressions so comical, physiognomies so jovial and profoundly happy, that I could not help sharing in their hilarity. Their eyes were creased, their mouths wide-spread and their nostrils dilated; they were grimaces to cheer up anyone's spleen. Those clownish masks were moving in zones that were rotating in an inverse direction, which produced a dazzling and vertiginous effect. Gradually, the drawing room filled with extraordinary figures, such as are only found in the etchings of Callot and the aquatints of Goya:[1] a pell-mell of character-

---

1 The reference to the prolific print-maker Jacques Callot (1592-1635) is particularly significant, given that Hoffmann's "Der Goldne Topf" was first published in *Fantasiestücke in Callots Manier* [Fantasies in the Manner of Callot], establishing the backbone of an ancestry of hallucinatory fantasy of which the French Romantic writers were well aware.

istic cheap finery and rags, human and bestial forms. On any other occasion I might have been disquieted by such company, but there was nothing menacing in those monstrosities; it was malice, not ferocity, that was making those eyes glitter. Only good humor was uncovering those disorderly fangs and pointed incisors.

As if I were the king of the fête, each figure came in turn into the luminous circle of which I occupied the center, with an air of grotesque compunction, to murmur pleasantries in my ear, of which I cannot recall a single one, but which, at the time, appeared to me to be prodigiously witty and inspired the most foolish gaiety in me.

At each new apparition, a Homeric, Olympian, immense and deafening laughter, which seemed to resonate in infinite space, burst forth around me in thunderous roars.

Voices that were alternately yapping and cavernous cried: "No, it's too funny; that's enough! My God, my God, how I'm amused! Stronger and stronger! End it! I can't take any more. Ho ho! Hoo hi! Hi hi! What a fine farce. What fine wordplay! Stop! I'm choking! I'm strangling. Don't look at me like that . . . or spin me around . . . I'm going to explode . . ."

In spite of those protestations, half comical and half imploring, the formidable hilarity was still increasing, the racket augmenting in intensity; the floors and walls of the house were lifting and palpitating like a human diaphragm, shaken by that frenetic, irresistible, implacable laughter.

So, instead of coming to present themselves to me one by one, the grotesque phantoms assailed me *en masse*, shaking their long clown's sleeves and stumbling in the pleats of their magician's robes, crushing their cardboard noses in ridiculous impacts, causing the powder of their wigs to fly away in clouds and singing extravagant songs with impossible rhymes in falsetto voices.

All the types invented by the mocking verve of peoples and artists were gathered there, but multiplied tenfold and a hundred times more powerful. It was a strange mob, the Neapolitan Punchinella slapping the hump of the English Punch in a familiar manner, the Arlequino of Bergamo rubbing his black muzzle against the floury mask of the French Paillasse, who was uttering frightful screams, the Bolognese doctor throwing snuff in the eyes of Père Cassandre, Tartaglia galloping on the back of a clown while Gilles gave Don Spavento a kick up the backside, and Karaghuez, armed with his obscene stick, fighting a duel with the buffoon Osque.[1]

Further away, the fantasies of droll dreams,[2] hybrid

---

1 All these are characters in French adaptations of the Italian *commedia dell'arte*, which became immensely popular in Paris in the seventeenth century, developing its own tradition there in fairground theaters and the Théâtre-Italien, its elements employed in hundreds of nineteenth-century vaudevilles.

2 *Songes drolatiques*, which I have translated as "droll dreams," recalls Honoré de Balzac's *Les Cent contes drolatiques* (1832-37), intended as a Rabelaisian imitation of Boccaccio's *Decameron*, although the author only completed thirty out of the projected hundred; the reference provides further confirmation of the liter-

creations, a formless mixture of human, beast and utensil, monks with wheels for feet and cooking-pots for bellies, warriors armored with crockery brandishing wooden sabers in birds' claws, statesmen moved by turnspits, kings plunged waist-deep in pepper-pots, alchemists with heads like bellows and limbs twisted in alembics, debauchees made of an aggregation of pumpkins with bizarre swellings—everything that the pencil of a cynic whose elbow in being jogged by drunkenness might draw.

All of that was swarming, crawling, scampering, leaping, grunting and whistling, as Goethe said in describing Walpurgisnacht.

In order to extract myself from the extraordinary crowd of those baroque individuals, I took refuge in an obscure corner, from which I could see them delivering themselves to dances that were never known in the Renaissance of the times of Chicard,[1] or the Opéra under the reign of Musard, the king of the intricate quadrille.[2] Those dancers, a thousand times superior

---

ary nature and substance of the supposed hallucination.

1 "Père Chicard" was a character who performed grotesque dances the masked balls of the Paris carnival in the mid-nineteenth century; he gave his name to an absurd style of dancing executed in a bizarre costume. The identity of the person who first donned the costume and performed the dance, inspiring numerous imitators, remains mysterious.

2 The composer Philippe Musard (1792-1859) was still at the height of his fame when this story was written, his pioneering "promenade" concerts—featuring hectic gallops and quadrilles as well as classical standards—were a great success all over Europe, still faintly echoed in the riotous "last night of the Proms" in London's Albert Hall every year.

to Molière, to Rabelais, to Swift and Voltaire, wrote comedies with an entrechat or a balancé so profoundly philosophical and satires of such a great range and such a piquant wit, that I was obliged to hold my sides in my corner.

While wiping his eyes, Daucus-Carola executed pirouettes and capers that were inconceivable, especially for a man who had mandrake roots for legs, while repeating in a piteous tone:

"It's today that it's necessary to die of laughter!"

O you who admire the sublime stupidity of Odry, the hoarse imbecility of Alcide Tousez, the idiocy full of aplomb of Arnal and the simian grimaces of Ravel, and who believe that you know what a comic mask is, if you had witnessed that Gustave ball evoked by hashish, you would agree that the most side-splitting comedians of our little theaters are good for sculpting at the corners of a catafalque or a tomb.[1]

How many bizarrely convulsed faces! How many blinking eyes, sparkling with sarcasm beneath their avian membranes! What gut-wrenching rictuses! What hatchet-slash mouths! What facetiously-dodecahedral noses! What abdomens swollen with Pantagruelesque mockery!

---

1 Charles Odry (1779-1853), Alcide Tousez (1809-1850), Pierre-Alfred Ravel (1811-1881) and Etienne Arnal (1794-1872) were all famous comedians who performed successfully on various Parisian stages in the 1840s; the reference to a "Gustave ball" is to an 1833 opera by Daniel Auber, with a libretto by Eugène Scribe, *Gustave III*, famous for its masked ball scene in the final act, which was sometimes performed as a independent piece and received a rave review from Gautier's friend and occasional collaborator Jules Janin.

Throughout that swarm of anguish-free night-mares, flashes of sudden resemblance of an irresistible effect were designed, caricatures to render Daumier and Gavarni jealous, fantasies to make the marvelous Chinese artists, the Phidiases of *poussahs* and *magots*, swoon with delight.[1]

Not all those visions were monstrous or burlesque, however; grace was also manifest in that carnival of forms; near the fireplace, a little head with peach cheeks and blonde hair was showing, in an interminable foot of gaiety, thirty-two little teeth the size of grains of rice, uttering bursts of shrill, vibrant, silvery laughter, prolonged and embroidered by trills and pauses, which traversed my eardrums and forced me to commit a host of extravagances by means of a nervous magnetism.

The joyous frenzy was at its highest point; nothing could any longer be heard but convulsive sighs and in-articulate gurgles. The laughter had lost its timbre and was turning to grunts; spasm was succeeding pleasure; Daucus-Carota's refrain was about to come true.

Already, several unconscious hashishins had fallen to the floor with the limp heaviness of drunkenness that renders falls devoid of danger; exclamations such as: "My God, how happy I am!" "What felicity!" "I'm swimming in ecstasy!" "I'm in Paradise!" and "I'm

---

1 Honoré Daumier (1808-1879), a printmaker in the tradition of Callot, and the illustrator who adopted the name Paul Gavarni (1806-1866), were both acquainted with Gautier; a *poussah* was a toy with a rounded base that returned automatically to an upright position if displaced, like a modern Bobo doll, while *magot* was a familiar term for an Oriental figurine of a fat ugly man.

plunging into abysms of delight!" were overlapping, becoming confused and drowning one another out.

Hoarse cries were springing from oppressed breasts; arms were writhing madly toward some fugitive vision; heels and the backs of heads were drumming on the floor. It was time to throw a drop of cold water over that hot steam, or the boiler would have exploded. The human envelope, which has so little strength for pleasure and so much for pain, would not have been able to support a higher pressure of joy.

One of the members of the club, who had not taken part in the voluptuous intoxication, in order to watch the fantasia and to prevent those of us who thought we had wings from passing through the windows, stood up, opened the piano and sat down. His hands, falling in unison, plunged into the ivory of the keyboard, and a glorious chord, resonating forcefully, caused all the rumors to fall silent, and changed the direction of the intoxication.

VI
Kif

The theme attacked was, I believe, Agathe's aria from *Der Freischütz*;[1] that celestial melody had soon dissipated the ridiculous visions by which I was obsessed,

---

1 Carl Maria von Weber's classic Romantic opera was first performed in 1821. Gautier would surely have been present when Hector Berlioz's French version was produced at the Paris Opéra in 1841.

like a gust of wind sweeping away deformed clouds. The grimacing larvae withdrew, crawling under the armchairs, where they hid in the folds of the curtains, uttering little stifled sighs; and again it seemed to me that I was alone in the drawing room.

The colossal organ of Freiburg surely did not produce a greater mass of sonority than the piano played by the seer—that was the nickname given to the sober initiate. The notes vibrated with such power that they entered into my breast like luminous arrows; soon, the aria played seemed to be emerging from my own body; my fingers agitated over an absent keyboard; the sounds sprang forth blue and red, in electric sparks; Weber's soul was incarnate in me.

When the piece finished, I continued by means of interior improvisations in the style of the German master, which caused me ineffable delights; what a pity that no magical stenography was able to collect those inspired melodies, heard by myself alone, and which I do not hesitate, although it is hardly modest on my part, to rank above the masterpieces of Rossini, Meyerbeer and Félicien David.

O Pillet! O Vatel![1] One of the thirty operas that I composed in ten minutes would have enriched you in six months.

The somewhat convulsive gaiety of the commencement has been succeeded by an indefinable wellbeing, a boundless calm. I was then in the fortunate period of

---

1 Léon Pillet was director of the Paris Opéra from 1840-47; he did not cover himself with glory in that role. Auguste-Eugène Vatel was then the impresario of the Théâtre-Italien.

hashish that the Orientals call *kif.* I could no longer feel my body; the bonds of matter and spirit were loosened; I could move by means of my will-power alone in a milieu that offered no resistance.

It is thus, I imagine, that souls must act in the aromal world to which we go after death.

A bluish vapor, an Elysian daylight, a reflection of an azurine grotto, formed an atmosphere in the room in which I saw indecisive contours trembling vaguely; that atmosphere, simultaneously fresh and lukewarm, humid and perfumed, enveloped me like the water of a bath with a kiss of enervating mildness; if I wanted to change location, the caressant air made a thousand voluptuous eddies around me; a delectable languorous possession of my senses and tipped me back on the sofa, where I collapsed like an abandoned garment.

I understood then the pleasure experienced, in accordance with their degree of perfection, by spirits and angels in traversing the ethers and the heavens, and how eternity might be occupied in Paradise.

Nothing material was mingled with that ecstasy; no terrestrial desire corrupted its purity. In any case, amour itself could not have augmented it. Romeo, as a hashishin, would have forgotten Juliet; the poor child, leaning over the jasmines, would have extended her alabaster arms in vain though the darkness at the height of the balcony; Romeo would have remained at the bottom of the silken ladder; and, although I am madly in love with the angel of youth and beauty created by Shakespeare, I must agree that the most beautiful girl in Verona would not be worth the trouble of disturbing himself, for a hashishin.

So I gazed with a placid, albeit charmed, eye at the garland of ideally beautiful women that crowned the frieze with their divine nudity; I saw the satin shoulders gleaming, the silver breasts sparkling, the little feet with pink soles soaring, and the opulent hips undulating without experiencing the slightest temptation. The charming specters that troubled Saint Anthony would not have had any power over me.

By virtue of a bizarre prodigy, after a few minutes of contemplation, I melted into the fixed object, and I became that object. Thus, I was transformed into the nymph Syrinx, because the fresco represented the daughter of the Ladon pursued by Pan. I experienced all the terrors of the poor fugitive, and sought to hide myself behind fantastic reeds in order to avoid the monster with goat's feet.

VII
Kif turns to Nightmare

During my ecstasy, Daucus-Carota had come in again.

Sitting like a tailor or a pacha on his neatly twisted roots, he attached flamboyant eyes to me; his beak clicked in such a sardonic fashion, and such an expression of mocking triumph burst forth throughout his deformed little person, that I shivered involuntarily.

Divining my fear, he redoubled his contortions and grimaces, and drew nearer, hopping like a wounded crane-fly or a legless man in his box.

Then I felt a cold breath in my ear, and a voice whose accent was familiar to me, although I could not specify to whom it belonged, said: "That wretched Daucus-Carota, who has sold his legs for drink, has stolen your head and put in its place, not a donkey's, as Puck did with Bottom, but an elephant's head."

Singularly intrigued, I went straight to the mirror, and I saw that the warning was not false; I might have been mistaken for a Hindu or Javanese idol; my forehead had been raised, my nose elongated to a trunk curved back over my breast, my ears were sweeping my shoulders, and, by an excess of inconvenience, I was the color of indigo, like Shiva the blue god.

Exasperated by fury, I set about pursuing Daucus-Carota, who was jumping and yelping, and giving all the signs of extreme terror; I succeeded in catching up with him and I banged him so violently against the edge of the table that he ended up returning my head to me, which he had wrapped in his handkerchief.

Content with that victory, I was about to take my place on the sofa again, but the same unknown little voice said to me: "Beware; you're surrounded by enemies; invisible powers are trying to attract you and retain you. You're a prisoner here; try to get out and you'll see."

A veil tore in my mind, and it became clear to me that the members of the club were nothing but cabalists and magicians, who wanted to draw me to my doom.

VIII
Treadmill

I got up, with a great deal of difficulty, and headed for the door of the drawing room, which I only reached after a considerable lapse of time, an unknown power forcing me to recoil one step in three. By my calculation, I took ten years to make that journey.

Daucus-Carota followed me, sniggering and muttering, with a false air of commiseration: "If he walks at that pace, he'll be old when he arrives."

I had, however, succeeded in reaching the next room, the dimensions of which seemed changed and unrecognizable. It was elongated, and elongated indefinitely. The light, which was scintillating at its extremity, seemed as distant as a fixed star.

Discouragement seized me, and I was about to stop when the little voice said to me, almost brushing me with its lips; "Courage! She's expecting you at eleven o'clock."[1]

Making a desperate appeal to the strength of my soul, I succeeded, by means of an enormous projection of will, in lifting my feet, which were clamped to the ground, and which I had to uproot like tree trunks. The monster with the mandrake legs escorted me and parodied my efforts, singing in a tone of drawling psalmody:

---

1 The story contains no clue as to who "she" might be, but if it is regarded as a sequel of sorts to "Le pipe d'opium," one might take an inference from that story.

"The marble is winning! The marble is winning!"

In fact, I sensed my extremities turning to stone, and marble enveloping me all the way to the hips, like the Daphné of the Tuileries. Half my body was a statue, like the princes of the Thousand-and-One Nights. My hardened heels resonated formidably on the floorboards; I could have played the Commander in *Don Giovanni*.

However, I had arrived on the landing of the staircase, which I tried to go down. It was half-illuminated, and acquired cyclopean and gigantic proportions in my dream. Its two ends, drowned in shadow, seemed to me to plunge into Heaven and Hell, two gulfs; on raising my head I perceived distinctly, in a prodigious perspective, superimpositions of innumerable landings, and staircases to climb as if to arrive at the summit of the tower of Lylacq;[1] on looking down I sensed abysms of steps, swirls of spirals and dazzling circumvolutions.

That stairway must pierce the earth all the way through, I said to myself, as I continued my mechanical march. *I'll reach the bottom on the day after the Last Judgment.*

The figures in the paintings looked at me with expressions of pity; a few agitated with painful contortions, like mutes who would like to give important advice on a supreme occasion. One might have thought that they

---

1 *Le tour de Lylacq* [Tower of Lylacq] is cited in several other stories by Gautier, sometimes coupled with the tower of Babel and sometimes with the destruction of Sodom and Gomorrah, and it is also cited in reviews and essays; he appears to have tried hard to add it to the lexicon of modern legendary lore, but it never caught on; he had much better luck with the Club des Haschischins.

wanted to warn me about a trap to avoid, but an inert and bleak force dragged me on. The steps were soft and sagged underneath me, like the mysterious rungs in the ordeals of freemasonry. The sticky and flaccid stones collapsed like the bellies of toads; further landings and further steps were resented incessantly to my resigned footsteps; those I had traversed replaced themselves in front of me.

That treadmill lasted a thousand years, by my count.

Finally, I arrived in the vestibule, where another persecution, no less terrible, awaited me.

The chimera holding a candle in its paws, which I had noticed as I came in, barred my passage with evidently hostile intentions; its green-tinted eyes were glittering with irony; its sly mouth was sniggering malevolently. It advanced toward me almost flat on its belly, dragging its bronze carapace through the dust, but it was not by virtue of submission; ferocious frissons agitated its leonine rump, and Daucus-Carota was exciting it as one does a dog that one wants to have beaten:

"Bite him! Bite him! Marble meat is a fine repast for a bronze mouth."

Without allowing myself to be frightened by that horrible beast, I passed on. A gust of cold air came to strike me in the face, and the nocturnal sky, cleared of clouds, suddenly appeared to me. A scattering of stars dusted with gold the veins of that great block of lapis-lazuli.

I was in the courtyard.

In order to render for you the effect that that somber architecture produced on me, I would require the brush with which Piranesi striped the black varnish of his marvelous copperplates; the courtyard had taken on the proportions of the Champ-de-Mars, and in a matter of hours had been bordered by gigantic edifices that cut out on the horizon a lacework of spires, cupolas, towers, gables and pyramids worthy of Rome and Babylon.[1]

My surprise was extreme; I had never suspected the Île Saint-Louis of containing so many monumental magnificences, which, in any case, would have covered twenty times its actual surface area, and I did not think without apprehension of the power of the magicians who had been able, in one evening, to erect similar constructions,

"You're the victim of vain illusions; this courtyard is very small," murmured the voice. "It is twenty-seven paces long, by twenty-five broad."

"Yes, yes," muttered the bifurcated abortion, "the paces of seven-league boots. You'll never arrive by eleven o'clock; it's fifteen hundred years since you departed. Half of your hair is already gray. Go back upstairs, that's the wisest course."

---

1 Giambattista Piranesi (1720-1778) was famous for his etchings of monumental architectures, including a series of "imaginary prisons" with huge subterranean vaults and monumental labyrinthine stairways, a probable source of inspiration for Gautier's fantastic architectures. His work was greatly admired by Thomas de Quincey, and undoubtedly influenced the visions recorded in the *Confessions of an English Opium-Eater* (1820).

As I did not obey, the odious monster wrapped me in the toils of its legs, and, aiding itself with its hands like crampons, towing me in spite of my resistance, made me climb back up the stairway where I had experienced so much anguish, and reinstalled me, to my great despair, in the drawing room from which I had escaped with so much difficulty.

Then vertigo took possession of me completely; I became insane, delirious.

Daucus-Carota was capering, leaping all the way to the ceiling, saying to me:

"Imbecile, I've returned your head to you, but I removed the brain with a ladle beforehand."

I experienced a frightful sadness, for, when I put my hand to my cranium, I found it open, and I lost consciousness.

IX
Do Not Believe Chronometers

When I came round I saw the room full of men clad in black, who were coming together with sad expressions and shaking one another's hands with a melancholy cordiality, like people afflicted by a common grief.

They said: "Time is dead; henceforth, there will no longer be any years, months or hours; Time is dead, and we're going to its funeral."

"It's true that he was very old, but I didn't expect this to happen; he was bearing up marvelously for his age," added one of the persons in mourning, whom I recognized as a painter, one of my friends.

I took the pipe from his hands, as I had done a few hours before, and began to inhale the intoxicating smoke, slowly.

A blissful laxity did not take long to take possession of me, and I felt myself becoming torpid, as I had in smoking the real pipe.

Until then my dream had kept to the exact limits of the habitable world, and repeated like a mirror the actions of my day.

I was nestled in a heap of cushions, and I tipped my head back idly in order to follow the bluish spirals in the air, which dissolved into a cotton wool mist after having swirled for a few minutes.

My gaze was borne naturally toward the ceiling, which was ebony black with golden arabesques. By virtue of gazing with the ecstatic attention that precedes visions, it appeared blue to me, but a harsh blue, like one of the flaps of the cloak of night.

"You've had your ceiling repainted blue, then," I said to Karr, who, still impassive and silent, had stuffed another pipe and was rendering more smoke than a stove-pipe in winter or a steam-boat in any season.

"Not at all, my son," he replied, putting his nose outside the cloud, "but you give me the impression furiously of having your own stomach painted red, by means of a Bordeaux more-or-less Laffitte."[1]

1 Château Lafitte, or Lafite, is an estate in Bordeaux, which became one of the foremost producers of claret when the Marquis de Ségur refined the method of production in the early eighteenth century, and it became a favorite at Louis XIV's court; it was owned by the Vanderberghe family when the story was written but later purchased by the Rothschilds. The surname Lafitte also became famous in the early nineteenth century as that of two pi-

"Alas, to tell you the truth I've only drunk a miserable glass of sugared water, in which all the ants of earth had come to slake their thirst, a swimming-school of insects."

"The ceiling was apparently bored being black, and has turned blue; after women, I don't know of anything more capricious than ceilings. It's a whim of the ceiling, that's all; nothing is more ordinary."

Having said that, Karr pulled his nose back into the cloud of smoke, with the satisfied expression of someone who has given a limpid and luminous explanation.

I was only half-convinced, however, and I had difficulty believing that ceilings were as whimsical as that; I continued to observe the one above my head, not without a slight sentiment of anxiety.

It was blue, as blue as the sea on the horizon, and the stars were beginning to open their eyelids with golden lashes; those lashes, extremely tenuous, extended all the way into the room, which they filled with prismatic sheaves.

A few black lines striped that azure surface, and I soon realized that they were the beams of the upper floors of the house, which had become transparent.

In spite of the facility one has in dream of admitting as natural the most bizarre things, all that commenced to appear a trifle shady and suspect to me, and I thought that if my comrade Esquiros the magician[1] were there,

---

ratical brothers, one of whom distinguished himself as a privateer during the American War of Independence.

1 The writer Alphonse Esquiros (1812-1876), author of the strange episodic novel *Le Magicien* (1838), who was later to be imprisoned for offending religion with his account of the life of Jesus, depicted

he would give me explanations more satisfactory than that of my friend Alphone Karr.

As if that thought had had the power of evocation, Esquiros suddenly presented himself before us, like Faust's barbet emerging from behind the stove. His face was very animated and his expression triumphant; rubbing his hands together he said: "I've been to the Antipodes and I've found the talking Mandrake."

That apparition surprised me, and I said to Karr: "Karr, can you imagine that Esquiros, who was not here a little while ago, has entered without opening the door?"

"Nothing is simpler," Karr replied. "One enters through closed doors, that's the custom; it's only badly brought-up people who pass through open doors. You know that one says as an insult that someone is a greater breaker-down of open doors."

I could not find any objection to make against such sensate reasoning, and I remained convinced that, in fact, the presence of Esquiros had nothing that was nor perfectly explicable, and perfectly licit in itself.

However, he was looking at me with a strange expression, and his eyes widened enormously; they were as ardent and round as shields heated in a furnace, and his body dissipated and was drowned in shadow, with the consequence that I could no longer see anything of him except his two flamboyant and radiant eyes.

---

as a social reformer, *L'Évangile du people* (1840). He was exiled after Louis-Napoléon Bonaparte's *coup d'état* in 1851.

Webs of fire and torrents of magnetic effluvia fluttered and swirled around me, ever more inextricably enlaced and tightening around me; scintillating threads ended at each of my pores and implanted themselves in my skin like hairs in a head. I was in a state of complete somnambulism.

Then I saw little white flakes that were traversing the blue space of the ceiling like tufts of wool carried away by the wind, or like a dove's necklace coming apart in mid-air.

I was seeking in vain to divine what it was when a low, curt voice whispered in my ear, in a strange accent: "They're spirits!" The scales fell from my eyes; the white vapors took on more precise form, and I perceived distinctly a long file of veiled figures who were following the cornice from right to left, with a very pronounced movement of ascension, as if an imperious breath were lifting them up and serving them as a wing.

In the corner of the room, on the molding of the ceiling, the form of a young woman was sitting, enveloped in an abundant muslin drapery. Her feet, entirely naked, were dangling nonchalantly, one crossed over the other; they were, moreover, charming, of a smallness and a transparency that made me think of the beautiful feet of jasper that emerge so white and so pure from the black marble skirt of the antique Isis in the Museum.

The other phantoms clapped her on the shoulder as they went past and said to her: "We're going to the stars, so come with us."

The shadow with the alabaster foot replied: "No! I don't want to go to the stars; I'd rather live for another six months."

The entire file passed by, and the shadow remained alone, swinging her pretty little feet and striking the wall with her pink-tinged feet, as pale and tender as the heart of a wildflower; although the figure was veiled, I sensed that she was young, adorable and charming, and my soul launched itself in her direction, arms outstretched and wings open.

The shadow understood my trouble, by intention or sympathy, and said in a voice as soft and crystalline as a harmonica:[1] "If you have the courage to go and kiss the person who was me on the mouth, whose body is lying in the black city, I shall live for another six months, and my second life will be for you."

I got up and asked myself whether I might be the victim of an illusion, and whether everything that was happening might be a dream. It was a final glimmer of the lamp of reason extinguished by slumber.

I asked my two friends what they thought of all that.

The imperturbable Karr claimed that the adventure was commonplace, that he had had several of the same kind, and that it was very naïve of me to be astonished by so little.

Esquiros explained everything by means of magnetism.

"All right, I'll go . . . but I'm wearing slippers . . ."

"It doesn't matter," said Esquiros. "I can sense a carriage at the door."

---

1 The term "harmonica" had not yet acquired its modern meaning; the reference is to a series of tuned strips of metal or glass fixed in a frame and struck with a hammer, like a xylophone.

I went out, and I did indeed see a cabriolet with two horses, which seemed to be waiting. I climbed aboard.

There was no coachman; the horses guided themselves; they were all black, and galloped so furiously that their rumps went up and down like waves, and a rain of sparks crackled behind them.

First they took the Rue de la Tour-d'Aubergne, then the Rue Bellefonds, then the Rue Lafayette, and after that, other streets whose names I don't know.

As the carriage went further, the objects around me took on strange forms; there were sullen houses crouched on the roadside like old spinners, wooden fences, street-lights that resembled gibbets closely enough to be mistaken for them. Soon the houses disappeared completely and the carriage was rolling through flat country.

We were traveling over a bleak and somber plain; the sky was very low, the color of lead, and an interminable procession of little slender trees ran in an inverse direction to the vehicle on both sides of the road; one might have thought them an army of broomsticks in retreat.

Nothing was as sinister as that grey immensity, which the thin silhouettes of trees striped with black slashes; not a star was shining, no wisp of light enameled the wan profundity of that demi-obscurity.

Finally, we arrived in a city, unknown to me, the houses of which, of a singular architecture, vaguely glimpsed in the darkness, seemed to me to be too small to be habitable. The carriage, although much wider than the streets it was traversing, did not experience any delay; the houses moved aside to the right and left like frightened passers-by and left the road free.[1]

After several turnings, I sensed the carriage melting under me, and the horses vanished in vapor; I had arrived.

A red light filtered through the interstices of a bronze door, which was not closed. I pushed it, and I found myself in a low room with floor-tiles of black and white marble and a stone vault. An antique lamp placed on a pedestal of violet breccia illuminated with a wan glow a recumbent figure that I took at first to be a statue, like those which sleep with hands joined, with a greyhound at their feet, in Gothic cathedrals; but I soon realized that it was a real woman.

She had a bloodless pallor, which I could do no better than compare to the hue of virgin yellowed wax; her mat hands, as white as hosts, were crossed over her heart; her eyes were closed and their lashes extended to the middle of the cheeks; everything in her was dead; only the mouth, as fresh as a pomegranate in flower, was shining with a rich crimson life, half-smiling as if in a pleasant dream.

I leaned toward her, placed my mouth on hers, and gave her the kiss that ought to revive her.

Her lips, moist and warm, as if the breath had only just abandoned them, palpitated under mine, and returned my kiss with an incredible ardor and vivacity.

---

1 This hallucinatory carriage-journey resembles the one made by the narrator of "La Morte amoureuse," published two years before "Le Pipe d'opium," which also features a temporary resurrection of a dead woman in a long dream.

Here there was a lacuna in my dream, and I do not know how I returned from the black city—probably riding on a cloud or a gigantic bat—but I remember perfectly that I found myself with Karr in a house that was neither his nor mine, nor any of those I knew.

All the interior details, however, and all the fittings, were extremely familiar to me. I saw clearly the fireplace in the style of Louis XVI the floral screen, the green lampshade and the shelves full of books at the corners of the mantelpiece.

I was occupying a profound wing-chair with earpieces, and Karr, his two heels supported on the rim of the fireplace, resting on his shoulders and almost on his head, was listening with a pitying and resigned expression to the story of my expedition, which I regarded as a dream myself.

Suddenly, the doorbell rang violently, and someone came to announce to me that a lady desired to speak to me.

"Have the lady come in," I replied, slightly emotional, foreseeing what was about to happen.

A woman dressed in white, her shoulders covered by a black mantle, entered with a light tread and came to place herself in the luminous penumbra projected by the lamp.

By virtue of a very singular phenomenon, I saw three different physiognomies pass over her face; for a moment she resembled Malibran,[1] then M***, and

---

1 The singer Maria Malibran (1808-1836), one of the most famous opera singers of her day, extolled by Gautier and many others; she had died in England two years before the publication of the story after falling from a horse. M*** might be the actress

then the person who had said that she did not want to die, and whose last words had been: "Give me a bouquet of violets."

But those resemblances soon dissipated like a shadow on a mirror; the features of her visage acquired a fixity and were condensed. I recognized the dead woman I had kissed in the black city.

Her attire was extremely simple, and she had no other ornament than a gold circlet in her dark brown hair, falling in ebony clusters along smooth and velvety cheeks.

Two little pink patches tinted the top of her cheekbones crimson, and her eyes were shining like globes of burnished silver; she had, in addition, the beauty of an antique cameo, and the blonde transparency of her flesh added further to the resemblance.

She stood before me, and asked me—a rather bizarre request—to tell me her name.

I replied without hesitation that her name was Carlotta, which was true;[1] then she told me that she

---

who performed as "Mademoiselle Mars" (Anne Salvetat, 1779-1847), cited in the preface of Gautier's *Mademoiselle de Maupin* (1835). The latter novel, published in 1835, had initially been commissioned as a biography of the notorious actress "Madame le Maupin" (Julie d'Aubigny, c1670-1707), but whether a novel can qualify, even metaphorically, as a resurrection is a matter of opinion.

1 Presumably the ballerina Carlotta Grisi (1819-1899), with whom Gautier was besotted; she made her debut in 1836 in London. Some time after the publication of this story Gautier was involved in the production of the ballet that made her famous, *Giselle* (1841), derived from a poem by Victor Hugo based on the same item of folklore as Alphonse Karr's "Les Willis." Carlotta apparently rejected Gautier's advances, but her sister Ernesta sub-

had been a singer, and that she had died young, that she did not know the pleasures of existence, and that before going to be buried forever in motionless eternity, she wanted to enjoy the beauty of the world, to be intoxicated by all sensualities and to lunge in the ocean of terrestrial joys; that she felt an exhaustible thirst for life and amour.

And, saying all that with an eloquence of expression and a poetry that it is not in my power to render, she wrapped her arms around my neck like a scarf and interlaced her slender hands in the curls of my hair.

She spoke in verse of a marvelous beauty, which the greatest poets awake could not have attained, and when verse was no longer sufficient to render her thought, she added the wings of music, and there were roulades and necklaces of notes purer than the most perfect pearls, tones of voice and threads of sound beyond human limits: all that the soul and the mind can dream of the most tender, the most admirably seductive, the most amorous, the most ardent and the most ineffable.

To live for six months, another six months, was the refrain of all her cantilenas.

I saw very clearly what she was going to say before the thought arrived, from her head or from her heart, as far as her lips, and I completed the verse or the song commenced myself; I had the same transparency for her, and she read my mind simultaneously.

---

stituted for her and was the mother of Gautier's two daughters, Judith (born in 1845) and Estelle (born in 1848).

I do not know where those ecstasies, no longer moderated by Karr's presence, would have stopped, when I sensed something rough and hairy passing over my face; I opened my eyes and I saw my cat, rubbing his whiskers against mine by way of a matinal congratulation, for dawn was filtering a vacillating light through the curtains.

It is thus that my opium dream finished, which left no other trace than a vague melancholy, the ordinary consequence of those sorts of hallucinations.

THE DOUBLE ROOM

by Charles Baudelaire

THERE is a room which resembles a daydream, a truly spiritual room, whose still, stale air is tinted with pink and blue.

Here the soul bathes in idleness, amid the aromas of regret and desire. There is something of the twilight here, in its blueness and its rosiness; it is as though one dreams sensuously during an eclipse.

The furniture extends itself, languidly prostrate. The furniture too seems to be dreaming, as if it existed in a state of permanent sleep, as all things vegetable and mineral do. The fabrics speak a language of silence, as flowers and daylit skies do, and sunsets.

These walls are undefiled by ugly paintings. Relative to the pure dream or the unanalyzed impression, specific and assertive art is blasphemous. Here the light is perfectly sufficient in itself, harmonizing with the delicacy of the shadows.

An infinitesimal hint of fragrance, chosen with exquisite taste, which carries with it a faint vaporous humidity, floats upon the air, lulling the drowsy mind as if it were a hothouse.

Hectic showers of muslin fall across the window and from the canopy of the bed, displayed like cascades of snow. Here upon this bed lies the Goddess, sovereign of dreams. Why is she here? Who brought her? What magical power installed her on this throne of dreaming and delight? What does it matter; she is here! I know who she is.

Those are the eyes which burn bright in the twilight; subtle and terrifying mirrors of the soul whose fearful malice I know so well! They draw, conquer and devour the unwary gaze of any who looks into them. I have made a study of them, those dark stars which command such curiosity and admiration.

What benevolent demon must I thank for thus surrounding me with mystery, silence, peace and perfumes? O bliss! That which we ordinarily call life, even when it can encompass happiness, has nothing to compare with this life beyond life which I have come to understand, and which I savor minute by minute, second by second.

No! There are no more minutes, there are no more seconds! Time is banished; it is Eternity which rules this place: an Eternity of delights!

But a heavy and terrible crash has thundered upon the door, and in nightmarish fashion I feel that I have been struck in the stomach by a pick-axe.

A Specter has rudely intruded upon the feast. It is some bailiff come to taunt me in the name of the law; or some shameless courtesan come to tell a tale of woe and add the trivia of her existence to the sorrows of my own; or perhaps some editor's errand-boy come to demand a manuscript.

The heavenly room, the sovereign Goddess of Dreams—the Sylphide, as she was called by the great René[1]—all their magic is dispelled by the crude hammering of the Specter.

O horror! I remember! I remember! Yes, this tawdry place of infinite tedium is indeed where I live. There are the ridiculous furnishings, dusty and bumped; the hearth devoid of flames and glowing embers; the sad windows where the raindrops have made patterns in the grime; the manuscripts scribbled-over or incomplete; the calendar marked with crayon to show the inauspicious passing of the days.

And that otherworldly perfume which exalted me with heightened sensibility is replaced, alas, by the stale odor of old tobacco, mingled with a sickening dampness. The rankness of desolation lies upon everything here.

In this narrow world, full to the brim with disgust, only one familiar object makes me smile: the vial of laudanum; an old and terrible mistress. Like all mistresses, alas, she gives too freely of her caresses and her treacheries.

---

1 Chateaubriand titled the first of his autobiographical memoirs *René* (1802), that being his given name, although he did not use it in his habitual signature.

Oh yes, Time has resumed control! The sovereignty of that hideous ancient Time is now restored, and with him has come his demonic train of memories and regrets, fits and fears, anguishes and nightmares, angers and neuroses.

I can assure you that every passing second now carries a strong and solemn stress, and that each one, leaping from the clock, says: "I am Life: unbearable, implacable Life!"

There is but a single second in a man's life whose mission is to bring good news—the good news, which strikes such inexplicable terror into everyone.

Yes, Time rules again; he has resumed his brutal tyranny. And he drives me on, as if I were an ox, with his duplicate threat: "Get on with it, churl! Sweat, slave! Live, and be damned!"

THE CLUB OF HILARANTS

by Charles Newill

THE door closed so firmly and so accurately that John Christie went down twelve steps of the staircase on the part of his body injured by Uncle Pycraft's boot.

Uncle Pycraft withdrew then into the room of the genteel Miss Milly, whose little heart was beating the charge; tranquilly, he emptied his cup of tea, uttered two or three grunts, which made his niece shudder, and finally went into his bedroom.

The blonde Milly was so stunned by the cavalry charge executed by her fiancé that she did not have the courage to request an explanation from her excellent uncle and guardian, the honorable Captain Pycraft; and yet she had a well-founded right to demand the reason for it, and for Pycraft's boot.

The captain had received John Christie five months ago, introduced into the house by the Reverend Mr. Maradan; he had welcomed with a very encouraging *oh!* the request for marriage that the young man had humbly presented to him. For four weeks John Christie had come to dine with them every Thursday. That very evening, which was a Thursday, John Christie, having had his share of an excellent York ham washed down with port, had come to announce to them that his uncle, Samuel Toots, the sheriff, had given him a position in his office.

By virtue of what supernatural and diabolical power had that news, which was nothing but good, produced on Pycraft the effect of a firebrand flung into a cask of gunpowder?

Why, suddenly forgetting the sacred rights of ancient hospitality, had he precipitated his future nephew into the stairwell and supported his retreat with a gesture customary in clownish choreography?

An impenetrable mystery.

As for John Christie, having received the blow, he traversed the Haymarket and went into the Oriental Tavern, where he ordered a glass of "half and half,"[1] served by a superb forty-year-old Mooress, who then came to sit down facing him on the other side of the table.

Horribly offended as a fiancé, John Christie had remained dignified and calm, as befitted a British subject.

"I've noticed," he said to the Mooress, in the tone of Hamlet's dialogue in the cemetery of Elsinore, "that the brain of the unfortunate Pycraft is becoming more deranged from day to day, like an old clock.

---

1 A mixture of mild and bitter ale; the term is used nowadays for various other mixtures, but not in a London pub in the mid-nineteenth century.

"Allah!" said the Mooress.

"Yes," John continued, who believed that he was only talking to himself, "there's something unhinged in his brain. I've surprised him making grimaces at his parrot. Then he suddenly starts uttering little bursts of laughter that resemble the whimpering of a puppy. If the marriage were made, I'd solicit a padded cell for him in Bedlam, and everything would be said and done, but my uncle will never consent now. Poor Miss Milly! What will become of her, I ask you?"

The Mooress, who was listening with her elbows on the table, exhaled a sigh that made all the glassware around her neck and in her ears tinkle, and winked at him tenderly—so tenderly that he blushed like a schoolboy.

When John Christie's alarmed modesty had recovered its equilibrium, he made the Mooress a gesture of the indignant Suzanne,[1] and the heiress of Abderham[2] went incontinently to seek adventure elsewhere.

John emptied his glass then, plunged his hands into his hair and absorbed himself in his reflections.

---

1 The eponymous heroine of the comedy *Suzanne* (1837) by Eugène Guinot and Joeph Duveyrier, alias Mélesville, waxes indignant in Act II, scene VII when publicly accused of being in love. The story was adapted as the grand opera, *La Chaste Suzanne* (1840) by Fréderic de Courcy and Pierre Carmouche, and novelized in the same year by Edouard Ourliac.

2 Abd-al Rahman was the Muslim leader defeated at the Battle of Tours by Charles Martel in 732, subsequently represented by the French as a turning point in history that began the gradual expulsion of the "Moors" from Frankish territory, and eventually from Spain.

At the twelfth stroke of midnight he quit the Oriental Tavern, as drunk as an American sailor on night-leave.

As he went past Uncle Pycraft's house he looked up, and showed his fist to the window placed at the left-hand corner of the first floor. It was that of the bedroom of the blonde Milly's ferocious guardian.

At that moment the door of the house rotated on its hinges, making audible a languorous little *miaow*; a black silhouette was outlined against the half-light of the wall; a key turned in the lock, and Uncle Pycraft, wrapped up to the nose in a capacious iron-gray cloak, slid like a rat along the row of houses.

In spite of his drunkenness, John thought he understood that the captain was going to fetch a doctor for poor Milly, suddenly and gravely indisposed; but that fear vanished immediately, for Uncle Pycraft was whistling between his teeth the march of the seventh dragoons. An uncle, however barbaric he might be, does not whistle the march of the seventh dragoons when his niece is in danger.

Freed of all preoccupation with regard to Miss Milly, John Christie then abandoned himself to suppositions as surprising as they were prodigious, which led him to follow the honorable captain at a distance.

Pycraft hesitated momentarily before cutting across Portland Place to reach Saint John's Wood, and the Brompton entrance.

John Christie was breathless with fatigue, emotion and half-and-half.

At that epoch—it was the middle of the month of June 1782—Brompton was a sort of obscure cloaca where a few paltry houses stood, islets of brick and somber verdure, scattered along a sunken road strewn with oyster-shells and rubble, something like the slope of the Butte Montmartre in 1800: the same desolate solitude by day, the same security by night.

Having reached the entrance to Brompton, Pycraft stopped dead, sounded the darkness with his gaze and slipped a pierced kernel between his teeth, from which he drew a thin sound.

Three seconds later, a little whistle responded to that signal, and a man emerged from the corner of a hawthorn hedge and approached the captain, with whom he exchanged a few rapid words in low voices.

John, who had slipped into the shadow of the hedge, saw the barrel of a rifle glinting in the hands of the man who was talking with Pycraft, but even though he strained his ears and made an acoustic funnel with his left hand he could only hear a fragment of the conversation:

"We received the new tubes yesterday."

"Ah!" said Pycraft. "How are they?"

"Very well-contrived. The major had the ingenious idea of fitting the mouthpieces of loudhailers to the openings; they're supple, light and very manageable."

"Has Doctor Sandby arrived?"

"An hour ago; we're only waiting for you to operate."

"Dewel?"

"Oh, I forgot. Dray was taken to Bedlam this morning. It appears that he tried to strangle Mrs. Dray a little when he went home last night."

"He came to the club in the evening?"

"Yes, and only left at two o'clock in the morning. He laughed a lot, poor Dray!"

"How many times?" asked Pycraft gravely.

"Four times."

"Too many! Far too many!" growled the captain, between his teeth.

The two men crossed the road then and stopped before the gate of a small brick house, the façade of which plunged into a ditch eight feet deep. An iron bridge led from the exterior gate to the door of the house.

The two men crossed the drawbridge and went into the house, which was as silent and black as the orifice of an oven.

John Christie waited for a cloud to pass over the disk of the moon in order to approach the house in his turn and examine it in detail.

In accordance with the usual plans of English cottages, and certain perfumes of lobster, John judged that the windows of the kitchen opened over the ditch. Those windows were barred, like those of the ground floor and the first floor. No light filtered from behind the windows. John decided to make a tour of the house, thinking that he might discover something on the side of the garden.

As he was going along the façade, there was an explosion inside, followed by a loud noise of breaking glass.

The senior clerk of Sheriff Samuel Toots was brave, but the cold of the night, fatigue and the torpor of drunkenness had sapped his courage considerably, which fell into his heels. No greyhound chasing a hare had ever run faster than the blonde Milly's Valentine when he was pursued by the seven-league boots of fear.

A quarter of an hour after his launch from Brompton, he precipitated himself into his room and fell on to his bed like an inert mass.

It was midday when his eyes, reddened and swollen by the previous day's excesses, opened to the sunlight.

While getting dressed, John drew up his battle plan.

It was obvious that the captain was part of the gang of forgers that had been making the detectives of London grit their teeth for six months. The little house in Brompton was the lair in which they delivered themselves to their culpable fabrication.

His first thought was to go and declare everything to his uncle the sheriff, but the thought of seeing the captain swinging at the end of a rope at Newgate immediately made him reject that idea. It was necessary, above all, to save Miss Milly from the shame of living with as great a criminal as Pycraft, and to free her from all complicity for the future.

John knew that the captain went out every day at about two o'clock to go for a walk in Hyde Park

He watched from a distance, and irrupted into the parlor, where Miss Milly was embroidering next to the window.

"Miss Milly," cried the nephew of Sheriff Samuel Toots in a voice full of conviction, "you're completely doomed if you don't have entire confidence in me." After consulting his watch he went on: "Miss, a boat is setting sail for Calais in an hour; the stage coach leaves for Edinburgh in twenty minutes; you know that it stops at Gretna Green. Would you like to go to France and remain"—here John hesitated and lowered his eyes modestly—"and remain Miss Pycraft, or become Mrs. Milly Christie before the hammer and anvil of blacksmith O'Kelly?"

Miss Milly darted a gaze full of tender compassion at her Valentine. The speech she had just heard could pass, with just title, for a fit of hot fever.

"Respond, Miss! Respond while there's still time," John continued, with a progressive exaltation.

"Master John," said Milly, in her mildest voice, "the sun is very hot at this hour of the day; I engage you not to expose yourself to it any longer today and to go home immediately."

"Oh, yes, yes that's it!" he said, in a plaintive tone. "You don't understand, and you doubt that my reason is very solid. Oh, unfortunate Miss Milly, if you knew, if I could tell you . . . No, no! I ought to keep quiet, it's your ignorance that is your strength, and will be our safeguard. But I shall watch over you, and snatch you from their claws by proving that they're . . ."

"What?" asked the pretty child, gently.

"Nothing, nothing! Au revoir, Miss Milly, au revoir!"

And John quit the parlor, gesticulating like a marionette.

Half an hour later he went into his Uncle Samuel's study.

The sheriff greeted him not as his sister's son but as a head clerk who has drawn the silhouette of Punch on the back of a report to the prime minister.

John allowed the storm to burst, and profited from a lull to ask his uncle to have him conducted to Newgate by one of his agents.

"To do what?" demanded the sheriff stupefied.

"In the present circumstances," John replied, "it's indispensable that I have a long conference with one of the most skillful thieves in the City, and it's equally urgent that you put at my disposal two of your most vigorous detectives."

"Speak! Speak, my dear John!" cried Samuel Toots, who, having always had faith in the intelligence of his nephew, glimpsed some mysterious and important affair.

"Do you have confidence in me, Uncle?" said John, whom the sheriff's movement had not escaped, and who wanted to exploit it to the advantage of his personal importance.

Samuel understood that he had given in too easily.

"I have confidence," he said coldly, "although I have not yet seen you at work."

"You'll see me soon, my dear Uncle."

"In sum, what does it concern? What have you discovered?"

"Forgery!" said John, laconically, in a low voice.

The sheriff rubbed his hands together as if to start a fire and immediately rang to give his orders on the matter of the two agents requested by his nephew.

"Just like that, you've picked up a trail?" he said, winking his left eye.

"Yes," said John, resolutely, "but I don't yet know whether the game is a wolf or a fox."

"Come on, come on, my dear John; be good to your old uncle, who loves you so much; just tell me . . ."

"Nothing, Uncle. I want to have the honors of the affair alone, for I intend to prove to you that I'm worthy of the honor you've done me by attaching me to your person."

"Master John!" said Samuel Toots, raising his voice. "Be careful! I can remember that before being your uncle I'm the sheriff, and that, as such, I have the right to interrogate you, to force you to speak!"

"Remember, Uncle," replied John, going to sit down tranquilly at his desk and commencing to sharpen a pen, "that if you interrogate me I will respond to you, under oath, that I know absolutely nothing."

Samuel Toots saw immediately that he had taken a false route. A cloud passed over his forehead—a cloud of wrinkles—and he clicked his tongue five or six times against his palate, like a wine-taster approving of a cask of Madeira. In Samuel Toots that was a certain sign of the most violent internal wrath.

John had known for a long time that his uncle had a character shaped like a star, and that it was dangerous to bump into one of the points of that star, but his reasons for resisting him were too strong.

Samuel Toots paced angrily back and forth in his study; that was his supreme resource in desperate cases. His anger descended then into his legs, like lightning along the chain of a conductor. He finally stopped in front of his nephew. He had passed from crimson to pale pink.

"John," he said, with a feline smile, "I'm going to give you a letter for the governor of Newgate; Fix and Knox are already waiting for you in the street. If you succeed I'll add an extra ten pounds to your salary from my own purse; if you fail, if you're playing games with me, I'll sack you as head clerk and throw you out as a nephew."

"Write to the governor of Newgate, my dear Uncle," said John, presenting him with the pen that he had just sharpened.

After having read the sheriff's note the governor of Newgate offered John a seat and waited for him to explain himself with regard to the thief he wanted to summon.

"It's a matter of a lesson that I want to take immediately," said John, "and I'd be very grateful to you, Governor, if you'd choose yourself the master rogue who can teach me most rapidly and efficiently to saw through an iron bar without making a noise and cut a window without breaking it. I won't hide from you that it's a matter of the salvation of the Bank of England and several important commercial enterprises."

The mocking smile that creased the prison governor's lips had engaged John to follow his request with that lie, the scope of which ought to justify the strangeness of his request.

A warder conducted John to the cell of a certain Frost, who was to be embarked the following day for Botany Bay. In exchange for twelve shillings, Frost put

John Christie in a position to execute a little breaking and entering very conveniently. Frost made the demonstration so clear, neat and precise that Samuel Toots' nephew felt sure of himself when he quit the bandit. In order to finish giving his pupil a high opinion of his merit, Frost had taken care to filch his gold watch surreptitiously.

However, the great resolutions of the fiancé of the blonde Milly were becoming less energetic by the hour, and it seemed less urgent to act. That was because the angelic image of Milly was shining like a sun between the silhouette of the captain and the shadow of his somber acolytes, and because, determined as he was to marry the niece of a hanged man, John was wondering deep down whether it was really necessary that the captain be hanged.

Those reflections brought him, via a gentle slope, to solicit an audience with Uncle Pycraft by means of a very respectful letter.

He did not have to wait long for a response. The captain had scribbled at the bottom of poor John's letter a sentence full of bitterness and disappointment:

Miss Milly Pycraft will never be the wife
of the nephew of Sheriff Samuel Toots.

Anyone but a man in love would have glimpsed in the wording of that refusal a world of suppositions and suspicions, but John only understood one thing: that all hope was lost. Then his policeman's instincts, which were slumbering in his heart, awoke with a start; the lover disappeared to give way to the detective. He was only separated from his beloved by the length of a rope, or the thickness of the hull of a vessel departing for Botany Bay. The doom of the honorable captain was irrevocably decided.

Three reports signed by Fix and Knox signaled further nocturnal excursions on Pycraft's part. John did not hesitate any longer. The expedition, comprising the two men of confidence lent by Samuel Topts and commanded by John Christie in person, arrived under the walls of the mysterious house in Brompton at ten o'clock in the evening on a moonless night.

Knox and Fix were armed with iron-tipped sticks. John had stuck a pair of pistols in his belt. The right-hand pocket of his carrick contained a diamond, a ball of wax, a little bottle of oil and three watch-springs.

At quarter past ten the captain arrived at the house, tripped the hidden spring of the gate and disappeared like a shadow at the far end of the footbridge.

"To work!" said John, resolutely, returning to his men.

Fix threw a knotted rope over the railings surrounding the ditch and moored it solidly to one of the bars.

"Remember my instructions," said John, in a low voice. "At the first gunshot, break down the door or come in through the ground floor window."

"Understood," said the two policemen, in unison.

John climbed on to Knox's shoulders and let himself slide down into the ditch. The frame of the kitchen window was raised, which simplified the work of the illustrious Frost's pupil greatly; but the grille was closed with a padlock.

John steeped one of his watch-springs in oil and attacked the ring of the padlock like an expert thief; it soon fell into his hand like an overripe pear. But the grille, rusted by rain, might have grated as it opened; a few drops of cleverly-poured oil bought its silence. It opened wide; John recommended his soul to God mentally and plunged in the darkness of the kitchen, murmuring Milly's name.

After having walked like a crab for a few seconds, John bumped into an open door, through which he slipped into a narrow corridor, at the end of which he encountered a staircase. The first step creaked under his weight. John remembered that Frost had recommended putting his shoes in his pocket on such an occasion, a maneuver that he executed immediately.

He counted thirty-two steps before finding a landing.

The house was as silent as the tomb of Ramses.

Extending his hands in front of him, John encountered a door-knob. There was no further hesitation; with his left hand he seized the butt of one of his pistols, and opened the door with his right

The room he entered was plunged in darkness. It was like a gallery, with a glazed ceiling that he divined by virtue of a blue transparent light.

John had already taken five or six steps forward when the door that he had left open behind him slammed noisily, pushed by the draught of air rising from the staircase.

Samuel Toots' nephew started and remained still, holding his breath.

When he had recovered his senses somewhat, he sniffed the air with an anxious astonishment.

That air was saturated with an insipid, bittersweet odor, traversed at moments by warm vapors and savage whiffs. At that moment, as if one of the witches of *Macbeth* had traced a magic circle around John with her broom handle, the most terrifying phantasmagoria came to animate the darkness.

Little orange or green flames, as shiny as topazes and emeralds, lit up in the night, which they illuminated with phosphorescent gleams. A hoarse yawn, as profound as the groaning of shingle on a beach, terminated by a sort of *miaow*, was audible four paces away from John, whose heart commenced to beat at two hundred pulsations a minute.

But that was only the prologue to the drama.

A strange staccato rustle, like something that might be produced by shaking a silky cloth, immediately came to break the silence that had followed the yawn. And a strangled, guttural, supernatural voice murmured almost in John's ear the words: "Sheriff's rogue!"

A cold sweat inundated John's temples, and his hair bristled on his head like a mane. He tried to launch himself forward, but his legs buckled after five steps and he stumbled in the void. Horror! His left hand settled on a warm, hairy body, and jaws seized the middle and index fingers.

Four seconds more of that inferno, and fear rendered John idiotic or mad.

Fortunately for Miss Milly's fiancé, all those terrors suddenly vanished, and reality was affirmed with the light.

A ruddy glow appeared at the other end of the gallery, through a glazed door ornamented with silk curtains.

John was in a menagerie; it was a matter of a young Javanese panther, a superb Brazilian parrot and an African monkey.

That mysterious house belonged to Doctor Sandby, the curator of the Natural History Museum and a corresponding member of eighteen scientific societies.

Completely recovered from his terror, John walked bravely toward the glazed door and lifted the corner of the curtain.

In the middle of a small oval room surrounded by wide low divans a strange apparatus stood on a marble table. That apparatus consisted of a lighted burner over which a stout glass retort was being heated, the tube of which was curved back under a bell plunged into a vat full of water. Two other leather tubes, as flexible as the pipes of a narghile, were screwed at one end to the top of the bell, which formed a gasometer. The honorable Captain Pycraft and the unknown man whom John had already seen on the Brompton Road, were holding the other ends of those tubes between their lips. Doctor Sandby, standing before the burner, was stimulating its flame with a bellows.

Pycraft's companion was panting like a hound returning from a hunt; his round eyes, open like archery targets, were fixed and glazed, his face livid; an idiotic smile was making his mouth grimace. It was quite simply horrible to see.

Pycraft was as red as a tomato, and his cheeks, inflated like those of a pibroch-player, seemed ready to burst. Suddenly, he let go of the tube, leapt to his feet, and a burst of strident laughter erupted from his broad chest.

John was petrified by astonishment. Meanwhile, the captain's burst of laughter was prolonged indefinitely, but it changed tone; from its initial explosiveness it became nasal and mocking.

The doctor then approached the honorable fellow cautiously, and laid him on the divan.

Only a diabolical pen could render the end of that scene exactly: the jiggling, the screeching, the hiccupping, the muted growling, and the clarinet giggles of the captain, who, after ten minutes of laughter and contortions, fell on to the parquet, as motionless and mute as a broken marionette.

"I've got it!" exclaimed John Christie, like Archimedes when he discovered his famous screw; and without waiting any longer he rejoined his escort, who were snoring in one of the roadside ditches.

The next day he went to his office as if nothing had happened between his uncle and himself, and had file number 37 brought to him, which bore on a yellow label the word: *Hilarants.*

All the documents that dossier contained were annotated in the hand of Samuel Toots, who had been following that affair for eight months with a zeal that resembled obsession.

This is what John learned after twenty minutes' reading:

In the year of grace 1772, John Priestley,[1] a chemist and chaplain to Lord Shelburn, found a new gas to which he gave the name *Nitrum flammans*. A few years later, while studying the properties of that gas, Priestley discovered its effect on the nervous system and nicknamed it "laughing gas."

The experiments gradually passed from laboratories into salons, where they were changed into hilarant séances. Then fashion got mixed in with it, and people inhaled the hilarant gas as they took coffee. Eventually, upmarket taverns in London would offer their regulars "exhilarating gas" every Monday.

---

1 The natural philosopher and theologian in question was actually Joseph Priestley (1733-1804) who served William Petty, Earl of Shelburne, as a librarian and archivist; his championship of free speech, his support for the French Revolution and his attempt to develop a "natural theology" in which the study of natural science would lead to a fuller understanding of the deity, and thus hasten the advent of the Millennium, led to his home and church in Birmingham being burned down by a mob; he was forced to flee via London to America. Nitrous oxide was one of a host of gases he isolated with the aid of the apparatus described in the story for collecting chemically-generated gases over water, preventing their dispersal and interaction with atmospheric gases, but he did not publish the work, confused by his results, and the experiments were not repeated in a disciplined fashion until Humphry Davy picked up the thread in 1798 at the Pneumatic Institute in Bristol, although Antoine Lavoisier would undoubtedly have carried it forward in Paris had he not been guillotined during the Terror. Davy, who was also an aspirant Romantic poet, was acquainted with numerous members of the Romantic Movement, including Charles Lamb, Coleridge and Shelley, and allegedly supplied them with nitrous oxide—and perhaps also with other psychotropic substances—in order that they could test its potential as a source of literary inspiration.

That lasted until the day when it was perceived that the inhalation of nitrogen monoxide was furnishing the halls of Bedlam in an alarming manner. The police intervened then, and the sale of "exhilarating gas" was prohibited, under the most severe penalties.[1]

The ordinance encountered recalcitrant laughers, however, who, unable to fight overtly, delivered themselves to their deadly passion covertly. Pycraft and Doctor Sandby were among that number. The former had been sentenced to fines four times; the latter had endured a fortnight in prison—and that thanks to the perspicacity and zeal of Sheriff Samuel Toots.

Enlightenment had just dawned in John's mind. The captain was avenging himself on the nephew for the uncle's persecutions.

John closed the hilarant file, consulted his watch—which marked two o'clock—and ran to Hyde Park.

The honorable gentleman was recovering from the previous evening's gas on a bench.

"All or nothing," murmured John, coming to sit down next to him.

"Hee hee hee, my dear captain," he cried, laughing with the same laughter he had heard in Brompton. "You seem less cheerful than you did last night. Ho ho ho!"

Pycrsft shuddered and shot him an oblique glance.

"How is dear Doctor Sandby? Very well, very well, no? Hee hee hee. His house is well-situated. One

---

1 This was, of course, pure fiction when the story was penned, but is an interesting anticipation of a historical pattern to be repeated in association with many psychotropic substances.

breathes such good gas there, hoo hoo hoo! My tongue has twisted! Such good air! Dewel! My head's splitting. My dear Mr. Pycraft. Can you imagine that my uncle has charged me with pursuing incorrigible hilarants of his acquaintance, and that I've spent my morning preparing an enormous labor. Ha ha ha! I shall track them, I shall annihilate them, my dear Pycraft; no one will even remember that they once existed in England."

The captain was livid.

"Ho ho! I'm a bachelor, you see! My time belongs to me, by day as by night. I have the legs of a stag, me, and flair! If I were married, my severity might perhaps be greatly relaxed . . . I might have disdained to occupy myself with those fellows . . . but as a bachelor, I shall be pitiless!"

"A bachelor!" murmured Pycraft, in a suppliant voice. "It's only up to you no longer to be one in two days."

"Really?" said John, radiantly

"Yes but on one condition . . ."

"Oh, my dear Pycraft," cried John, hurling himself into his arms, "I would never have the courage to cause pain to such a cheerful uncle!"

A week later, to the minute, Miss Milly became Mrs. Christie, and Uncle Pycraft departed for Lahore, where he went to take command of a regiment of Sepoys.

John, who had friends in the East India Company, had solicited and obtained that command for him.

Pycraft was the President of the Club of Hilarants, the last one that existed in England. The association, which had existed for fifteen years, vanished into smoke after his departure.

THE DOCTOR'S HALLUCINATIONS
A Moving Terrain. The Danae Delusion.

by X. B. Saintine

IN accordance with the doctor's own indication, we had been occupying a private booth in a small restaurant of the second order, but the first choice; physicians know about that, and in that regard, at least, one can trust their experience and their conscientious observations.

The dinner, in which iced champagne had taken the place of other wines—that was another of the doctor's prescriptions—was approaching its conclusion, and we were beginning to chat with our elbows on the table, when he returned of his own accord to our previous conversation on dreams and visions. Knowing that I kept a journal of my dreams, he asked me whether I had classified them by order—from which I had carefully refrained, great God!

He spoke to me first about "lucid dreams"—*clara somnia*—during which the mind retains all its power of dedication and even invention.

Poets have been known to make verses, and mathematicians to have solved problems during those sorts of dreams, which are also called "psychic," the soul enjoying its complete liberty therein, during the complete slumber of the senses. In a contrary order, there are "hyperesthetic dreams," in which the senses are solely dominant, and excessively, as if unchained in the absence of the mastery of logic.

"In the great class of hyperesthetics," he told me, "we first distinguish the 'symptomatics,' whose character is not so much passionate as persistent. Hippocrates, and Galen after him, had already called attention to them as providing an excellent diagnostic in maladies, hence the name of symptomatic. In order to inform us, those dreams proceed by the law of contraries. If, during your sleep, my friend, you frequently participate in good meals, if you dream about cooking, feasting and food for three days running, consider yourself warned; your habitual alimentary regime is insufficient, or one of your digestive organs is only fulfilling its functions imperfectly. Thank God, I think that neither you nor I will dream about Pantagruelesque feasts tonight . . . to your health! . . . and to mine!"

He held out his glass.

"Your symptomatic dreams, Doctor, are reminiscent of a mirage, which, in the midst of the desert sands, presents water and shade to unfortunates extenuated by thirst and heat."

"Let's not get confused, my dear friend; a mirage is only manifest to open eyes; it's a hallucination, not a dream, and before we arrive at hallucinations, let me

take up my theory of dreams again. After the symptomatics come the 'symplegadics';[1] they are disordered
dreams in which the senses and the imagination collide,
in which several dramas are mixed into a single one:
complicated, monstrous dreams with neither head nor
tail, in which the nightmare rightfully takes its place.
But you're right, to the devil with these big words,
which even the Greeks, who furnished them, don't
understand. For me, what springs evidently from my
observations is that in a dream, a man is doubled; the
body and the soul are able to isolate themselves from
one another, or recombine in conditions quite different
from the normal state."

"Bravo, Doctor!" I exclaimed. "Now you've arrived
at recognizing my theory of *the second life*."

"If it is a theory," he replied, smiling, "it might
well, like my theory, lack common sense—but pass for
the second life, and even the third, which I'm very far

---

1 I can find no remaining evidence of the term *symplégadique*—
which I have transcribed straightforwardly into English as symplegadic—having been used as a medical term in France, but it
might well have been deployed by the botanist and physician
Timothée Puel (1813-1890) and pioneering contemporaries who
attempted to catalogue the medicinal properties of native plants.
On the other hand, it might have been invented by the author,
who used it elsewhere. If he really had consulted a physician about
the matter, that supposed expert might have improvised it on his
own account. The etymology of the term is obvious; it comes
from the story of Jason and the Argonauts, who encountered the
Symplegades, or Clashing Rocks in the course of their adventure,
so-called because they smashed together when anyone tried to pass
between them. The English adjective symplegadic does exist in a
few commentaries on that story.

from renouncing, even though I'm a member of the Académie de Médecine."

The dear doctor took a few sips of the wine that I had just poured for him, seemed to abstract himself from his reflections for a few seconds, and then smiled again.

"Since we've come back to this terrain, in exchange for your two hunts, I'll tell you about two odd little accidents of my youth, which, I believe, with a few developments, might furnish two curious chapters for your journal. It's up to you to recognize your property and to classify them as seems good to you."

And immediately, he launched into the first chapter.

"The most audacious traveler," he said, "has never traversed a bolder, stranger, more moving and more stirring route than the one I came to travel one day—yes, a day when I frayed a passage above a dense, compact human crowd that took the place of a parquet: a veritably mosaic of living, grimacing, convulsed heads, rolling terrible eyes and each vociferating louder than the next. On such a path, the most skillful equilibrist wouldn't have been able to take ten paces without stumbling, for along with the heads, arms were agitating, bent and stiff, terminating in closed fists, similar in their movement to the swaying of gastropod tentacles—or, rather, the multiple limbs with which hideous cephalopods are equipped. If, as a poet, you prefer mythological comparisons, imagine a thousand or twelve-hundred heads of Medusa with their serpentine tresses.

"In spite of those heads, those arms, those eyes, those cries and those fists, all of which were menacing me simultaneously," my savant friend went on, "I continued walking, still upright. My feet sank into their bushy tresses, slid over the curve of foreheads, clung on to the angular projections of shoulders, and I, strangely enough, whose nature shares nothing with that of a lion, did not feel for a moment the dread of danger—not even that of the harm I might cause. Tell me, doesn't that have a complete resemblance to a dream?"

"Wasn't it one?"

"No; everything was real in the contact of my feet with those heads and shoulders, and without worrying overmuch about it, I walked there as if on rugged terrain with a few fissures, that's all."

"What, then, Doctor, inspired you to such audacity?"

"Fear, my friend—the fear that sometimes gives birth to heroes. I launched myself across that scabrous route without any other preoccupation than that of fleeing—and not fleeing a peril, but a simple emotion.

"I was a medical student then; all my studies were marching ahead, and valiantly, I dare say; only operatory science still found me a rebel, in revolt. Twenty or a hundred times I had tried in vain to watch some unimportant operation. Meanwhile, my pusillanimity threatened to ruin my future.

"One morning, I was following the visit to the Hôpital de la Charité when our illustrious professor announced to us for the following day a surgical operation on number 17 *with a new apparatus*. Number 17 was a little man with a grim and harsh physiognomy. That physiognomy did not inspire any compassion in me, and by virtue of its very unpleasantness it suited me.

"I got up at first light, resolved not to weaken this time, to watch the operation, not only in such a way as to get a good view, but in order not to desert my post. I was in the process of keeping my word.

"The Amphitheater of the Charité presented the form of an immense funnel equipped with steps from the top to the bottom of its perimeter. I went down to the bottom of the funnel. When I found myself facing the operating table, so close that I was almost touching it, I sat down on the narrow banquette, toward which converged, necessarily, all the steps of the enclosure, soon garnished with numerous students, because of the announcement of the new apparatus.

"Not a single place remained vacant; the last arrivals were forced to give one another a leg up in order to make use of the window-sills, for want of anything better; the doors were obstructed by a triple rank of spectators, like the entrance to the orchestra stalls of our theaters on days of grand performances. And I, literally plunged and submerged at the bottom of the funnel, like Cain in the final circle of the Dantean Inferno, got ready, with sweat on my brow, finally to commence my course in human suffering.

"A little door opened facing me. Preceded by the hospital interns, like a consul by his lictors, the professor made his entrance, to the sound of applause. He said a few words about the operation and about the new apparatus, showed the instruments, with a clear and rapid comment on each one. Then two orderlies brought the unfortunate number 17, enveloped in the sad gray overcoat that is the uniform of the place.

"At the sight of him, I shuddered, but without losing courage. However, that physiognomy, which had only inspired an antipathetic sentiment, was ennobled, as at the approach of martyrdom. While he was being stripped of his only garment, the poor fellow paraded over all of us a gaze imprinted with such a dolorous resignation that it seemed to me that the knife prepared for him had just plunged into my chest. He was then laid on a thin mattress; his wrists were drawn toward his feet and secured by solid ligatures . . .

"I did not see any more. I had already commenced my terrible ascension of the steps; a violent nervous shock had simultaneously shaken within me the organs of intelligence and given incredible strength to those of locomotion. A blind movement impelled me forward, whatever obstacles there might be; I would have confronted a battery of cannons. I could no longer see clearly; I believed that I was traversing a phantasmagorical terrain, that an enchanter had strewn grimacing heads and contorted arms in my path.

"Thus I accomplished that terrible climb, thus I traveled intrepidly that moving route strewn with reefs, and above all with punches—for when I recovered my senses in the street, in the open air, I was bruised. The next day, my legs and my body were black with contusions.

"Such is, my dear friend, the exact story of my odyssey across the great amphitheater of the Hôpital de la Charité in Paris. To enlighten you more fully on the provocative causes of that unusual manner of travel, read *Recherches sur les hallucinations* by Szafkowski, and especially the works of the savant Alfred Maury . . ."[1]

"My dear Doctor, I prefer to hear your second chapter."

"Good!" he said. "Another glass of champagne to make us forget the amphitheater of the Charité and poor number 17."

After a moment of silence, he continued: "This time, it's no longer a matter of a hospital scene; it's my turn to transport you into a land of enchantment, into the midst of a voluptuous tableau, and even slightly libertine—which might appear strange to you on the part of a grave practitioner like me, but are we not in a private booth? The lady at the counter won't know anything about it; furthermore, I'll be brief in my descriptions in order not to put your modesty and mine to too long a proof."

That beginning of the second chapter caused me to prick up my ears. The doctor emptied his glass, filled it again himself, as if distractedly, and, holding it up at eye level, he spoke:

"For you, as for me, it's determined that today will be entirely consecrated to memories of youth. My

---

1 *Recherches sur les hallucinations au point de vue de la psychologie, de l'histoire et de la médecine légale* (1849) by Louis-Rufin Szafkowski. The physician and scholar Alfred Maury (1817-1892) was an important contributor to nineteenth-century exercises in the hypothetical interpretation of dreams, and a significant precursor of Sigmund Freud, although his writings covered a wide range of subjects, including oft-reprinted studies of *Les Fées du moyen-âge* [The Enchantresses of the Middle Ages] (1843) and *La Magie et l'astrologie dans l'antiquité et au moyen âge* [Magic and Astrology in Antiquity and the Middle Ages] (1864).

youth, when I evoke it, seemed to arrive in a direct line from Villemomble, near Paris, where my father had a country house. So, I was at Villemomble, and I was collecting plants in the little wood that surrounds it and is linked to those of Rainey, when the air suddenly seemed to be separated before me into globules absolutely similar to the ones rising from the depths of this glass, except that, instead of rising they were descending. They were descending like a fine granular rain of little transparent yellow pearls.

"That yellow tint was gradually accentuated in its gleam and vivacity; soon, further revived by the warm rays of the summer sun, filling the atmosphere of the wood, the globules began to vibrate, to swirl pell-mell like myriads of midges, and to vanish into a general flamboyance, in the wake of which their golden gleam was attached to all the objects living or inanimate, that surrounded me.

"Around me, nature seemed to be entirely the work of a goldsmith; gold shone on the foliage of the bushes and thickets, as on the grass and the pebbles of the paths; all the flowers were buttercups; the birds had golden eyes and golden plumage; flies and insects were transformed into flying nuggets; one might have thought that the mines of California and Australia had come of their own accord to show themselves above ground; it was a complete Eldorado.

"A few paces away, an immense tree loomed up, as rutilant as the other trees but distinguished among them all by gigantic pods that hung down all the way to the ground. I approached and I opened one of them;

to my profound surprise, I found on the satin parchment of the sheath, separated from one another by a light partition, graciously folded up and arranged in rows like haricot beans in their pod . . . yes, I found . . . I'll give you a hundred guesses! . . . women, my dear friend, charming young women!"

"What! Women in pods?" I exclaimed.

"And blondes, of course—more than blondes, since the material of their tresses was pure gold. That is the way things were in the country to which I had been suddenly transported; the women there grow on trees, on trees of the leguminous family, as you've divined; there's no need, moreover, to take the trouble of shelling them.

"As I recoiled, bewildered and confused, almost frightened by the sight of that marvelous discovery, all the pods hanging down toward the ground opened spontaneously, by dehiscence, as we botanists say; the pretty fruits of the enchanted tree, detaching themselves from their envelope, were launched to the right and left, bounding and falling back, like the seeds of the balsam tree when their capsules burst; an army of sylvan nymphs surrounded me, all in a costume that only mythological habitude and great warmth can authorize. Holding hands with one another, some formed groups worthy of antique sculpture, true living tableaux that did not lack golden frames; others performed dances before me, whose choreography the foremost ballet master of the Opéra would not have disavowed. I had never found myself at a similar fête . . . but enough details."

"Why, Doctor, why? Anyway, this time, you won't deny that this really is a matter of a dream?"

"A dream? No, a poisoning."

I started in my seat. "A poisoning? What? How? In the middle of a wood, when you were only thinking about collecting plants?"

"Exactly. But let's go back a little. In imitation of our skillful novelists and our imperial prosecutors in their speeches, I had to establish the facts first in order to keep your curiosity alert, saving the explanation of the cause for later. Now, in order to discover the cause of the principal, and even unique, event of my second chapter, it's necessary to return to my first chapter, as you'll see . . . but let's drink! A storyteller, like an orator, has a right to a glass of sugared water, for which champagne can substitute, after all, and even with a certain advantage."

The waiter had just brought a third bottle; I filled the doctor's glass, and he continued.

"Since my famous affair with number 17 in the amphitheater of the Charité, I had been much preoccupied with hallucinations, and, having concluded my medical studies, I chose as the subject of my thesis hallucinations provoked by the ingestion of certain vegetables. I was the first to identify their logical, philosophical and therapeutic development . . .

"Listen carefully. First, the narcotic substance acts upon the senses, which then react upon the imagination; the latter, violently overexcited, renders to the physical machine the shock that it has received therefrom; it's a reactive shock . . . a reactive shock, you understand . . . and then between the two components a sort of entente is established, a harmony, an equilibrium: an order within the very disorder. Hallucinated eyes see externally, as well as in the plastic state, which only exists in our mind, and in the dream state; hence the visions and apparitions, gracious or terrible, the visual tricks that abuse you . . . but that's my thesis that I'm passing before you, my dear friend, when I only wanted to tell you . . . what did I want to tell you, then . . . ?"

He put his glass down on the table, after having emptied it in a single draught, and then filled it again, still distractedly.

"Ah! I have it! Well, my dear, not content with making observations and theorizing, I experimented on myself; I sampled opium, datura, mandrake and hashish; I subjected myself to the action of all those powerful anesthetics, mysterious enchantresses, which opened the doors of unknown paradises or frightful infernos by turns . . .

"When I was on the point of sustaining my doctrines before my judges in the Faculty, in the matter of narcotics, it only remained for me to make the intimate acquaintance of henbane, a wild plant with hairy leaves and yellow flowers striped with purple, perhaps excessively calumniated, in my opinion, for although it makes one pay a little dear for the fêtes it gives, it gives splendid ones, or at least complete.

"Henbane, the henbane with which I had not yet experimented, I had just encountered in the little wood of Villemomble. For love of the art, I had chewed its leaves, its stem and its roots, albeit with precaution—I knew how poisonous the plant was with which I was dealing . . .

"A quarter of an hour later, I was prey to the delusion . . . the Danaë delusion! That's the name that the famous Boissier Sauvageot . . . or Sauvage . . . gave it.[1] Then, in the wake of my vision of leguminous women, I was seized by a violent headache . . . that diabolical cephalgia I think I still have . . ."

The doctor put his hand to his head and searched for the bottle that was already three-quarters empty, but I had caused it to disappear. Evidently, iced champagne was not as inoffensive for him as he had claimed.

He continued his story anyway, mingling it with rather vague reflections.

"As I returned to Villemomble, my gracious houris, who had suddenly changed into aged witches covered in spangles and tinsel, accompanied me as far as the entrance to the village, vociferating insults addressed to me and blasphemies.

"Having arrived at my father's house, I had difficulty recognizing it, so magnificently was it gilded from top to bottom. Inside, everything, furniture and personnel, was glistening under gold; the cook had a golden apron; the manservant was braided with gold on all the seams of his waistcoat; even my father, instead of his fine gray beard, had a long golden beard, which reminded me

---

1 François Boissier de Sauvages de Lacroix (1706-1767), a friend of Linnaeus who attempted to compile a classification of diseases modeled on the latter's classification of biological species, also carried out early research on mental illness.

of the sign of a certain silk-merchant in Paris. I was laid down in golden sheets after being made to take a footbath in liquid gold at forty degrees.

"Finally," continued the dear doctor, whose tongue was thickening increasingly, ". . . fortunately, I have a solid head . . . I prescribed myself two grains of lemonade . . . no . . . two grains of emetic in a pint of lemonade . . ." He interrupted himself, and said: "Why do you have two heads . . . ? The next day, I could no longer see anything but yellow . . . dark yellow. The day after, bright yellow, the color of champagne . . . hang on, where's the bottle?"

"We've drunk enough, Doctor."

"Perhaps you're right." And, after having looked piteously at his empty glass, he turned toward me: "Beware of champagne, my dear friend; it too is a hallucinator."

And my savant doctor did not take long to fall asleep.

THE PORTALS OF OPIUM

by Marcel Schwob

I had always made every effort to avoid living a regulated life after the fashion of other men. The endless monotony of repeated and habitual actions exasperated me. My father having left an enormous fortune at my disposal, I had no desire but to live life to the full, but neither sumptuous houses nor luxury carriages attracted me. The frenzy of hunts and the indolence of spas were equally unappealing to my restless mind: it was all too little. Men live nowadays in extraordinary times, when the novelists have shown us all the facets of human life and have revealed the underside of every thought. How can one help but be utterly tired of commonplace sentiments and experiences? Is it any wonder that many of us allow ourselves to be attracted towards the gulf where shadows mysterious and unknown remain? Is it any wonder that some are possessed by a passion for the exotic and the sublime research of new sensations, or that others are eventually overcome by a broad compassion which extends itself over all possibilities?

My various pursuits had created in me an extravagant curiosity regarding human life. I felt a painful desire to be alienated from my own existence, so that I might sometimes be a soldier or a merchant—or the woman that I saw passing by, shaking her skirts—or that lightly veiled young girl who just now entered a tea-room and had half-lifted up her veil to bite into a cake, before pouring water into a glass and relaxing, with her head bowed.

Given all this, it is easy enough to understand how I came to be haunted by curiosity as to what lay behind one particular portal.

There was in a remote district a high gray wall, pierced only by railed openings set at a great height, with false windows palely drawn upon its implacable surface; and set in the base of that wall on the uneven ground, devoid of any peepholes through which one could obtain a glimpse of what lay within, was a low door set in an arch. It was sealed by an iron lock in the form of coiled serpents; and crossed with green bars. The lock and the hinges were rusted. In the long-deserted street the nettles and thistles had sprouted in clusters about the threshold, and the door was mottled by whitish flakes like those on the skin of a leper.

From time to time, my dull walks brought me to that silent street, and I addressed the question of the puzzling door. Were there living beings behind that mysterious portal? What extraordinary existence might be led by those who passed their days in the shadow of the great gray wall, cloistered from the world by the little low door which one never saw standing open?

One evening, while I was wandering among the crowds, looking for curious individuals, I remarked a little old man with an odd limping gait. He had a red handkerchief dangling from his pocket, and he continually struck the pavement with a twisted cane, as though with derision. Under the gaslights this figure seemed perpetually striped by shadow, and his eyes sparkled so greenly that I was irresistibly reminded of the image of the door: I became instantly certain that he had some connection with it and that he had been through it.

I followed that man. I could not know for certain that he had anything to do with my puzzle, but it was impossible for me to act otherwise—and when he reached the end of the deserted street where the door was, I was illuminated by one of those sudden presentiments that sometimes take hold of us, and I felt that I had a perfectly clear idea of what would happen.

He knocked twice, or perhaps three times, on the door. It turned on its rusty hinges, without grating.

I did not hesitate: I sprang forward. I stumbled over the legs of a beggar who was sprawled out along the wall, but whom I had not seen. On his knees he had an earthenware bowl, and there was a tin spoon in his hand. He lifted his stick and cursed me in a raucous voice, but I paid no heed. The door was silently closed again, behind me.

I found myself in an immense gloomy garden, where the weeds and brambles sprouted to knee-height. The ground was soaked, as though by continual rain; it seemed to be soft clay, to judge by the way it clung to my boots at each step. I groped my way forward through the gloom, towards the muffled noises which the old man made as he went on ahead of me. I soon saw a crack of light; there were trees in the distance upon whose branches paper lanterns were hanging, giving out a faint and diffuse reddish light. The silence was less profound now, for the wind seemed to breathe slowly in the branches.

On approaching closer, I saw that the lanterns were painted with oriental flowers and that they described in the air the words:

HOUSE OF OPIUM

Rising up before me was a white house, square in shape, with long narrow windows. Drifting from within came the sound of slow discordant music, whose rhythm was beaten out by drums, and overlaid by the chanting of dreamy voices. The old man paused at the threshold and turned towards me, gracefully shaking his red handkerchief, and I accepted his gestured invitation to enter.

In the corridor beyond I met a thin yellow creature, clad in a loose robe; she too was old, with a shaky head and a toothless mouth. She ushered me into a rectangular room, with white silk stretched over its walls. The hangings were decorated with vertical black stripes, rising as far as the ceiling

I saw before me a carefully-organized assembly of lacquered tables. A thin flame was smoldering in a lamp of red copper; there was a porcelain pot full of a grayish paste, a number of pins, and three or four pipes with bamboo stems and silver bowls. The old oriental woman rolled some paste into a pellet, mounted it on a pin and melted it in the flame. Then, placing it carefully in the bowl of the pipe, she tamped it down and sealed it with a plug.

Without pausing for reflection, I took the pipe and lit up, and I took two puffs of an acrid and poisonous smoke, which instantly stupefied me.

Although there was no sense whatsoever of any transition, I saw passing before my eyes the image of the door, and the bizarre figures of the old man with the red handkerchief, the beggar with the bowl and the old woman in the yellow robe. The black stripes upon the wall seemed to become magnified in width as they approached the ceiling, and to diminish nearer to the floor, in a kind of chromatic scale of dimension—which, it seemed to me, could be heard resonating in my ears. I seemed to hear the sound of the sea—of waves which broke in rocky grottoes, explosively driving out the air with their mute blows. The room seemed to have turned topsy-turvy, although I had had no impression of movement; it appeared to me that my feet had taken the place of my head and that I was lodged upon the ceiling. Eventually, I suffered a complete annihilation of my activity; I desired only to remain eternally where I was, and to continue that experience.

It was then that a panel slid aside somewhere in the chamber, through which there entered a young girl like none I had ever seen before. She had a body powdered with saffron and eyes upraised towards her temples; her eyelashes were decorated with gilt, and the shells of her ears were delicately limned in pink. Her teeth, which were as black as ebony, were spangled with constellations of tiny fulgurant diamonds, and her lips were painted blue. Thus decorated, with her skin spiced and painted, she had the aspect and the scent of those Chinese ivory statues which are curiously pitted and enhanced with gaudy colors. She was naked to the waist; her breasts hung down like two pears, and a brown skirt checkered with gold floated above her feet.

The desire for strange experience which had taken hold of me became so violent at that moment that I hurled myself towards that painted woman, groveling before her. Each of the colors of her costume and her skin seemed to the hyperesthesia of my senses to be a delicious sound in that harmony which enveloped me; each of the gestures and the poses of her hands was like some rhythmic element of a dance, infinitely varied, of which my intuition somehow understood the whole.

I said to her, pleadingly: "Daughter of Lebanon, if you have come to me from the mysterious depths of opium, stay, stay . . . my heart desires you. Until the end of my days I will nourish myself on that unparalleled drug which makes you appear before my eyes. Opium is more powerful than ambrosia, because it bestows the immortality of the dream, rather than the miserable eternity of life; more subtle than nectar, because it creates beings so strangely brilliant; more just than all the gods, because it reunites those who are made to love one another!

"But if you are a woman born of human flesh, you are mine—forever—because I would give everything that I have to possess you . . ."

She fixed upon me those eyes which glistened between her golden eyelashes, came slowly closer, and sat down in a casual manner which made my heart beat faster.

"Is it true?" she whispered in my ear. "Would you give your fortune to possess me?" She shook her head incredulously.

I can assure you that madness had me completely in its grip. I snatched my check-book from my pocket. I signed a blank check and threw it across the room; it fell upon the parquet.

"Ah!" she said. "But would you have the courage to become a beggar in order to be with me? It seems to me that I would like you better then. Tell me—do you want that?"

She began to undress me deftly. Then the old oriental woman led in the beggar who had been beside the door when I entered; he came in hastily and when he had put on my discarded vestments he took himself off again. As for me, I put on his patched cloak and his underclothes full of holes, and took up his stick, his spoon and his begging-bowl.

When I was thus clad, she said: "Go!" And she clapped her hands.

The lamps went out, the panel fell back into place. The girl summoned by the opium vanished. Amid the vivid confusion of the walls I saw the old man with the red handkerchief, the old woman in the yellow robe, and the hideous beggar dressed in my clothes, who threw themselves upon me and pushed me into the mouth of a dark corridor. I passed through it, and was drawn on through a maze of sticky tunnels, with viscous walls to either side of me. An inestimable time flowed by; I lost track of the hours—I seemed to be dragged along interminably.

Then, all at once, white light flooded over me. My eyes quivered in their orbits; my eyelids were screwed up against the sun.

I found myself sprawled before a little low door set in an arch, sealed by an iron lock wrought in the form of coiled serpents and crossed with green stripes: a door identical in every way to the mysterious door through which I had passed before, but set in an immense whitewashed wall. An empty and desolate country extended before me; the grass was parched, the sky was deep blue and cloudless. Everything was unfamiliar to me, including the heap of dung which lay beside me.

I was lost—as wretched as Job and as naked as Job—in that place behind the second door. I pounded on it, I shook it, but it is as firmly closed now as it ever was. My tin spoon rattles against my empty begging bowl, hollowly.

Oh yes, opium is more powerful than ambrosia, bestowing upon life the eternity of misery; it is more subtle than nectar, corroding the heart with such vitriolic cruelty; it is more just than all the gods, punishing the curious who have desired to violate the secrets of the beyond.

Oh, exceedingly just, subtle and powerful opium!

Alas, alas, my fortune is laid waste—alas, alas, my wealth is lost!

THE OPIUM SMOKER'S DREAM

by Pompon[1]

IT was our first banquet. In fourteen years, since Saint-Cyr, hazard had scattered us throughout the garrisons of France, but recently Captain Chambenoit, the theoretical father of the promotion, had had the good idea of reuniting us at Grand-Vétour, so that at eight o'clock in the evening we numbered about a hundred and fifty—the others had died under Prussian bullets—gathered, glasses in hand, around an iron trestle table.

There were cries, onomatopoeias and provoked memories: a formidable merry-making that evoked bursts of laughter to shake the windows. For myself, Chambenoit having absolutely convinced me that it was necessary to deliver a speech over dessert—a *laius*—I was not without a certain anxiety; in order

---

1 "Pompon" has been employed as a pseudonym by more than one French writer, but it is difficult to identify the one who employed it frequently in *Gil Blas* and *La Lanterne* in the era when the present story was published.

to chase away an apprehension and give myself courage, Chambenoit never ceased refilling my glass with Champagne, and I emptied it with conviction. Well, when one is not an orator . . .

On the white tablecloth, the crystal, the pyramids of fruits and the candles in the candlesticks took on vague forms; the moustached faces of my comrades smiling at me as in a dream; I found that life was beautiful and that the truffles smelled good, when Chambenoit suddenly gave me a terrible clap on the shoulder and cried: "Over to you! Go, old man, and spout well!"

And I went, and I spouted. I believe, by Saint-Georges, that I even did so in verse. I recalled the old school:

> *Sunday in Paris, a day of true apotheosis,*
> *The heart overflowing with marvelous pleasure,*
> *We saw the future, all sunlit and rosy*
> *Through a plume that masked the eyes.*

And I adjured my comrades always to rally in future to that annual banquet, that promotion dinner.

> *Wherever our destiny might take us,*
> *That day, we'll be as young as in the good times,*
> *And we'll find again in spite of the years,*
> *The gaiety of old, when we were twenty.*

Oh, my lads, what enthusiasm! I don't know whether I was speaking the language of the gods, but the entire audience stamped its feet. My comrade embraced me, weeping tenderly, and toasts were drunk to the poet! I was the poet, and I drank, and stood up, and shouted in a Stentorian tone in order to dominate the applause.

"What a success, eh!" said Chambenoit. "Are you happy?" Chambenoit had a thick tongue.

"Yes," I replied, "but it lacks air . . . I'll say more; it lacks women."

"Well, come and smoke a good pipe of opium."

And without giving me time to reply, in the midst of the hubbub, cock-crows and patriotic songs, my friend took me by the arm and we slipped away.

Outside, the cold night air finished me off; the tremulous and extenuated street-lights of the Palais-Royal were oscillating, reflected from the wet roadway.

Here we are in the Rue des Petits-Champs—is it really the Rue des Petits-Champs? We turn into one or two black side-streets, and I find myself in front of an immense palace, the windows of which on every floor are scintillating with light behind closed Venetian blinds. We lift a sculpted silver hammer and suddenly, as if by enchantment, the door opens. We go up a broad stairway covered by a carpet from Smyrna. In the stair-well, emerging in the midst of rare flowers and green plants, a large statue representing Truth Emerging from a Well bears a torch terminated by a globe of pink glass, which casts a soft light over the surrounding objects.

We arrive on the first floor; Chambenoit lifts up a door-curtain and pushes me forward; I am literally dazzled, In a drawing room blazing with light, fifteen costumed women are extended on large sofas in the most various attitudes—attitudes that mirrors reflect to infinity. In the center of the room, a fountain sends a silvery spray into the air, which falls back melodiously into a marble basin. Where am I? In the Occident or the Orient? Gathered in that fête are the most bizarre individuals and the most varied nationalities. Here is a Spaniard in a mantilla, with very short blue satin dress, with legs admirably molded in blue silk stockings with embroidered sides; there, a Circassian allows immense black tresses to fall to the floor, in which pearls are distributed; elsewhere, an Arab with a coppery complexion, like an orange, is wearing a rich costume of red silk, braided with gold. What is particular about those costumes is that one might think that there is only a single clasp to open or button to unfasten for them to fall to the floor. All of that, moreover, is indecisive, scarcely outlined in a lilac light of apotheosis.

And while I try to collect myself in the midst of that tale from the *Thousand-and-One Nights*, the Circassian advances toward me, gazing at me with two large dark eyes, which burn my marrows, and without a word, smiling with a mysterious air, a callipygian gleam, draws me irresistible in her wake, in a halo of sensuality.

Here I am in an Oriental room, lying on a bizarre divan in the form of a silver seashell supported by a swan. The Circassian, on her knees beside me in an adorable attitude, lights an opium pipe. I close my eyes, weighed down by the wine fumes, and the dream commences.

. . . A very soft blue sky, over which little clouds with baroque forms are running, resembling lubricious amours with swollen cheeks drawn in pursuit of stars, with naked arms where dimples are nested and the miles of supernatural beings who know nothing of life except its intoxications.

And while the poignant notes of a quietly-played waltz vibrate, women come from the harems of the sky, from voluptuous distant paradises, to descend in spirals through the ether like Tintoretto angels and fly furiously around me, brushing me with their wings. And that friction, as warm and perfumed as the caress of a fan, causes me a sensation of infinite sweetness.

Scarcely have they touched the ground, executing before me an ideal dance on the tips of their roseate feet, than they suddenly vanish into the azure, leaving behind them a kind of wake of troubling odors.

Now, gradually, the pink clouds disappear like gauze curtains, successively lifted, and I see under high Moorish porticos, filing along stairways of marble, the cortege of the queen. First come black Nubian heralds clad in tiger skins, with white robes striped with red, and then priests with long beards and high headdresses, miters of bizarre form, majestic and mocking, like the pontiffs with the faces of fauns who officiate in Tiepolo's charnel-houses; and then Nubian warriors, with bows and arrows over their shoulders and long streamers of lacy red cloth floating over their scattered hair; and then, finally, the queen, draped in a royal mantle, the Egyptian lining of which has concentric strips forms a kind of radiant halo for her. Against that backcloth, her beautiful semi-naked body undulates, powerful and languorous, with a lascivious motion of the hips, projecting above banderoles knotted very low down.

The orchestra of the cortege is playing a lively and joyful tune with a regular, automatic rhythm, with chords of an indescribable pride or a heart-rending tenderness, overlays and complications of sounds, and abrupt changes in measure which disconcert me at first and then grip me entirely. There are themes that unfurl infinitely, simple to begin with, which gradually become lost in an inextricable tangle of crazy embroideries or distant variations. From time to time a melody surges forth, imperiously savage and passionate, with unexpected decelerations and bizarre transports, which stop abruptly, leaving me ready to faint.

The march continues, generous and proud, languishing at times like a woman's adieu, only to resume more resolutely and more wildly. Gradually, the measure accelerates, and, in the surges of the brass instruments of the loud orchestra, hook the tumultuous desires of a pause of flesh, joy and intoxication. The rounddance gallops more rapidly and more sonorously; something akin to human screams, plaints or sobs are heard. Carried away in that turbulence, I do not know whether I am dying of pleasure or of pain . . .

And in the distance, haughty and disdainful, very straight on her throne, like a Hindu deity, the queen provokes me with the delight of her eyes, by means of irresistible appeals of her hands, raised or joined in lascivious and demanding poses. She exhorts me to climb up to the idol, to tear away those golden banderoles that hide her encircled nudity and seize in my clenched hands those breasts, whose palpitation is like the wing-beats of two captive birds, and to bathe in the profound waves of her titanic hair.

Her eyes are shining delectably, like fascinating water, through the velvet fringe of her lashes. It is her who now advances slowly, and her divine mouth comes toward my kiss. I have the perfume and savor of her flesh on my tongue. Our lips unite, and the brass of the orchestra is unleashed in a hurricane, in a sonorous tempest, the superhuman chords of a great triumphant air bursting like a thunderclap, which, after that supreme cry, gradually diminishes, fades, and dies away . . .

The opium pipe is extinct. The dream is over, I open my eyes again. Crouched beside me, in a grotesque attitude, my bare-headed ruddy companion, the pearls hanging ridiculously from her unkempt hair, is looking at me with satisfaction, with the humble and flat smile of a whore.

"Well, my darling," she says to me, in a hoarse and husky voice, "have you had a beautiful dream?"

O atrocious awakening, which brings one back from artificial paradises!

"Here," I cried, "I hold you in horror; take your louis and get away!"

And I go home, very sad, and heart-sick, through the dirty passers-by, the black streets, the sordid fiacres and the muddy causeways, having never felt all the ugliness of real life as intensely as after that sublime dream.

And the next day, I had a hangover.

Damned Chambenoit!

OPIUM AND SMARA

by Jean Lorrain

Opium

THE Javanese servants had provided each of us with a small pipe crammed with greenish paste. A negro dressed entirely in white, who suddenly appeared between the tapestries, lighted each of them in turn with brightly-glowing charcoals from a small silver brazier. Seated in a semi-circle on cushions set upon the Asian carpet, with our hands resting on squares of embroidered silk or Persian velvet, we smoked in silence, concentrating our whole attention on the progressive effects of the opium.

The company gathered in the studio, which had earlier been so noisy, had now fallen into silent meditation. At Ethal's signal, the agile hands of the Javanese had unbuttoned our waistcoats and loosened the collars of our shirts in order to facilitate the effects of the drug. I was seated next to Welcome. Maud White—whose figure, freed from restraint, moved sinuously beneath her black velvet peplum—was stretched out beside her brother. The English formed a separate group, already subdued by the increasing oppression of the narcotic. Still seated in her armchair, rigidly encased in her armor of precious stones, the old Duchess of Althorneyshare was the only one present who was not smoking. Pipe in hand, Ethal was still caught up in the comings and goings, giving orders.

All the candles in the chandeliers had been extinguished. Only two had been replaced and relit, burning brightly in the middle of the room. Their flames lit up two opposite corners of a carpet laid out there, about which the negro had distributed flower-petals. He had strewn them around like a shower of rain, and had then retired.

Candles and flower-petals! One might have thought that we were at a solemn wake. The smoke from our pipes ascended in bluish spirals. A dreadful silence weighed upon the studio. Ethal came at last to stretch himself out between Welcome and myself, and the ceremonial dancing began.

In the mute and heavy atmosphere of that vast vapor-filled hall the two Javanese idols began to sway on the spot, the rhythmic movements of their feet extending through the length of their bodies into the contortions of their arms. Their extended hands seemed boneless and dead.

Standing in the midst of the flower-petals, in the spectral glow of the two candles, they feverishly crumpled the wool of the carpet beneath their hammering toes. Their legs glistened from their narrow ankles to their slim thighs in a flux of transparent gauzes. They were now wearing strange diadems on their heads, like conical tiaras, which made their faces seem triangular and intimidating.

While they silently shook themselves, with slow and cadenced undulations of their entire bodies, the scallop-shell breast-plates slipped gently from their torsos, and the jade rings slid along their bare arms. The two idols gradually divested themselves of their garments. Their finery accumulated at their feet with a light rustling sound, as of seashells falling on sand. The tunics of white silk followed the slow fall of the jewelry. Now, as they stood on tiptoe, very slender in their exaggerated nakedness, it was as if two long black serpents shot forth from the cones of the two diadems had begun a delicious and lugubrious dance within the bluish vapors.

The sound of snoring was already audible, but amid the plucked petals the naked idols continued to dance.

All of a sudden they took hold of one another at the waist, twirling while tightly interlaced, as though they had but a single body with two heads . . . and then they suddenly evaporated. Yes, evaporated, like smoke—and at the same time the hall was filled with a new light.

A whole section of the tapestry was moved aside. Dressed as a stage, Claudius's model table appeared: cold and waxed like a parquet floor, lit from behind by the pearly and frosty glow of a wan nocturnal sky.

It was a sky padded with soft clouds, against which stood out the sharp and black silhouettes of roofs and chimney-stacks: an entire horizon of chimney-pots,

118

acute angles and attics, formed in salt and iron filings. In the distance, the dome of Val-du-Grâce could be seen. It was a silent and fantastic Paris, as seen by a bird in flight—the same panorama that could be seen from Claudius' windows, framed like a stage-set by the skylight of his hall.

Above this improvised stage, as if sprung from a dream, a whiteness appeared: a flocculence of tulle or of snow, something silver and impalpable. This frail whirling thing, which leapt and fluttered delicately beneath the moon, in the ennui of that corner of a deserted studio, was the slender naked form of a dancer.

She spun around in the mute air like a winter snowflake, and nothing disturbed the fearful silence save for the soft pitter-pat of her footfalls. Were it not for the silky rustling of her tulles she would have seemed supernatural in her transparence and thinness. Her legs like slender stems, the rigid projection of her bosom, her pallor blue-tinted by the moonlight, and her astonishingly fragile waist combined to give her the appearance of a phantom flower: a phantom and perverse flower, funereally pretty. The scenery of Parisian roofs and chimneys completed the illusion. It was some little ghost strayed from Montparnasse or Belleville which danced there, in the cold of the night. Her flat yet delicate face had the ghastly charm of a death's-head; long black hair descended to either side of her head, and in her hollow eyes there burned an intense alcoholic flame, whose blue ardor made me shudder.

Where had I seen that girl before? She had the slenderness of Willie and the smile of Izé Kranile, that triangle of ironic pink flesh revealing the hardness of enamel . . . oh, the shadows playing about those shoulder-blades . . . it was as if the skeleton were showing through beneath the platitude of her breasts!

All around me, the rattle of heavy breathing emerged from somnolent chests, but they were no longer snoring. My head was heavy, and the moistness of icy sweat was all over me . . . and the snowflake danced on and on.

She flared up suddenly in a flash of violet, as if bathed in projected limelight . . . and instantly flew back up into the sky as the chimneys and the roofs invaded the studio. They were now in the friezes and in the bay-window dazzlingly lit by the same flash of light. It was as if the invisible houses beneath the roofs and chimneys had suddenly surged up from the ground—and I was lying, among my Asian cushions, on the pavement of a street in the middle of a deserted Paris.

No, not Paris, but at a road-junction in some lugubrious suburb: a place bordered with newly-built houses as yet uninhabited, their doors boarded up and their grounds concealed, stretching into the distance. It was a cold and frosty night. The sky was very clear, the pavement very hard. I had a harrowing impression of absolute solitude.

From one of the streets, all of whose buildings were white, two horrid louts were emerging. They wore velvet coats, linen jackets, red handkerchiefs tied around their necks, and had vile fishy profiles beneath their high-peaked caps. They hurtled forward like a whirlwind, dragging with them a struggling woman in a ball gown. A sumptuous fur-lined cloak slid from her bare shoulders. She was blonde and delectable, but her face could not be seen and I dreaded that I might recognize it. The violent scene was utterly noiseless.

I could see nothing of the silent and brutalized woman but her lustrous back and the soft blonde hair at the back of her head. The two thugs were gripping her tightly by the arms. She had fallen to her knees, paralyzed by terror. I wanted to call out, to run to her aid, but I could not: two invisible hands, two talons, took me by the throat also. Suddenly, one of the bully-boys knocked the woman down, pressed her face to the ground, and knelt on top of her, sawing at her neck with a cutlass. Blood spurted out, splashing the green velvet pelisse, the white silk dress and the delicate golden hair with vivid red. I woke up, choking hoarsely on my stifled cries.

The other smokers were all around, sleeping heavily, with their faces contorted. The tapestry had fallen back into place over the studio skylight. The night was dark. The two candles were still burning, but the greenish light they emitted was distorting the faces. What a sight they were, those stretched-out bodies! Ethal's studio was strewn with them. We were not like that to begin with; whence came all these cadavers? For those people were no longer sleeping; they were all dead, just so many corpses. A veritable human tide of cold green flesh had risen to the flood and broken like a wave . . . but an immobile wave, cast at the feet of the Duchess of Althorneyshare—who still remained, rigid, with her great eyes wide open, seated in her armchair like some macabre idol!

121

She too was greenish beneath her make-up; it was as if the purulence of all the bodies heaped at her feet cast a humid glow upon her flaccid skin; her corruption was phosphorescent. Her diamonds had become so livid that she now seemed to be embellished with emeralds, like some bloated green goddess—and in her hieratic face, the color of hemlock, only the gleaming eyes remained white.

I watched that abomination. The ancient idol—so stiff that she seemed to be on the point of breaking up—was leaning over the body of a young girl prostrate at her feet: a supple and white cadaver outstretched upon the floor, of whom nothing could be seen but the back of the head. The back of the head was blonde and broad, like that of Maud White. Althorneyshare, with a sinister mocking laugh, put her voracious mouth to the nape of the neck as though to bite it—or, rather, to suck at it like some vile cupping-glass, for in her haste the teeth had fallen from the rotten gums.

"Maud!" I cried, brought bolt upright by anguish—but it was not Maud after which the horrible hunger of the idol was lusting, for in that same instant I saw, shining in a violet halo, the smile and the oblique expression of the tragedienne. Her mysterious mask was all aflame in that aureole above the horrid Althorneyshare . . . and everything faded away into the shadows, while a familiar voice murmured in my ear:

"The chastity of Evil is in my limpid eyes."

It was her voice—the voice of Maud White!

Smara

At this point, the sequence of my memories is disrupted.

I sank into a chaos of brief, incoherent and bizarre hallucinations, in which the grotesque and the horrible kept close company. Prostrate, as if I were being garrotted by invisible cords, I floundered in anguish and dread, oppressively ridden by the most unbridled nightmares. A whole series of monsters and avatars swarmed in the shadows, coming to life amid draughts of sulfur and phosphorus like an animated fresco painted on the moving wall of sleep.

There followed a turbulent race through space. I soared, grasped by the hair by an invisible hand of will: an icy and powerful hand, in which I felt the hardness of precious stones, and which I sensed to be the hand of Ethal. Dizziness was piled upon dizziness in that flight to the abyss, under skies the color of camphor and salt, skies whose nocturnal brilliance had a terrible limpidity. I was spun around and around, in bewildering confusion, above deserts and rivers. Great expanses of sand stretched into the distance, mottled here and there by monumental shadows. At times we would pass over cities: sleeping cities with obelisks and cupolas shining milk-white in the moonlight, between metallic palm-trees. In the extreme distance, amid bamboos and flowering mangroves, luminous millennial pagodas descended towards the water on stepped terraces.

Herds of elephants were on sentry duty, using the tips of their soft trunks to gather blue lotuses from the lakes for the gods. This was the India of Vedic legend, far beyond mysterious Egypt. At times, when we were passing overhead, strange idols stood guard upon the banks of rivers and pools. Some were angular, some cut by hatchet-blows out of solid granite; they were seated, with their hands on their knees, their petrified watchdog heads staring down into the water. Quadruple rows of teats covered the torsos of others. Some had a glitter and radiance about them, as if they were all newly forged; others seemed covered in leprous sores, so old that they no longer had faces. One had a nest of interwoven serpents crawling under the armpit; another, so beautiful that it seemed musical, had a brow gemmed with stars.

Among those idols, at prayer by the light of the moon, were the kneeling faithful; among these worshippers there were beasts as well as men.

Three matrons with heavy hips and ripe breasts were washing their linen at the foot of a Sphinx. Their hands were wringing out and beating the mysterious laundry, and the water trickling out of it was stained with blood.

One of those laundrywomen resembled Princess Olga, another the Marquise Naydorff; I did not recognize the third. An opossum, at prayer in the shadow of a Buddha, appeared to be the ghost of Meinherr Schappman: like Ethal's friend from Berlin, his careful paws were picking over a string of opal beads . . .

And a whole procession of storks, perched on a high wall beside a Turkish cemetery and silhouetted by the night, looked up as I passed overhead, and mocked me with their beaks.

Now we were flying over marshlands. All of a sudden, the hand that was carrying me released me.

Sticky walls . . . greasy ground . . . a choking and insipid darkness . . .

I was in a crypt whose vaults were oozing, lying in a strangely moving mire, which rose up in places and plunged into depths in others. It was like a warm tide, dreadfully thick and fluid, in which my rocking body was bogged down. There were silky murmurs, light rasping sounds . . . I know not what unnamable things brushed against me, an obscure crawling sensation extended from my legs to my back, vile warm breath scarified my flesh . . . and then, under my groping hands, I felt the horror of little fat and hairy bodies, all of them shifting, wriggling under and over me . . .

For a few moments, flaccid wings fluttered against my face; then frightful kisses from little pointed mouths, whose teeth were tangible, settled on my neck, on my hands, and on my face. I was a captive of hopeful caresses, my entire being tortured with cunning little bites until I lost my strength. From top to toe I was prey to innumerable blood-suckers: fetid beasts shared my body between them, insidiously violating the entirety of my naked form.

Suddenly, in the gloom which had become greenish, I saw the singularly bloated faces of the two Javanese servants, laughing mockingly. They floated in mid-air, disembodied, like two transparent varnished bladders, whitely diademed. Percolating from their half-closed eyes, as if shining through two slots, was a dead and greasy gaze. The two bladders laughed, while four hands without arms came towards my face: four soft and cadaverous hands, menacing my eyes with their sharp fingernails, splayed like claws at the ends of long golden cigar-cases.

And by the light of the two ghostly faces, I saw what a frightful enemy it was that had conquered my flesh. A whole army of enormous bats—the heavy and fat bats of the Tropics, of some vampiric species—was kissing my body and sucking my blood. The caress persisted, sometimes so precisely that I was forced to quiver with atrocious pleasure. Enfeebled, close to some climactic spasm, I stiffened in order to shake off the pullulation of that collective kiss; and as I did so something hairy, flaccid and cold entered into my mouth. Instinctively, I bit down on it, and it filled my throat with a sudden spurt of blood: the taste of some dead animal was bitter on my tongue; a tepid gruel adhered to my teeth.

It caused me to wake up . . . at last!

An alkaline burn was pricking my nostrils; a hand clapped a refreshing wad of damp linen to my temples; there was hurried movement all around me, and the half-sleep from which I was slowly emerging was penetrated by the noise of comings and goings, of voices . . . and I opened my eyes.

Ethal was kneeling beside me. Into the disorder of the studio, invaded by the morning light, came a draught of cold air from an open bay-window. It revived me. One of my hands was between those of Sir Thomas Welcome, who was slapping my palm. The anxious eyes of Maud White watched me considerately over the shoulder of her brother.

"He ought never to have smoked," opined Sir Thomas.

In the sullenness of the sad and dusty studio, the first light of dawn was the last gasp of the orgy. In the morning light the tapestry had faded to the color of urine, the busts were cadaverous, the flower-petals were a stain upon the carpet, and all along the chandeliers wax had clotted into green stalactites.

Everyone was preparing to leave. The English, brought to their feet by the negro, retired stiffly, with closed and sinister faces; they almost had to be inserted by force into their overcoats. Maud, reassured, wrapped herself in a long pelisse of straw-colored silk. Set upright on my cushions, I sipped the water tinted with arnica which Sir Thomas gave me. What pity there was in those huge bright eyes looking down at me!

"Let's go," said the Irishman, offering me his hand. "We can leave now." Monsieur White also offered a supportive hand. While we were saying our goodbyes I saw that Maud had a ring on her finger set with two big black pearls surmounted by a ruby: an enormous trefoil of gems, which I had seen on Althorneyshare's finger before the smoking-session began . . . and Maud's eyes were as fresh as water, the pallor of youth restored to them!

The Duchess was leaving Ethal's rooms at that very moment. Trailing waves of cerise silk, rustling with gold lace, bundled up to her ears, and recently patched up. Powdered and freshly replastered, her old satyr's face was smiling in the midst of a cloud of white lace.

"Time to go," she said—and left, leading away the brother and the sister.

"We must do the same," insisted Thomas Welcome. "The morning air will make you feel better. Do you want me to take you home?"

"The Duc de Fréneuse has his coupé," Ethal put in, brusquely.

"An open carriage would be better. I won't take you along the Bois—we'll take the quays, following the Seine." As Claudius made a careless gesture, he added: "Monsieur de Fréneuse lives in the Rue de Varenne and I am at the Hôtel du Palais."

PARISIAN ORGIES

by Jane de La Vaudère

A S desperate as Fiamette, André had rented a modest room in a furnished house and, trying to vanquish his pride, had returned to the editorial offices of newspapers where he had left copy. Here, he was kept waiting for two hours nursing fallacious promises; there he had been sent away, asking him to come back in a few weeks. In any case, no one read, no one had the time to read, and no room remained to insert all the articles he sent out on a daily basis. A few editors of more modest periodicals had deigned to scan André's reports or short stories, and had returned them to him, admitting that his excessively literary genre would put off the ordinary clientele of the paper.

One evening, having dined on a bread roll and a glass of milk, the poet sought a refuge with Chozelle, who welcomed him as if he had seen him the previous day.

The Master was attending scrupulously to his toilette.

Standing in front of a table laden with small pots and mysterious instruments, rounded or pointed, he was making delicate use of pencils, pastes and pads, effacing a wrinkle, accentuating a shadow, reddening or blue-tinting here and there. On the shelves there were lotions for widening the eyes, foams of crimson and ceruse white for heightening the complexion, oils for making the skin supple, unguents and balms for the hands and concentrated perfumes with delicate floral tints in crystal vaporizers.

Jacques, bare-chested, had just finished depilating himself, and he was passing a powder-puff scented with vervain over his shoulders and chest. A black satin corset was waiting on a chair, in the company of long mauve silk stockings and fluffy garters.

In spite of his sadness, André could not help smiling.

"These . . . feminine objects are for you?"

"Certainly. I've always protested, you know, against the carelessness and ugliness of men's garments. I'm setting a good example.

"Who will know?"

Slightly nonplussed, Jacques replied, warily: "Well . . . you, for a start . . ."

"It's necessary not to count on me for propaganda. I'm a savage, you know."

Chozelle shrugged his shoulders.

"We'll civilize you. Here, a mist of white heliotrope in a cloud of Chypre—that makes an appreciable mixture."

He turned his back on the poet, who was obliged to press the rubber bulb of a vaporizer and spread the perfumed mist over the Master's back and shoulder-blades.

"Pass me that mauve lawn chemise . . . oh, and my little gold chain with the talisman; I have a mania for fetishes and amulets, you know."

Mechanically, his soul in mourning, André obeyed Chozelle, who blew kisses to himself in the mirror, rounding his arm and raising the little finger in a precious fashion.

"Are there going to be women?" asked the poet, with the vague desire to numb himself, to drown the memory of defunct intoxications in other intoxications.

Jacques turned round indignantly. "Women? It's quite enough to have to put up with them at the theater! Have I ever taken you among women?"

"In sum, where are we going?"

"That's true—it's two months since you quit me and you don't know anything about my life. We're going . . . but you're not thinking of accompanying me dressed like that, I suppose?"

"I've taken a room nearby; it will only take me ten minutes to get dressed."

"Go on, then—and be beautiful."

Chozelle took André to the house of a friend of Defeuille's, very luxuriously installed, who hosted . . . esthetic soirées. The room into which the newcomers were introduced was surrounded by low divans with gilded amours on marble pedestals, holding electric sheaves, in the corners. Other amours, kneeling or re-cumbent, were presenting baskets of fruits and flowers.

Pipes and thin green pastilles were disposed on trays. A few opium-smokers were already installed for the fiction of amour, forgetfulness or oblivion.

Heating long needles in the flame of a pink wax candle burning beside them on little tables, they introduced them into the paste, which fixed a light ball thereto, and then garnished their silver pipe. The ignited opium cooked slowly, sending clouds of acrid smoke toward the ceiling, where the shadows of the dreams evoked were designed.

André felt a surge of joy. He would be able, then, to intoxicate himself, to forget, to drown his dolor in morbid fiction!

"Come on, Jacques," said Defeuille. "We're only waiting for you."

Chozelle shook his fingers, made a tour of the room, naming each guest, who returned his handshake idly. The bruised eyes had disquieting gleams, the hands, laden with rings, were agitating in feverish impatience. A little to one side, the androgyne couple only seemed to be living for one another A single pipe served for two ecstasies, and interlaced fingers bore it from the lips of one to the lips of the other.

There were very young men there, almost children, who had curious and frightened gazes, an expression of disgust and pride, dread and audacity. Their curly heads, blond or brunette, reposed on velvet cushions; their voices had a strange resonance and their vague, murky, disquieting ideas retained nevertheless a destructive charm.

The perverse nonchalance, and the cruel and cold complication of all those crackbrains troubled them reciprocally with passions and morbid desires.

Children passed by, throwing rose petals into glasses of champagne, which they presented to the guests. André emptied his in a single draught and asked for more, his soul anguished and tortured by amour.

"I see, young friend," Jacques observed, "that you're in an excellent disposition. You'll see that one doesn't get bored here."

Smokers were agitating on the divans. Hallucinated gazes were scintillating or dying, ecstatic pupils moving upwards in the nacre of the eye, and sighs occasionally escaped from panting throats. Breasts inflated, under soft silk shirts, arms apart as if to seize the shadows of dreams. A few sleepers with features contracted by a mysterious terror seemed to be creatures of nightmare, the exhausted participants in some macabre round-dance.

The flames of the pink candles vacillated under feverish breaths, and it seemed to André that the gilded amours were agitating on their pedestals. But that was certainly a hallucination produced by the first puffs of opium that rose to his brain. He was lying on a divan and had cooked the green paste, following the example of those surrounding him. A pain drilled his temples, and he thought that a clod of earth was rising beneath his skin. The impression was disagreeable; he was unaccustomed to it, and an initial nausea followed his effort. But the alert passed and he recommenced, wanting to numb himself at any cost.

There were young men there from good families, gone astray, handsome lads devoid of scruples, sick people, madmen and cunning individuals avid for fame. The mystery with which the latter surrounded themselves, the scorn that they affected for the bourgeois and women, made an aureole of strangeness for them, and in a land where nothing any longer surprises anyone, they could inflate the poisonous mushrooms of their souls "esthetically."

Even more so than at Defeuille's dinner, attitudes were free and mannerisms singularly provocative.

Chozelle, however, had disappeared with a dozen young men. André remained in the company of the smokers and a few knights of doleful countenance who were drinking silently. Acrid smoke drowned the electric jets, which no longer illuminated any more than vague Argand lamps in a distant fog.

The poet no longer knew what was real in that décor; his imagination wandered in the troubling fields of dream. It seemed to him that magical eyes were shining like embers in the night, and that Chozelle's stryges and empusas were descending from the ceiling to kiss him on the lips.

Those caresses had a viscous and bitter flavor; disgust nauseated him. The larvae and the vampires, which like blood, spread out, and, fleeing the trenchant edge of the sword, populated the shadows. He told himself that they were not spirits but fluid coagulations that one could cleave or destroy, and tried in vain to get up in order to chase them away.

However, he added, mentally, with a residue of lucidity, *human thought creates what it imagines; the phantoms of superstition project their real deformity into souls, and live the very terrors to which they give birth. The black giant extending his wings from the Orient to the Occident, the monster that destroys consciences, the frightful divinity of ignorance and fear—the Devil, in a word—is still, for an immense multitude of children of all ages a terrible reality.*

At that moment, he saw, distinctly, membranous wings, terminated by claws, palpitating above him, and a fleshless face with hollow orbits and a lipless mouth leaning over his.

The hallucinations of opium, he told himself, *are not playful. Everything that overexcites sensibility leads to depravity or crime; tears summon blood! Great emotions are like strong liquor; making habitual use of them is abusing them. Now, any abuse of the emotions perverts the moral sense; one seeks them for their own sake, one sacrifices everything to procure them; they erode the heart and crush the skull!*

He waved his arms to drive away a colossal toad with red pustules and phosphorescent eyes, which had just leapt on to his breast. For a minute he was suffocating, but then the monster disappeared.

Continuing to analyze his impressions with a singular clarity, he observed, mentally: *One arrives at the deplorable and irreparable absurdity of committing suicide in order to admire and pity oneself in seeing oneself die. Manfred, René and Lélia are type specimens of perversity all the more profound because they rationalize their un-*

healthy pride and poeticize their dementia. The light of reason does not illuminate insensible things or closed eyes; or, at least, it only illuminates them to the profit of those who can see. The word of Genesis, Let there be light! *is the victory cry of the intelligence triumphant over darkness. That word is sublime because it expresses the most beautiful thing in the world, the creation of intelligence by itself.*

André, who had closed his eyes, opened them again, and his gaze fell upon one of the torch-bearing amours. Was it another hallucination? He distinctly saw the child move, hang the electric tulips on the wall and descend from his pedestal, shaking off the gold powder that covered his skin. The other amours did the same, and, holding one another by the hand, led a farandole around the smokers.

Their bodies shone under the gilt, they laughed, and sometimes let themselves fall on to divans.

André lifted the little pipe to his lips again, and a freshness descended and ran through his veins. He felt a great wellbeing invade him; a thousand new thoughts whirled in his head. He smoked and smoked again; then he spoke in a voice steeped in tears; an extraordinary sensibility gripped him, as if all his other sensations had dissolved, saturated in an immense desire to weep.

He tried to get up, but an intolerable pain drilled his temples. Everything around him was spinning: the tables, the drinkers, and the amours sighing on a bed of roses and gold powder. Specters agitated, laughing. Then he heard his voice, which had a sound like a cracked bell, and he did not understand what he was talking about. He was increasingly duplicated, his thinking and reasoning being witnessed, mute, gagged and confused, the decline of the other.

The doors opened very wide, and he saw Chozelle advancing again, dressed as a woman, and displaying, under a short skirt, his mauve silk stockings. Other men followed in analogous disguise, causing gauze corsages to seethe over flat chests, rounding out the biceps of wrestlers while simpering, and quivering like voluptuous gypsy women.

It was too much. André was seized by frenetic, inextinguishable laughter, and then everything was abolished within him.

The fay of opium is a mistress who refuses herself at first, but soon lavishes her lovers with the most intoxicating caresses. Almost every day, having finished his work, the poet plunged into the hallucinating inebriation. Thus, his nights, populated by phantoms, did not have the banal bitterness of reality. He lived a double life, caressing in dreams a smiling and faithful Fiamette, who did not sell her kisses, but put her soul on her mouth in order to offer it to him, like a flower in a virginal cup that no other lip had brushed.

But the young man's nerves were exacerbated by that game; he had continual vertigos, stiffening in the street in order to maintain a firm stride, and sometimes, on the sly, leaning on walls in order to recover his strength. His memory, once marvelous, had lacunae; he often required a fatiguing mental tension to recall the simplest things. In those dispositions, he put up a vague resistance to Jacques' caprices, whose demands took on an increasingly aggressive character.

They went out at hazard, when the sun's rays, like golden baldrics, striped the narrow streets of the quarters of vice and misery. They went past sordid boutiques, abattoirs black with coagulated blood where quarters of meat hung from iron hooks, along with the livers and hearts of cattle with huge protruding blue arteries. Water from flower pots dripped on their heads and "seamstresses" leaning out of mansards laughed on seeing them shake themselves like dogs under the overly impetuous jets of their watering cans.

But Jacques welcomed those feminine whims without amenity and fled toward more discreet dens of misery, eclipsed behind the door of some hovel that stood ajar, while André continued walking at random, searching for he knew not what: appeasement or dolor, visions of idylls or murder.

In the mills of Montmartre, Pascal tried to stun his young friend, showing him masquerades à la Gavarni, displays of women for the taking or for sale on tumbrils decorated with flowers and pennants, collapsing the naked flesh, as in pedlars' trays offered to lovers of spicy delicacies. Neurasthenic corteges of Bacchus and Pan blew pipes and ran out of breath behind the laughing beautiful girls, and a wind of dementia caused the plumes of barbarian chiefs and enchanted Lohengrins to oscillate, in the midst of a crowd drunk on cries and animal odors.

Volleys of laughter became so loud that the orchestra sometimes stopped, losing the key and the measure.

There were Romans with naked arms and proud torsos, slaves with strides impeded by chains, their hands bound; and torturers brandishing pincers, boots and flesh-tearing scissors. Hindus dressed in white, Talapoins coiffed with cords and beautiful Moorish women tinkling with barbaric jewels were delivering themselves to epileptic tremors while awaiting the principal procession. Under the raw light of electric tulips, all the neuroses of the Parisian festival passed by, supremely made up.

As at the Folies Perverses, androgynous couples were circulating, enlaced, and in the near effacement of sexual nature, the thought of disquieting anomalies took increasingly deep root.

Journalists were taking notes, collecting fruitful publicity; demi-mondaines were showing off their jewelry, more enthusiastic for renown than homages. Only the artists and the models were really amusing themselves, without posing, happy with their well-earned success. And there truly was an entire bouquet of pretty girls there, with fine limbs and breasts offered in voluptuous cups.

"Take your choice," said Pascal. "Life is short and you're still young enough to be loved for yourself. I can see gazes fixed on you, and they're not grim. If you wanted . . . !"

"No," sighed André. "I don't have the heart for pleasure . . ."

"Bah! Try anyway."

"I wouldn't know what to say. Amorous words freeze on my lips . . ."

"They'll love you more for it, disdainful beau!"

"Isn't it better to love than to be loved?"

"Pooh! Those are big words for very little. An hour of sweet embrace doesn't commit you to anything. One drinks from a cup of flesh as one drinks a little amontillado from a cup of crystal when one is thirsty, and one goes to sleep without regret. There's no question here of sentiment, and the girls with firm breasts who offer the wine of amour don't want you to give them your soul in exchange. They wouldn't know what to do with it, poor things!"

"I believe, friend, that you're mistaken. A woman requires even more tenderness than caresses, and her laughter is always near to tears."

"Poet!"

"Perhaps . . . and even more so today than yesterday, because I'm more unhappy."

Pascal shrugged his shoulders. "Go back to your Fiamette, then."

"No. I don't want to. I can't."

"Because you love her too much. When I told you that amour only makes people do stupid things."

The bays of the great hall of the Moulin Bleu[1] had been converted into boxes decorated in a bizarre and charming fashion. Women were emerging from floral

_____

1 Evidently the Moulin Rouge, where the Bal de Quat'z'Arts was held after 1893, the author presumably thought a substitution appropriate, as she had in the satirical transformation of the Folies Bergère into the Folies Perverses.

sprays, showing a corner of their nudity, and the corollas of roses were mingled with the corollas of breasts, summoning the butterflies of the kiss.

At midnight the procession was organized, in which Gaul, Egypt, India, Assyria, Persia, Phoenicia, etc. were all represented. Prehistoric times were rendered with a fortunate abundance of imagination, and an ironic fantasy that always attained the unexpected.

There were Hindu pyres there, surrounded by bayaderes with gauze langoutis, tragic mourners and Brahmin sacrificers. Egyptian houses, boats of flowers, gallant guinguettes, Byzantine palaces and prehistoric grottoes offered women of all colors, all sellers of lust.

The Moloch of *Salammbô* reared up in a corner, gigantic and terrifying, and the faint sounds of kisses departed from niches where cardboard gods raised their murderous arms. The priestesses of amour, always ready for sweet sacrifices, only had to disturb their jewels to offer their flesh to caresses.

A young man of almost supernatural beauty was leading the Phoenician bull, and prostitutes threw him flowers, begging for a glance from his wild velvet eyes.

André could not help admiring the harmonious arrangement of everything, and if the lover was still suffering, the artist, fond of beautiful forms and beautiful décor, experienced a secret contentment. He did not admit it, however, fearful of Pascal's skeptical smile, and his slightly humiliating consolations of a man blasé with regard to the promises and the disappointments of the heart.

"You see," said the artist, "the man who is in love is like a torture victim turning on that wheel. Every foreseen turn brings the same tortures. Amour is always similar, and he does not pardon his victims."

He was pointing at an enormous wheel on a cart preceded by barbarians clad in animal skins, armed with steel blades to butcher the body. All around, the condemned charged with chains were groaning; two supple young women were agitating the curls of their hair in the flames, and the heads of virgins, freshly severed, opened their languorous eyes on the ends of golden pikes. A Buddha mounted on a frog brought up the rear of the cortege.

Pascal had dragged André to supper. Installed beside a pretty girl of fifteen, he was frightfully drunk, and had no idea how he was going to get home. Only the sound of a soft voice remained in his ear, and he had discovered in a pocket of his carnival costume a red poppy similar to the one that the child was wearing in her hair.

In that epoch the disciple had a very regrettable adventure.

Jacques had the custom of going to a mysterious location, elegantly perverse, about which he only spoke in a low voice, with alarmed and glorious expressions of very pleasing effect.

A considerable number of those equivocal establishments exist in Paris, which the police tolerate because important people frequent them and the scandal of an arrest would have a great resonance. The descents of the law are thus only habitual in houses of the second rank, the more modest clientele of which cannot protest.

Outside, nothing denounces the special seductions of the place. Honest shop windows display, through transparent curtains, a few rows of tables and a counter where a woman of mature years—the only one in the place—is enthroned. Pale esthetes are drinking bitter wines the color of mahogany or amethyst, and chatting politely about one thing and another. At the back, a felted door that closes of its own accord gives access to a luxurious and barbaric salon, which recalls those of brothels. No pretty women, alas, but a display of special absurdity. English types, above all, flock there, displaying the awkwardness of tall clergymen in frock-coats, with varnished shoes and rings with large bezels on every finger. There are also aggressive bulldog faces with ears devoid of lobes, surprising baboons, flaccid individuals with bloodshot eyes and idiots with the faces of cut-throats, flashy foreigners and lunatics.

At midnight, the fête begins, and the program scarcely varies. As among Defeuille and his friends, the interpreters of the "drawing room comedies" decked out in feminine costumes, put on abundant curled wigs with reflections of gold or flame, rub themselves with ceruse, oils and balms with subtle essences, to give themselves the illusion that they are exactly what they scorn. Very young men truly resembling women, who almost have the right to be proud of their slim stature and their large dark-ringed eyes, are the most surrounded, the most pampered.

Full of resignation, André laced the Master's corset, fastened his mauve satin garters and fixed verbena cushions to all the futile hollows of his feminine armature.

Jacques stretched his arms, struck poses, and smiled at himself in the huge mirror with three faces, in which he could see himself generously.

"Am I at my best, this evening?" he asked, pinching his ear-lobe, after having passed a moist finger over the eyebrows in order to fluff up the velveteen.

"You're full of seduction, dear Master."

"Why don't you want to be one of ours, my child?"

"I don't know," the young man murmured, with a discreet irony. "I don't have the vocation."

"Alas, in spite of my lessons, I haven't found in you the docile pupil for whom I was searching. You don't have the soul of the divine androgynes who, alone, bring some charm to life! If you were even a faithful companion, a submissive and comprehensive disciple!"

Resigned, André did not riposte; his brow was dolorous and his thought vague, almost always blurred by the abuse of narcotics, and Jacques softened.

"It would be so pleasant, however, to be only one, only to exist for that ardent union of heart and soul! Look, the scarab of this clasp is scratching me, and this whalebone is digging into my ribs . . ."

"Yes, Master."

"This evening, I'm no longer, and better, than your Master, I'm . . . but why that hangdog face? Are you ill?"

"Indeed . . ."

And the young man, paler than the ceruse paste the covered Jacques' cheeks, let himself fall into an armchair, experiencing something akin to a shock to the heart, followed by the breakdown of a poorly-greased machine.

"What's the matter, then?"

"If you'll permit, this evening I'll stay at home."

"No, I want you to come with me, in order that I can lean on your shoulder and mirror my eyes in yours. You'll inspire me with a few harmonious verses on the grandeur of our absolutely superior esthetic mission. Here, get my clothes, and put this gold powder in your hair."

André had therefore known, after many other nostalgic gatherings, the rendezvous of the Labybird, the honest cabaret with the banal provincial front window. He had witnessed, in an elegant stupidity, the gallant tourneys of florid knights; then, drunk on peppery wines, mingled with extracts of tuberose and acacia, his soul still capsized by his opium dreams, he had lost the notion of time.

Old readings came back to him, especially that in which Petronius recounts in the *Satyricon* the debauched life of Rome. Pigs crowned with myrtle and roses had the same curiosities and strange ruts as our enervated Parisians. In hospitable houses open to amorous passers-by, one glimpsed, between placards, indecisive nudities, brief couplings to the chords of barbaric music. There were disquieting incubi with the heavy finery of courtesans, plastered with white greasepaint, primped and perfumed, asexual individuals, plump and unhealthy, with wide empty eyes circled with kohl.

Those scenes, cut out in the quick of ancient mores, were almost the same as those played out there in paltry fashion for a few initiates. Adulterated joys of Sodom, unrealizable desires of new sensualists, disgust of a decrepit civilization, unconsciousness of vice become necessity, all the aberrations of our modern literature are found in the *Satyricon*, and André remembered its enticing debauches and erudite hysterias.

In his sleep, he now saw singular things: an elevated throne rose up before him, enameled with polychromatic tiles, encrusted with beryls and opals. Sprawling on the steps were adolescents with naked, imprecise forms, with slender limbs decked with jewels, and Jacques, seated on the broad seat, caressed them one by one, and then cut their throats slowly without a muscle in his face twitching. Blood spattered the steps; the bodies, in brief spasms, rolled down one after another.

His jaundiced, parchment complexion striped with wrinkles, his gaze fixed with cold cruelty, Chozelle reddened his hands in that work of butchery, lingering over warm touches, in the perverse joy of the agonies that he had determined.

Then there were other scenes, lascivious dances of naked young men, whose loins undulated under girdles of sardonyxes and emeralds, whose necklaces spat sparks, swarming over flat chests like chameleons of flame.

And a hermaphrodite detached himself from the group, displayed pale limbs, of a perfect beauty, and

146

mimed Salome's dances before Herod. André thought he was seeing Fiamette, but a mutilated, strange, vengeful Fiamette.

It was not only the swooning dancer that was reanimating the senses of an old man by means of sighs and soft flesh, quivering with lust; it was Sin itself, an adorable, hybrid and venomous corolla, swelling for the annihilation of a race.

Fiamette—for it was her—mounted the steps of the throne, bent over the tetrarch, offered him her scarcely-emerged breasts, the nipples of which were bleeding, and the enlaced couple disappeared in swirls of mist, and then flew away, to be lost in the ceiling, while André uttered a cry of rage.

And other hallucinations, after a moment of anguish, populated his semi-slumber.

From time to time, he emerged from his nightmares, exhausted, worn out, his thought capsized in terror, and he heard, above the noise of poorly closed bedrooms, the dull, regular and feverish shock of arteries that were beating madly beneath the skin of his neck.

"André, I assure you that this russet wig would suit you marvelously, and this girdle of peridots with the enamel scarab would fasten without difficulty around your loins. You can sing to us, in a soft voice, the amorous chants I've taught you. Do you want to?"

"Leave him alone; can't you see that he's drunk and can't hear us."

"Then let's put these gold lamé veils on him ourselves."

Jacques took André in his arms, and the disciple, continuing his dream, allowed himself to be undressed without resistance. Under the rain of flowers that submerged him, he heard, confusedly, the light plaints of syrinx flutes and ewe-skin drums, the fury of sistra of iron and ivory, and he thought he was at a Roman orgy in which the games would unfold in floods of wine and blood.

He was Heliogabalus, and the Priests of the Sun were dancing before the obscene symbol of the Black Stone, brandishing torches whose perfumed drops were falling all around him. He did not refuse the adorations, conscious of his august role, and smiled while an entire people prostrated themselves, awaiting a word from his painted lips.

The priests of Cybele kissed him on the corner of his lips, and invited him to take part in the fête of voluptuous Nature.

He was lying on a very low bed in the form of a gondola, his breast and legs naked, with a curly wig that covered his forehead. Cassolettes were burning beside him, and he was rolling the pink beads of a coral necklace between his fingers. His eyes filled with an incessant mirage, he respired warm aromatic smoke that exasperated his desires, and he felt procreated for the advent of the androgyne intermediate between woman and man: the definitive triumph of the principle of life. He thought that he had both sexes, and he rejoiced in the idea of engendering himself in the glory of his omnipotence.

Supplicant arms were extended toward him, however; if he disdained the caresses, he did not repel them, generous in his triumph, and his hallucinated gaze was lost in a tumult of shimmering silks and gemstones in which fragments of flesh blushed.

Jacques leaned over him, and hugged his shoulders more and more narrowly, while a slave fanned them with a large flabellum. And there was a softness that the disciple would not have dared to suspect. His thought floated randomly; he no longer imagined other delights.

"My child of election," said Jacques, "how I'm quivering in sensing you here, in my power without revolt. You have finally understood the goal of your existence, the mystery of your destiny, and nothing will separate us henceforth." He did not cease kissing his eyes, hugging him, palpating his body with a nervous impulsiveness, similar to a delirious crisis.

The slave agitated the flabellum more limply in the thickened air, and the golden wax candles let their burning tears fall on the white tunics of the priests of Cybele, kneeling as for a sacrifice.

Docile, André allowed himself to be manipulated. Then there was a noise in the corridors; the witnesses suddenly rose up to the ceiling, and everything disappeared in floods of mist.

The disciple recovered consciousness under a rude fist that was striking him, and an unknown voice enjoined him to put on his clothes, which men were throwing at him disdainfully.

He got dressed, without understanding, as if in a dream. It was only later that he learned that a police raid had disturbed the esthetic fête at the Ladybird cabaret.

He was incarcerated, along with the proprietor of the establishment, but thanks to Chozelle's influence, he only spent a few days in prison.

THE MALAY

by Jean Richepin

POOR as I was, and so poorly dressed, but with my good twenty-five-year-old arms under my jacket, I'll be damned if I feared unfortunate encounters, even in that sinister quarter where I lived among the worst riff-raff in London. The most cunning and boldest rogues saw immediately, judging me at a glance, that there wasn't much to clip from me—might as well say nothing—and that the nothing in question would, in case of an attack, be vigorously defended. Thanks to which, and also to a certain knowledge of English slang, I could take a bath of poverty and rascality, in total security, whenever I wanted, in the mud of that underworld, reputedly so dangerous.

I was, therefore, if not anxious, at least a trifle astonished on the day when I noticed that I was being followed, positively followed, but the strange individual whose face, gait and costume had said to me the other night: "Hey! De Quincey's Malay!"

He did, in fact, resemble in a miraculous fashion the fantastic apparition described in the *Confessions of an Opium-Eater*: the same emaciated face, simultaneously pale and tenebrous; the same hallucinated gaze; the same exotic rags; the same spectral stride; and also something unspecifiable, almost inexpressibly dream-like and symbolic—as if within that wanderer all of Asia, ecstasized by opium, surged forth, and as if the individual, visible and tangible, and hence real, was nothing himself but one of the fugitive clouds taking on substance in that ecstasy.

Yes, thus he had appeared to me the other night, that strange individual—on the night when I had gone to pay a visit to one of the palaces of "just, powerful and subtle opium," as De Quincey the Visionary puts it.

A somewhat lamentable palace, however! A kind of cupboard above the back room of a shop, with a wooden divan for its only furniture. It reminded you of a sentry-box—and what a stink the ten or twelve unfortunates lying on the floor exhaled, from their greasy and damp rags, their sweaty bodies, in that close room with the low ceiling, overheated by the large flame of a gas-jet! But a palace all the same, inhabited by emperors and gods, a palace whose bare walls stirred incessantly in the most magical and paradisal décors.

"Hey! De Quincey's Malay!"

Yes, that was exactly what I had said—or, rather, thought—on seeing the strange individual enter, and then sit down facing me, and in following him, a few moments later—but a long, long time—through the course of interminable voyages in which he was my guide, silent and enigmatic, through all the floras and faunas, all the architectures and crowds, all the multi-colored lights and tenebrous sensualities of the most marvelous and monstrous Orient.

To such an extent that on awakening, on returning from my magical pilgrimage, when I had found myself once again on the wooden divan, between two heaps of human flesh like two cadavers, a scarcely-resuscitated cadaver myself, observing that the strange individual was no longer there, I had doubted that I had ever seen him other than in a dream, through my memories of reading De Quincey, as an evocation of the opium.

But no! Here he was, alive, apparently solid, no longer an apparition of smoke—since, that morning, in the open air, walking through the swarming crowd, every last trace of smoke had evaporated from my brain. I was in full possession of my faculties, my perception clear and my senses sharp, my eye as bright as a basilisk's. And he was there, the Malay; it was really him!

Certainly, the first time I had turned around a little while before, obscurely troubled by a gaze drilling into the back of my neck, and I had seen the man following me, I could have believed it a reflorescence of my nocturnal dream—all the more so when, abruptly, the man disappeared into the crowd, vanishing like a furtive and fulgurant vision.

The second time, however, half an hour later, he presented himself to me face to face, in the manner of someone seeking to recognize and be recognized. It is true that then, again, when I mechanically closed my eyes to avoid the extraordinary glare of his, he had disappeared as if he had been swallowed up by the ground. Nevertheless, I was sure of not having been, this time, the victim of a persistent hallucination.

Furthermore, during the last half hour, it was neither once nor twice but a good ten times that I had been haunted by him. Sometimes, I sensed him at my heels, of which I made certain by turning my head. Sometimes, I almost bumped into him at a street corner. Sometimes, I rubbed shoulders with him in the eddies of the crowd, where I had him for a neighbor for a few strides, his arm brushing mine with a quasi-communicative pressure, and his eyes, his nostalgic eyes, burning with fever, trying to enter into a mute dialogue with my own fugitive eyes.

Finally, now, I could no longer maintain the slightest doubt as to the reality of his presence. The tailing, closer and closer, less and less concealed, had reached the point at which, in the bar into which I had gone to escape the pursuit, the man had come in behind me and, on the empty bench where I had sat down, the man had come to sit down beside me.

Immediately, of course, I stopped avoiding his gaze and turned to face him squarely, frowning, my expression hostile, teeth clenched, nose to nose.

His face suddenly expressed a profound sadness. Two large tears ran down his cheeks. Then, gently, he placed a hand on my breast, and began to speak—or, rather, to whisper—in a language that I did not understand, but in an extremely musical and seductive voice. One might have thought him a child singing like a bird.

Not knowing how to respond, I asked the barmaid for two glasses of whisky, and offered one of them to the stranger. He wet his lips with it, then gave it back to me with a gesture telling me to finish it, and that he wanted to do the same with mine. That was a politeness customary in the low taverns of London, and I complied.

After which I said to the man in English: "Now that we're friends, tell me what you want and why you've been following me as you have."

I saw in his large desolate eyes, however, that he did not understand what I had said. I was, therefore, obliged, like him, to resort to sign-language. This time, he understood.

From the folds of his belt he took a long silk ribbon, which he unrolled in front of my face, asking me, by means of gestures, to read the characters that were inscribed on it. At the same time he explained to me, still by gestures, but quite clearly, that the inscription represented an enormous and fabulous treasure of gold and precious stones. He expressed gold by pouring out, between his thumb and index-finger, imaginary coins that accumulated in cascades. He signified precious stones by making his fingernails shine, polished like onyx, and blinking his eyelids very rapidly, within the fissures of which his eyes flashed and sparkled like diamonds.

I demonstrated that I had missed nothing of his mute discourse, and he seemed delighted—so delighted that he flung his arms around my neck and embraced me, weeping, as if he had gone mad.

155

I had, however, paid close attention to the silken ribbon, and I had recognized that the characters were Sanskrit, of which I possessed a vague knowledge: not enough, certainly, to translate the exceedingly long inscription, but sufficient to decipher a few scattered words. I pointed them out to him with my finger and mimed their meanings. One meant "king," which I interpreted by the simulation of a crown on my head. Another signified "sky," and another "earth," which were easy for me to render. Finally, one word recurred frequently, which signified one of the mysterious names of the god Shiva. I happened to know that the word is represented in Hindu architecture by a certain hieratic design. I traced the outline of that design in the air, after having touched the word on the silken ribbon.

From these various identifications, the man must have imagined that I understood the entire inscription, and that undoubtedly struck him with terror. So, at least, I judged on seeing him suddenly throw himself at my knees, frightened, his hands trembling, like a criminal begging for mercy. At the same time, he resumed his bird-like twittering, but this time with extreme volubility, and in an exceedingly shrill tone, which was deafening.

Unfortunately, I was not the only one who was deafened. A drunkard who was sleeping in a corner was woken up by it, and rushed at the poor devil, who was still prostrate.

I tried to launch myself to the unfortunate fellow's aid, but he thought, on the contrary, that I was joining in with his aggressor and falling upon him. Admittedly, the three of us composed, on the ground, an incomprehensible amalgam. At any rate, by the time I found myself sitting astride the drunkard, the other had decamped.

With one bound I was in the street, searching for him—but in vain, as one might imagine. Agile, slippery and furtive as he was, how could I tell where that human eel had replunged into that human mud?

I was never to see the strange individual again.

In the opium den, to which I returned in an attempt to obtain some information, I got none. The man had only been there once, on the night when I was there myself.

Who was he? What did he want with me? What did the inscription on the silk ribbon represent? Why did he want to make me, in particular, party to it? And then, why that terror at the idea that I was able to translate it? Was that exile in possession of a fabulous treasure? Had he stolen it? So many questions without answers!

And how many hypotheses I formulated, with regard to that bizarre adventure, as marvelous and absurd as a dream!

That it was only a dream I have not believed for a long time, having had before me so much evidence that proved its visible and tangible reality during those few hours of my life. But today, through the distant mists of the past, when I find that admittedly-implausible story in my memory, I sometimes wonder whether the powerful and subtle opium is as just as De Quincey claims, and whether it is not instead a very mischievous demon, which amused itself with me by parading me for an entire morning through the mirages of a hallucination as consistent as life itself—for I forgot to mention that I never found the bar in which the scene had unfolded again either.

And yet, what a tableau it all makes, distinctly outlined in vigorous colors, in the museum of my memory!

THE GREEN GOD

by Gabriel de Lautrec

MATHIAS CORBUS was at the rendezvous on the edge of the wood. It was the hour when the street-lights were being illuminated and the other life of the city was beginning. After a few minutes, he saw Jean Derève arriving, and both of them, after having consulted one another, descended toward the river by way of sloping streets, through the new constructions that were springing up in those parts.

"If it is necessary to believe historians, the exodus of peoples always takes place from east to west, in the direction of the sun. It seems that humankind, a natural product of the warmth poured out by the star, incessantly marches with it in order to remain under its vivifying influence for as long as possible. Our most ancient memories show us nations, still assembled in families, descending from the high plateaux of Asia when the soil became insufficient for the increased number of human beings. Invasions of barbarians covered Europe successively, and the flow of hordes, like a tide, unfurled over the plains of the continent to come to die definitively, on the beaches of Brittany and Spain, against the other tide of the ocean. But after centuries of apparent repose, the movement recommences, and bold navigators, departing for gold or glory to discover new worlds, are only precursors.

"Like peoples, cities, in their march, follow the course of the sun. Paris develops in that direction, and also that of the river, the two being fortunately parallel on the road of progress. It is natural that one descends more easily than one moves against the current of a watercourse. That is also an influence. The former, however, is the stronger. When they are united their accord gives a perfect result. Everything in the city goes from east to west. Even the lightning obeys that strange commandment. The storms accompany the Seine. It is toward Auteuil and Passy that new houses are constructed. The center of the city, which was once marked by the Place Royale, is moving westwards every day. Life on the boulevards is gradually abandoning one extremity for the other. It is necessary to see in such facts not the manifestation of pure chance but the application of laws as inherent to humankind as its own existence.

"How easy it would be, if one wanted to do it, to multiply those relationships and establish mysterious correspondences that might become clearer by comparison! It is not child's play, but an effort toward unity. It is no use being an observer, if one is content to collect innumerable observations without seeking the connections between them. On the contrary, the person who

160

begins to perceive that everything is similar is marching on the road to truth. At every step his thought penetrates one of the secrets of nature. It glimpses the great secret, the simplicity and the harmony.

"The puerilities of the ancients sometimes have the same profound meaning as the modern visions. Empedocles compares the Earth to a vast animal of which forests are the hair and the divine sea the sweat. Evidently, such comparisons sin in that they take as reality one of the objects of comparison and want the other to be identified with it, instead of supposing that the two are different projections of the same law. But it is also necessary to admit, in those phrases, more than wordplay. We make Paris the heart of the world without expressing anything by the vocable other than a striking analogy. How do we know that there isn't a more rigorous similarity?

"One can, for instance, look at the maps of Paris found in the carriages of the circular railway as little images rotating around their object. The red line of the limit gives the strange form of a heart, with a regular depression at the corresponding point, turned, moreover toward the west, as if drawn by the sun. A puerile assimilator might pursue the comparison, which does not go very far. The mountains and the woods, and the river, the great artery, lent themselves to ingenious reasoning. The idea, following its route, falls into paradox, but is it not sufficient for astonishment that one can find such pretext for the game, which seems plausible.

"Nothing is known. The world is infinite, but the same forms ought to appear at all the levels of infinity.

We must be for some what others are for us. The animalcules that live on the surface of our body doubtless, surely, have glorious civilizations, and inexpiable wars for the possession of the area between two pores of our skin. Reflections of that nature enable scorn for the infantile brain of a Napoléon. Earths surged forth from the sun like globes of fire cool slowly, and the crystallizations produced at their surface are the dwellings, temples and palaces of human beings, with their silky and emotional life. The same phenomena appear on the sparks sprung from our hearth during the brief moment, relative to their magnitude, before they become grains of cold ash, like the dead moon in the sky.

"We only know the beings that are on the scale of our eyes. Animalcules do not suspect the personal reality of our body. Nor can we say anything about the immense body on the surface of which we agitate childishly. All hypotheses remain plausible and are lost, one after another, in the void of our thought. But it would be strange if our body alone were endowed with consciousness and other assemblages of material elements were all deprived of it, for the entertainment of our pride."

Jean Derève and Mathias Corbus had passed Les Invalides, saluting in passing the bridge of arches of alliance launched in honor of barbaric borrowers of the north and had taken the Boulevard Saint-Germain at the Pont de la Concorde. Paris was animated in the special atmosphere of the evening. They approached the warm streets where youth exasperates its desire to live and numb itself in the light, far into the night. They passed groups of students and artists, accompanied by young women, some of whom were pretty.

"The pretty girls, launched into voluptuous circulation every day, head for this quarter in small numbers, because it forms a city within the city, less Parisian than provincial, with its floating population and its sellers of the illusions with which twenty-year-old appetites are content. The future advocates or physicians, a little sad to have seen the old brasseries disappear, play at house and manille with women who are often also from the provinces, and who populate that Babel in which the unfortunate confusion of languages reigns. Observers who reappear, by virtue of a slightly perverse taste, in the milieux through which they once passed, note one evening by chance the face of a charming young woman whom they will not find the next day, rapidly abducted. Those who remain, in growing old, take on a redoubtable aspect.

"More interesting forms are encountered in painters' studios. But again, the good models present irreproachable parts of the body more often than faces. It is better then to contemplate a marble, for the body only has its flower of expression in the smile and the gaze. All beautiful bodies are similar. It is the eyes that change them, and the lips that allow the various souls within them to become transparent. It is difficult for a man to die of regret for a beautiful form if he has not initially been seduced by the special charm of the face, and by the play of physiognomy that enables a woman to be herself and not a random other. In spite of the philosophy of Plato, what attaches us to the beloved is not beauty, but *her* beauty. That is so true that everyone searches eternally for the same features. The man who has been abandoned turns round when he perceives on passing, even ugly, someone who reminds him of the lost gesture. It is possible to remain indifferent to the most authentic grace that is not that of yesteryear.

"And how few heads really have an expression! One ought not, it is true, reason from merchants of pleasure. It is too easy, by taking illusory examples, to demonstrate that amour is an illusion. Glimpsed in the evening, under artificial light, some of them, at least, seem to have a personality. The hair and the hat, the different usage of make-up or speech separates one from another, and can, for a few minutes, stimulate special curiosities in the human beast. But with what amazement one observes, on awakening after the good or bad night, that, taking advantage of the obscurity, a demon expert in facile jokes has come to place on the shoulders of the occasional lady, in exchange for yesterday's face, the same colorless and banal head. They are all the same when morning comes. It is an observation made by young men whom the rigor of fate condemns, as well as their sentimental idleness, to similar amours. But they perceive subsequently that those women, fortunately, are not all women."

The two strollers had sat down, fatigued by a true voyage, on the terrace of a noisy café. The interior light spread out violently over the sidewalk. Young women were circulating between the tables. Fragments of witty conversation could be heard from neighboring groups.

Mathias Corbus and Jean Derève leaned back, the soul abandoned like the body in the nonchalance of a public bath. They summoned a waiter, who brought them coffee and beer.

"You mentioned Saint-Maur," said Mathias, "and you expect me to reveal to you, more explicitly than him, what secret of dreams is included in the usage of poisons. You desire that they transport you to the ideal realm where existence is happy and the game of personality becomes facile. I disapprove of those procedures. Too numerous are those who demand from accursed substances an embellishment of life, however illusory. The attempt can be profitable, however, if it is not excessively prolonged.

"Some people are idle or dare not develop their power. One day, by chance, under a new influence, they sense that they are living differently. It is not, believe me, merely to savor a dubious pleasure, of which one is never sure, that one should make such attempts. It happens that an unusual shock suddenly shows a person his soul. Morphine and opium enable an unknown sensibility to surge forth from the depths. What a temptation for the man to whom those new emotions are revealed! What a desire to rise, if not without danger, at least without effort, above surly life! 'It's necessary to be intoxicated,' as Baudelaire says, 'by wine, opium or poetry.' But the man who is intoxicated ceases to be himself, in the good as well as the bad sense.

"The dream is evidently to conciliate enthusiasm and clarity, to retain the direction of one's being and at the same time to abandon oneself to charming influ-

165

ences. A very difficult accord, I fear. Perhaps only those are right who do not care about obtaining from poisons an increase of their energy but who only seek enchantment and forgetfulness. Too frequently, life is a bad dream; and one ought to be indulgent to the invalids who demand the liberating opium loudly. Existence easily becomes sinister when one has some sensibility.

"The man who does not arouse the ardor of a profound passion drags himself along lamentably. Fortunate are martyrs and saints! Fortunate is the cenobite who prays in the cold silence of the cell and sobs toward God! All those of us who agitate in a puerile manner do not even succeed in the miserable enterprise of amusing ourselves. For my part, I am interested in certain things, and I spend my days appropriately. I regard myself as satisfied, because I am not ambitious; and I have not found unhelpful, in order to give myself at intervals a different vision, and seize various aspects, the usage of certain drugs, of which my curiosity has, in any case, never made me a slave. But it would be infantile to allow oneself to be mastered and to live under an influence. I have sampled all intoxications, but I have known, by contrast, at other times, the charm of asceticism. And I have become capable—this alone is important—of suggesting to myself the most various states of soul, simply by the exercise of my will. I have told you that additives are only profitable in order to learn to do without them.

"They are numerous, and their choice varies in accordance with countries and people. Women take morphine, and so do physicians, on occasion. It is the unfortunate remedy for insupportable pain. But the danger is that one contracts therefrom a mortal malady whose course is interrupted. I am also repelled by the surgical procedure. I believe that opium smoking, with its immobile dreams, is better suited to idle socialites. It also possesses navigators from Oriental lands, who have retained after their return the habits acquired out there. But the material difficulties are an obstacle to the diffusion. Furthermore, the initiation is rather slow. That last inconvenience is not unique to opium. It has saved many hesitant individuals.

"The people have wine and alcohol, of which it is better not to speak.

"You know that in Ireland, ether is propagating rapidly, completing the annihilation, by new means, of the vague inhabitants of that country.[1] The drug has primarily physical effects. It gives an extraordinary lightness of body and mind. Perhaps you have occasionally eaten strawberries dipped in ether. But the insupportable and persistent odor hardly permits a correct man to give himself to that vice; everyone perceives his mania. I have a horror of manifestations and involuntary confessions. In any case, it seems to me that there can be no question of drinking ether. The

---

1 Ether-drinking became something of a craze in Ireland in the 1880s before it was curtailed by law in 1891, when ether was classified as a poison and strict controls introduced on its sale and distribution. Modern sources suggest that it was popularized by a physician named Kelly, who marketed it as a medicament, and was widely taken up in a backlash against the Temperance Movement, allowing people who had "made the Pledge" to get drunk without having to consume alcohol.

taste, even dissimulated by mixtures, is disagreeably intense. I believe that one obtains sufficient impressions by sniffing a flask. The brain is rapidly affected and one arrives without difficulty at the state of fortunate semi-consciousness in with everything around one is blurred, in which sounds and visions are metamorphosed and attenuated, although our senses, instead of losing their acuity, acquire an astonishing and seemingly fragile sensibility.

"Although ether is in the first rank among the accursed beverages, it is improbable that opium, of which I have spoken, can be known in its real effects by the usage of laudanum. The complicated apparatus of smokers would be inexplicable if a few drops of liquid had the same virtue. That is undoubtedly not the case. It is necessary to smoke the resin, in the Oriental fashion. Our mores do not permit that easily. And I conclude therefrom, for everything has a cause, that the usage of the poison necessitates certain habits that we do not have. It is suited to the temperaments of hot countries, where the soul willingly follows the slope of torpor. The liquid extract scarcely provokes anything but visual impressions, or, rather, an amusing deformation of vision. All stupefiants, in any case, by means of the dilatation of the pupils, act in that regard to a greater or lesser extent.

"I believe, moreover, that a person who uses one or another of those substances habitually, will not experience very different effects if he tries a new one in passing. Sensitivity exasperated in a certain direction retains a tendency to the same awakenings. A hashish-eater taking opium or ether one day, by virtue of necessity or curiosity, will have that day, as usual, a hashish intoxication.

"I don't know whether that observation has been noted before. I don't believe so.

"One can also observe that it is dangerous to mix. That increases immeasurably the unfortunate impression that results from the absorption of various wines. The most deplorable of my memories is of that nature. I had sampled Indian hemp with a morphinomane that I did not know as such. The modifications of his self, of course, from the picturesque viewpoint, were those of morphine, but the nervous disturbance was multiplied tenfold. He had a frightful crisis. I believed seriously that he was going to die. He swore to me that he would never have the fantasy of renewing that experiment. It was sufficient.

"You have present in mind the accounts of Baudelaire and Théophile Gautier. They are excellent studies of the cult of the green god. There are curious pages in the work of Alexandre Dumas père that are amusing. I suspect him of having employed hashish to amplify some of his descriptions, for example, the grotto of Monte Cristo. I shall talk to you shortly about the imaginative influence that renders the substance dear and redoubtable to litterateurs and musicians. But the notes that they have left, or the works that they wrote with that obscure unavowed collaboration, are, from all points of view, documents more precious, although not technical, than the brochures of physicians on this subject. That is because it is absolutely necessary in order to describe such effects, to have experienced them oneself. There does not exist in any language a true poem of amour having as its author a man who had not loved.

"Physicians, practical men, have only been able to note and utilize one bizarre property of the poison, the prodigious overstimulation of the sensation of hunger. It is very discomfiting to go to dinner, especially the first time, after taking hashish, with people who are not habituated to eating it. With a moderate dose one can, for instance, render appetite to consumptives. Another excellent influence might also be produced in the latter case, by which I mean a general excitation of vital activity. But how many physicians, men of science, are interested in what might be called, in science, experimentation? They prefer to employ their time searching for hypothetical microbes or serums that it is necessary to hasten to take, while they cure by fashionability and suggestion.

"There is no lack of benevolent subjects for the experiment. The vice is very contagious. One finds the green poison in a great many pharmacies, of course, but in the same way that one does not procure remarkable wines from the usual merchants, it is not always the perfect drug. The inferior product, however, well-prepared and in good condition, produces sufficient effects. Certain inhabitants of the city, of bourgeois and calm appearance, go in search at regular intervals if their provision of dreams. In their souls, without a doubt, the visions of Hoffmann and Poe pass. There are aulic councilors haunted by the green demon.

An extract in pill form can also be replaced by a liquid extract. The formula was given to me, in fact, by a pharmacist who had doubtless succumbed in serving the passion of others. He lives in the vicinity of the Arc de Triomphe. He gave me a bottle that I left to another of my friends, not daring to make use of it myself. The pharmacist was the most colorless man I ever saw. Under the smiling and indulgent gazes of his pupils, he poured a few drops from the green bottle over a sugar lump, which he absorbed with an expression of joyful ecstasy. Then he went through the streets looking for popular celebrations, searching for material for his dream, entirely happy, giving the impression of being slightly mad.

"People sometime also use flower-heads of the plant, which are smoked. There is an old herborist's shop in a narrow street near the Seine, at the back of a courtyard. But it is necessary to be skillful to distinguish, by smoking the leaves, French and Indian hemp. That usage is, moreover, not always excellent. One experiences impressions similar to those given by smoking tea. I do not know what effects an extract of tea put into pills has.

"But let us note that it is necessary not to think—and one ought to add, by any formula of persuasion—of returning to the normal taste of tobacco a pipe that has known, even if only once, the charm of Indian hemp. It will retain for the rest of its life an abominable bitterness. One must resolve no longer to fill it with other leaves than the accursed ones. You can see there, without effort, a symbol of passions that poison one's soul forever. Let us note that in order to please the old moralist who slumbers, with his spectacles and his head on his breast, in the depths of the soul of each of us."

During Mathias' discourse, the animation of the street had died down. The café became deserted. A few belated couples were seen on the terrace exchanging inferior amorous words. The two conversationalists got up. Two o'clock had just chimed. They walked along the boulevards. That is when the glimpsed banks of the Seine and the Cathedral recall Victor Hugo.

"Are you sleepy?" said Jean Derève.

"A sage is never somnolent. That axiom is found in book six of the Bhagavata, paragraph thirty. It won't rain tonight. We have eternity to sleep."

Jean Derève smiled. "May the Eternal put on our lips, before sealing the sepulcher, a strong dose of opium or hashish!"

"No, dreams are only produced in moderate sleep, and death is probably a profound sleep. It's true that one cannot foresee the effects exactly in accordance with the measure of the poison. Some are astonished and do not experience any result. The influence depends greatly on the present disposition. It's also necessary to distinguish between the different forms: jam, extract or leaves. Gautier speaks about the jam, a mixture with a perfumed vehicle. It has a slightly sickening taste. In that form, hashish only has a very attenuated influence, slothful, so to speak. It is, I think in those conditions that the Orientals use it. But everything is transformed by temperament. The native of Indo-China smokes an opium pipe lying on a mat, which is sufficient to give birth to his somewhat animalistic dream. Thomas De Quincey, the man of the North, the Englishman with robust nerves—because he was English, albeit slightly mad, being a poet—felt deprived when he did not have a large carafe of laudanum on his work-table.

"The observations that I have been able to make all bear upon people using pills. That is the most convenient form. One can easily carry with one the pretext of the dream; and it's truly an amusing problem to pose that so many visions can be enclosed in a globule of green paste. They really are, since, once the globule is absorbed, they go to deploy in our brain, displaying to our inner vision a crazy, charming, colorful pantomime. The effect is rapid or slow, and is not produced, in any case, in everyone. For some, who are refractory in one way or another, there is only a bizarre shock, a brief and painful disturbance of the brain. Or, again, the impression lasts, but is purely physical and utterly unbearable. There are nervous tremors, convulsions of the eyes and inarticulate moans, indicating a profound suffering. One stops at a first experiment, with the sentiment of having had a narrow escape, like tobacco smokers to whom the first cigarette gives vertigo. Those accidents are rare, and for habitués they are produced no more frequently than the others for a habitual tobacco smoker. It requires very unfavorable circumstances, an already existent malaise, or an exaggerated dose. With elementary precautions, they are never produced.

"Among all sorts of experiments there are bad cases. Only reasoning from them is taking rare exceptions for the rule. Does the opinion of an inexperienced smoker make the law for tobacco? Does a person whose stomach only accepts milk cut with mineral water have the right to affirm doctorally that drunkenness does not exist and that Bacchic poets are liars? And that the drunkenness of wine, moreover, must be crude, and devoid of charm besides?

"That is the error into which I saw a talented young novelist, known for well-written, modern works of fortunate development, fall one day. He witnessed a séance at which I was present, which was deplorable. Two neophytes were ill. One suffered a malady of the stomach with sharp crises, accompanied by vertigo. The other was a very advanced morphinomane. The novelist, whose unique and only observation it was, never wanted to admit that it was not inclusive. He wrote thereafter a chapter of a book in a definitive tone. It would have been pointless to sustain to him that he would only have the right to give a serious opinion after other observations made on normal individuals. Bacon's laws, for him, assuredly, were a dead letter. He did not suspect that, for science, the isolated fact does not exist. I conceived vehement doubts after that about the verity of his books and the documentary value of his descriptions.

"For normal temperaments, in a period that lasts from a few minutes to a few hours and ends up being limited similarly in the same person, the effect arrives suddenly. It is a seizure of the sensibility as abrupt as it is absolute, a kind of reasoned vertigo, for wanting it, one can remain master of oneself and assist one's folly. The patient is well aware that he is dreaming, but like a traveler sitting in an enchanter's carriage, who can direct it on condition of not getting out of it. You did not have to make a great effort to divine that, a little while ago, as well as relating notes made on others I was talking about myself. There is no impression newer and more moving than that of having the soul gripped by that poison.

"The first day that I used it was one of the best days of my life. My incredulity underwent the strangest of revelations. I had been walking for a few hours with the old poet Lélian,[1] who died five or six years later. It was time to go back. My furtive intoxication went back an hour or two, and I was waiting, with a slight anguish, to be alone with my impressions. There was no other symptom apart from that expectation.

"That evening, the Bohemian genius had received 'a few golds,' as he put it, and I accompanied him toward the Montagne Sainte-Génevière, where he lived, lavishing the most virtuous advice on him as we went. He listened to me, shaking his head like a bald bear with the greatest gravity. He recognized the wisdom of what I was saying. The moment had come to astonish public opinion by the sober rigor of his life. What a pity to spend nights drinking in order to ruin oneself. He was going to return immediately to his room on the fourth floor of a modest house.

"We walked on. With his cloak, his vast hat and his staff, he resembled a grim shepherd. Our silhou-

---

1 In Paul Verlaine's classic study of *Les Poètes maudits* (1884), the author includes himself under the anagrammatical pseudonym "pauvre Lélian."

ettes became rather vague under the moonlight in that old quarter. I remember that in one narrow street that rose up in pointed cobblestones between two rows of Medieval houses, I arrived at accents whose eloquence would have made the most hardened sinner dissolve in tears. Without taking account of it, I was under the influence that had arrived.

"We separated on the poet's threshold, after great protestations. He closed the door with a gesture that I divined, in the vestibule, to be Roman. And I drew away, in the moonlight, which outlined in black the gables of the facades on the descending route, refraining from turning round, divining that he was watching, from behind the furtively-reopened door, for me to turn the first corner in order to go impenitently to his culpable pleasures. With our fine assurance, in that solitary and nocturnal décor, like two people who are not dupes but are putting on a very good semblance, we had played a charming scene from an Italian comedy.

"I would not have employed that expression if the property of the poison were not precisely to solemnize all encounters and give them a theatrical appearance. A majestic fever takes possession of you. The slightest incidents take on an infinite value. Has it not happened to me, lying in an armchair, to spend long minutes contemplating a ceiling rose, finding an inexpressible grandeur in the vision of those ordinary but regular designs? Music, beautiful verses heard, and the landscape, all acquire a profound charm. Life becomes amusing and easy. It is as if the hand of a mage has passed a fresh new color over everything. A pretext is not even necessary. Each wave of intoxication that rises to the brain evaporates in evocative clouds. And there is at the same time, as in dreams, the unexpectedness of images, the repose, for a few hours, of effort, and a playful activity, in a divine torpor. Imagine that folly is striking your head, slowly and repeatedly, with a golden hammer.

"It is the same mental disposition as in a dream, with, it is true, the inconvenience of the artifice employed. If one could create such a state of soul naturally, one would be similar to the gods. I've often thought what joy that ability would give us. The mysterious law of dreams has not been studied sufficiently. But remember the most beautiful ones you have had. No real voluptuousness approaches it. Suppose now that, without losing the charming insouciance, you were capable of directing your impressions, and that, above all, you were not at the brutal mercy of awakening. For men endowed with that admirable genius, it would then only be a matter of overturning the usual order of existence. One would spend upright the few hours necessary to physical life; but once the tasks were accomplished, everyone would plunge back into the evocative night, like a fatigued worker who sees every evening the door of an unknown palace opening, of which he is the king.

"The direction of dreams!

"If it is true that in slumber, we only rediscover, in a bizarre and new order, the impressions of the previous day, we could make from those known elements an unusual masterpiece, as painters and sculptors have borrowed the head or the wings of some vulgar beast in order to create a chimera that does not exist. And how do we know that our eyes are not given to us to see and our ears to hear the scattered colors or sounds with which we compose, when night falls, the painting or opera of genius? The persistence of the soul and its slight consciousness, when it is liberated from exterior things is perhaps the one proof of our immortality. It allows us to comprehend that we are still alive, that we are respiring with an ardent and sure breath, even and especially when we have folded over our thought the darkness that protects us, as a child sleeps in a bedroom with closed windows, which the noises of the street cannot reach, and which a discreet lamp populates with dreams. But it is evidently necessary only to speak of people with sufficient mastery of their obscure soul to be able to read the pages of the book that the crowd cannot open. For the majority, sleep is a brief but absolute death; and if they have dreams, they are anxious about that abnormal phenomenon. Thus, animals, except for a few superior ones, do not dream.

"That freedom from matter, that communion in sleep with a divine soul, was the origin of belief in prophetic divinations. The soul of the Earth was revealed to sleepers in the lair of Trophonius. The state of dreaming is superior to that of wakefulness. It is better to see with closed eyes, to hear without ears. It is a superb joy to observe that the organs can disappear without the rest of us being annihilated.

"But of all that mystery I can only retain one sole verity, the absence of effort, the spontaneity, the rapidity of thought, the supple unfurling of visions. It is in that respect that the intoxication of which we speak can be compared with usual dreams. The voluptuousness that it provides is also a liberation. Certain essential stages can be noted, however, in the duration of that joy, for it is easier to observe and abstract the laws of the waking dream than the other. The first impression is a frank and intense gaiety. On the evening that I told you about, after quitting the poet, in the exquisite décor, I had fits of silent laughter, as after an amusing act well played. And it was by that bizarre and excessive hilarity that I recognized being henceforth under the impression.

"Although the manifestations vary with diverse temperaments, few people escape that absurd nervous laughter. A man exuberant in the normal state then becomes redoubtable. He will make a series of puns to supply all the bearers of almanacs for ten years, even in the most obscure provinces, with old French gaiety. In many people, moreover, that period is the entire crisis. It is also necessary that they be capable of some awakening. Stupid souls feel nothing. Malevolent souls, on the other hand, even in that first phase, are frightfully revealed. I have had in hashish, without provoking them, confidences painful by virtue of the sudden light that they cast on the dirtiness of certain consciences that I knew vaguely. The intoxication is, at any rate, favorable to frankness. But intellectual intoxication ought to be redoubted by all those whose soul is vile. Moral ugliness is reflected as if in a magnifying mirror. Let such people remain in silence and in their obscurity. I see there a magic realm the door of which is eternally closed to them. They will not know the charming and veritable effect of hashish.

"It would be puerile to remark that people denuded of intelligence are even more denuded of it, although they astonish themselves at that moment; or they say vulgar things. On the contrary, nothing is as amusing as conversation with people of agreeable commerce. Everything favors the blossoming of a particular humor. The beginning is a slightly feverish expectation, mingled with incredulity. One is unaware of the effects. One does not know from which direction the seductive demon will come, and one looks furtively at the doors, and the mirrors that are the doors of the occult. Everyone is slightly arrogant.

"The tendency exists to make fun of the credulous who anticipate unusual things. One makes jokes at their expense and one laughs—except that the laughter gradually takes on a special quality and rings with a new timbre. The person who does not suspect it suddenly finds that he is under an unusual influence, with the vehement and grateful desire to cry: '*Ecce deus!*' He is not alone; his fit is contagious. The craziest visions emanate from the most futile incident. A charming good grace lends itself obligingly; any word pronounced takes on unexpected significance. It is the bizarre impression noted by Thomas De Quincey, for whom, in opium, the mere words 'Roman consul' evoked Roman armies, triumphs and all the grandiose apparatus of legends and paintings.

"The soul is at the mercy of its dreams and the imagination. External vision is subject in that regard to bizarre modifications. One looks at one of one's neighbors; one is astonished to see his face and to find it irresistibly comical. One starts to preach to him, with a gravity agitated by spasms, the necessity of changing his face as soon as possible. I have heard some hashishins make speeches with an incoherence and an abundant fantasy that would have made the fortune of a fairground barker, but it is like a light froth that gradually fades away and vanishes. The conversation is all verbal acrobatics. The wordplay is entangled and enchained with an unexpected logic that seems dazzling. Exuberant joy, a veritable physical sensuality, is betrayed by profound respirations and colored faces. The cheeks are dolorous and the eyes haggard.

"That period is variable in duration: an hour or two, sometimes a whole evening or an entire night. The fatigue that flows is proportionate. Observe, in any case, that it is difficult to render an accurate account of the duration. In hashish, as in opium, space and time are deformed. For philosophers, space and time, simple *a priori* forms of sensibility, do not exist in themselves. They are convenient forms for disposing our impressions, which contract or extend to the desired dimensions. An insect that lives for a day has an existence as long as that of a carp or a crow. Everything is relative. We cannot count the minutes except by means of the successive thoughts that we have had. A dreamless night appears to us as rapid as a lightning flash. We know, on the other hand, that some nocturnal vision, which we believed to last for hours, unfurled in a second. Joyful sentiments, and above all painful ones, permit us to measure our life. They are the white or black milestones that reveal the road traveled; and the more urgent those sentiments are, the fuller and more real the moment seems to us.

"But how much more rapid our march is between the white markers than the black ones! Eternities go by in hours of waiting behind the curtain of the window, while listening for the advent of the noise of a distant carriage, which increases, which is going to stop, and with always goes past our house. Those hours do not have the same duration as those that fly by at the feet of a beloved woman, saying puerile things to her.

"Is not the flow of time always equal, and the fall of the sand in the hourglass no more hasty or retarded? In hashish, sudden visions succeed one another with such rapidity that we believe that we live years of joy in a minute. For how long are you plunged in that ocean with golden and voluptuous waves? How many waves have brushed you, lulled you, and carried you away tumultuously? You look at the clock. Its hands do not seem to have moved. One can lead one's existence at the pace one wishes. The man who has a passion for living beauty or for art has lived more in one day than the bodies with monotonous gestures that we see passing indistinctly in the street have in their entire terrestrial presence.

"And like time, space, which is correlated with it, since it is measured by time, acquires a rare elasticity on those occasions. I have retained the memory of evenings when, after a distant séance, I was returning home on foot. What fatigue! The route stretched desperately. I thought about Petit Poucet in the forest, who saw a red window shining through the distant trees, and who went toward the light without ever being able to get closer to it. Add that, in order to climb the steps of my staircase, it would have been advantageous to me to have borrowed his boots, each step being, in my imagination, at least a meter high. It also required, in order to move, even with that difficulty, a certain impetus.

"In the first experiments, it often happens in certain subjects that all the functions of relation are suspended. Later, one gets used to it, one can come and go, but still with unusual impressions that give one a slightly astonishing gait. With experience, one corrects them, knowing their falsity. They gradually disappear as one achieves more self-mastery. There is, in any case, a surprise in any initiation, from all viewpoints, which subsequently loses its novelty."

The two companions had run aground in a restaurant near Les Halles, and while chatting, gazed through the cigarette smoke at the noctambulatory figures scattered in the air around them. There were young women in quest of amour who were contenting themselves with a supper. Men in worn garments were drinking with them. Some ordered complicated drinks with a weary expression. At the back of the room three musicians around a piano remained silent for a moment; then their hands took the violins with a sudden decision. The notes of a waltz departed furiously, then languished, and shreds of the melody were heard through the appeals of drunkenness or disputes. Sometimes, two women enlaced one another and danced to the music, and then returned to their places. The ceremony continued with the passage of a saucer in a solicitous hand through the scantly charmed audience, into which coins clinked. There was a repose, and the same ritual was celebrated with the same details.

The timid daylight appeared, as if through a fog. The large windows became pale with a diffuse light. Shadows could be seen passing by on the sidewalk.

"The second period," Mathias Corbus continued, "is announced by a calming in the laughter and the games. The conversation is more discreet. Profound thoughts, or those thought to be, supplant the puerile fantasies. It is the moment when people amuse themselves constructing philosophical systems and cosmogonies. Everything seems easy. The mind plays with ideas, or ideas play with the mind. Nothing troubles the serenity. It is an assembly of gods around the nectar and the ambrosia, letting fall in a slow and rich voice words imprinted with solemnity. And each member of the audience, in fact, believes himself to be a god. One experiences a disdainful pity for vain usual cares.

"That ecstasy, in some people, takes on a contemplative form. They follow an interior image, the colors and lines of which have no equivalent in real life, or, rather, take the present sensation—sound, décor or perfume— as a theme. I have memories. One evening was spent at a good classical concert, in which I heard a triumphal march, so majestic and so moving that my heart was oppressed and, in order not to cry out with delight or faint with joy, I was obliged to go outside to respire the appeasing night air. Another time, in a drawing room whose furniture was pure Louis XV—that is the style of hashish—I had a conversation with a woman whose garments, appearance and smile were miraculously harmonious. No more was necessary. They were impressions of absolute art.

"But equally, when one is fortunate enough to encounter intimate friends, one abandons oneself to the discussion of fine subjects. One thinks that no one has ever had such imagination, richer verbal treasures, such ease in navigating among arguments and images. Things said appear to be admirable, even the charm disappears. It sometimes happens, as in dreams, that one follows brilliant thoughts, delighted by having conceived them, and one sees them gradually fade away and lose their luster as one awakens, to be reduced, in the broad daylight of consciousness to some absurd or childishly grotesque phrase. That is rare. The interest often remains, in an indecent or vulgar fashion. It is the tendency of hashish to give substance to the strangest conceptions.

"I was so gripped, that day, by the material effect of the poison, that I did not have the strength to open a drawer for sheets of paper, and I noted the pantomime on the envelopes of letters that happened to be under my hand. When I reread them, there were twenty written leaves, with tedious and infantile repetitions, fragments of verse, refrains, an entire mass that I had to eliminate in order to reduce the work to five or six pages, crazy but amusing. You will find the fragment in a volume of poems in prose that I published, almost all the pages of which were written under the same inspiration.

"In the beginning, one is still too troubled to make a reasoned usage, but after some time the manifestations differ. The classic crisis no longer existing, one steers the excitation in the desired direction. If one eventually gets the habit—I don't advise you to acquire it—and you want to furnish a considerable effort at a certain moment, absorb a pill in the evening. Renew the dose two or three hours later if the effect is insufficient. Have a light meal about half an hour later and set to work. You will be fortunate to retain for three or four hours a light tendency, a facility of elaboration, an ease in thought and phrase that you have never known. Everything that you do will be extraordinarily interesting for you. If it is a work of science, the most arid research will have flavor. If it is a matter of poetry, new images, a source of joy, will crowd before your eyes. It is important, as I have indicated, to reread what you have written later. You will find such incoherencies in what had enthused you that they will make you smile. But passages will remain that you would not have composed without metaphors and visions whose color survives.

"You might raise the objection of the dangers. To take the written page and compose—for what I have said also applies to music—under an influence is to risk impotence in the normal state. That rule is not absolute, for the impetus acquired persists even beyond the moment. And then, the habitués will reply that it does not matter, if they find better inspirations. There remains the physical peril and the disturbance of the heart or brain to dread. But that is the ransom.

"Do not listen to the donkeys who do not want any intoxication, even of genius. They reproach Musset for his intemperance, without wondering whether it was not the exaggeration and the fatal consequence of a disposition useful to his work. Posterity will not know that the poet was a drinker. He had the penalty of his passion, he will have the merit. Strictly speaking, he was a martyr, if you wish. And if one is conscious that the poison is developing within us, perhaps, an unknown virtue, which has not been revealed, what true artist would not accept to see his life abridged, if he had the assurance, by means of that offering, that he would create the beautiful form and realize his ideal?

"The objection would be the same, and more forceful, for disinterested employment. The person who only seeks pleasure will experience the baleful effects of hashish more than another, since he abandons himself to his impressions instead of directing them. It is impossible that a good fortune of that nature should not be expiated. Prudence can attenuate the bad consequences, but it is rare that one will not experience them, one day or another, by virtue of an exaggerated dose or an unfavorable disposition, I knew one unfortunate who suffered heart palpitations for several weeks after his first experiment, like those soldiers of amour who are mortally wounded in the first battle. Some people are unlucky.

"I came out of a house one evening in order to return home in a state of confusion that did not leave me the strength to hail a cab to transport me. As each vehicle went past I represented to myself in advance the intense effort that I would have to make in order to summon the coachman, open the door and give my address, all with sufficient calm that the man would not think me insane. It was necessary not to think of it. All that I could do was walk like a somnambulist straight ahead, on a route that unfurled like a veritable Calvary. Oh, the torture of sensing one's thoughts vagabonding and fleeing! There is no worse torture for a self-controlled man who does not want to abandon himself.

"As I marched, it appeared to me that, from one minute to the next, my heart was going to stop beating, for physical pain was mingled with mental apprehension, or that I was about to be overwhelmed by a misfortune that was following me. I was like those unfortunates who say to themselves: 'One more effort, one more step. If I get as far as that, I'm saved . . .' And the anguish was renewed, with alternatives of better and worse, for there is a rhythm in hashish, and terror comes in successive waves after moments of calm. I asked myself, without daring to reply, at what blessed station my torture would come to an end.

"But often, having returned home, I did not find repose. I have spent frightful nights imploring slumber, sensing my brain congested and terrified by my heart. Sometimes, it beat as if to burst. Sometimes, with cold sweats, I lost it beneath my hand. My breast was as motionless as that of a corpse. And as it is necessary that the bizarre, even in the tragic, never loses its prerogatives, I was desolated by the idea that it would be impossible for me, in spite of the most laudable contortions, to put an ear to my breast in order to ausculate myself.

"One can, however, attenuate those tortures, which come from a sort of vertigo of the stomach. It is necessary to take astringents. I have seen people experience good effects by eating a lemon. Cold water is also a good remedy. But the best remedy is to reassure oneself by thought that the malaise is, fundamentally, not dangerous and will soon pass. The most radical treatment would doubtless be never to take hashish again.

"What is one to do? It is futile to want strange sensations if one is not disposed to expiate them. Every man who is preoccupied with living an intense life commits, if one still supposes that kind of reasoning, a sin that must be punished. What joy is not redeemed by a pain? The sovereign law of equilibrium is never found in default. Who can tell whether there is not a mysterious appeal in dread itself? Danger is seductive because it is redoubtable. It would truly be too good if one could play with weapons and philters without risking death. Then again, one ought to congratulate oneself on proofs from which fear dissuades vulgar souls. But the tortures of hashish, like those of opium, are very little for the man who has had the joys.

"I am talking about profound joys. Among all those who seek them, only a small number have known them. As well as moderation, certain safeguards need to be in place. But it is possible, at times, to enter the forbidden country. One of my finest memories is that of an excursion by carriage, along deserted streets—for all my landscapes are of cities—with forgotten women, one evening in May. They were singing softly, and their voices, very banal, suddenly became divine. We were passing over a bridge. I had the sudden, absolute vision of snowflakes falling around me. The sadness of that unreal snow in the warm night, the music of the songs, and the silent décor of the houses, all carried me far away. I have never had a moment more perfect in my life. One might have thought that we were going, murmuring, beneath falls of white wings, to the burial of a Pierrot who had died of amour, in order to put Basque tambourines and fans in wreaths on the funeral cart.

"Such hallucinations are rare. There are others that I cannot recount. The story would only have meaning for initiates. One must also refrain from the poison in painful hours, for it amplifies all the scenes and different states of the soul. But go, after having absorbed it, to a concert or to contemplate a painting. Go for a walk in a well-ordered park or an unexpected forest. Have light around you, especially candlelight, smiles, beautiful gestures bright and silky garments. Hashish is a lover of luxury, as well as a diabolical sower of fear. Infernal forms, if you are not careful, will haunt your nights. You will believe that you are immured for eternity in a sepulcher, with phosphorescences grimacing in the blackness around you.

"But more frequently you will find yourself in a series of red rooms with hangings and candelabras. You have arrived for a celebration and you know that soon, a strange ceremony will take place. The figures around you are majestic and their appearance has an old-fashioned elegance. But the details, even ridiculous, have a sovereign value. You hear music coming from neighboring rooms in gusts, from an opera of genius is which human anguish and joy are summarized. However, you are not without anxiety. A mystery hovers. You look furtively at the hems of dresses with Watteau pleats with the apprehension of seeing a cloven foot.

"It is a true demon that is haunting you, but what a marvelous demon! You believe that no initiation is more profound. The soul, if only in illusion, is open to sensations of intense life, and by means of its almost infinitely increased faculty of imagination, sees things in a new light. It moves through the world with the intuition of unsuspected relationships. And curiosity awakes, which counsels going toward that unknown. Is not lack of energy often, perhaps even always, the consequence of the lack of interest that one finds in existence and its manifestations. One can, with the occult aid of bizarre gods, acquire the habit of activity. The ecstasy of certain hours reveals to our minds sudden and magical verities, in the real meaning of the word.

"But that is sufficient. You have interrogated me. It was a nocturnal conference. Here is the morning, which will dissipate the clouds in which our conversation has gone astray."

They emerged from the smoky room, which had become livid by contrast with the frank clarity outside. On the sidewalk, an exquisite torpor gripped them. They went around piles of vegetables and roses. A few groups of noctambulists, in the middle of the street, were buying flowers. Ragged individuals with sly smiles awaited sous that had gone astray. The life of the day woke up to the din of carts. And there was an impression of moving through perfumes, under the oblique gaze of the rising sun, with the elastic fatigue of a happy night of insomnia, toward the refreshment of repose.

THE PHANTOM OF OPIUM

by Louis Latourrette

EVERY evening, at about eleven o'clock, she arrived at the smoking den—one of those smoking rooms in the vicinity of Passy, paltry in their mock-Oriental décor but disquieting because of the strangeness of their mysterious clientele. By that entitlement, Parisian smoking dens can even seem more suggestive than those of the great cosmopolitan centers of opium. In China, the habitués are too uniform, in the type of the intoxicate heavily enslaved by his unique and maniacal vice; in the ports too, one finds similar colonials dazed by an irremediable need, more demanding every day, and every day more especially imperious. In Paris, those slaves of the divine drug are the minority in the smoking dens. What one sees there, above all, are the deranged or the curious, who do not belong to opium yet, but who come to request, feverishly, forgetfulness of a dolor, a disappointment or a remorse, or a stimulant toward some rare and unfamiliar dream. They do not love opium yet for itself, for its harm, like the slaves of the terrible poison, but because it is a remedy for them. They are under the influence of damnations more poignant than that of avid thirst; and their various eccentricity, being more pathetic, is thus more attractive than the bleak parity of the unfortunates concentrated to deadly delight.

The smoking den in question is the most reputed in the capital for its relative luxury and the excellent quality of its stupefacients. With the opium, in fact, all the facilities of ecstasy and marvels are delivered there: hashish, morphine, ether and alcoholic beverages aromatized by the most intoxicating essences of the poppy.

She was a young woman, scarcely twenty years old, very pretty, of a characteristically northern aristocracy with her fine pale features, her bright golden hair, her cold blue eyes and the svelte tall delicacy of her body. Her bearing was that of a proud patrician, her elegance somber and impeccable. In the same way, her jewelry was remarkable because the limpid virginity of numerous diamonds shone uniquely therein. A proud and enigmatic sadness chilled that seduction.

She came every evening into a large banal drawing room, the only woman among twenty men, who were assiduous in their attendance. She entered, distant in her indifference, stepping over the bodies of smokers extended on mats without repugnance for the gasps of some and paying no attention to the deliria of others. She went to her selected place and lay down on a mass of rich cushions. A little Annamite maidservant attached to the establishment hastened to bring the pipes, the pots, the needles and the minuscule lamp with the wan gleam of a night-light, called so picturesquely by an English poet "the lantern of the brothel of dreams." Immediately, the young woman inhaled the soothing smoke greedily, not with the slow sensuality of pleasure but with the impatience of the fidgety, who desire rapidly from opium its numbing effect and extraterrestrial lucidity.

Rapid and numerous, hastily ignited by the little Annamite, the pipes succeeded one another, until the smoker, her eyes vague, was immobilized. Sitting up among the cushions, she gazed at us without seeing us; and we, from our mats, prey to the inferno of our blissfulness, admired that young woman like an image of the gracious and impassive demons of nirvana, so pretty, so pale and so blonde, with eyes of glacial morning.

A Chinese adolescent of ambiguous charm, intoned in a very low, singing voice the poetry of the divine Li-Tai-Pe; and the exquisite harmony of the words of genius, incomprehensible for us, seemed to us, in our enchantment, to be a mysterious psalm devoted to that mysterious deity. As for her, she did not hear it; her eyes were fixed on a sublime void.

More than all my companions I was intrigued by that adherent of the accursed cult. We did not know anything about her; the personnel of the smoking den, interrogated, could not tell me anything. Who was she, I asked, why did she smoke? So young, what crime or disaster could she have to forget? When her beauty and her wealth guaranteed her the most complete human felicities, what inconceivable desire for infinity tempted her, which she was seeking in fallacious opium?

She came every evening for four months.

Doubtless my curiosity about her would have remained without result, if one of us had not brought one evening an exasperated smoker, the young Prince Ourantcheff. As he came into the drawing room he perceived the strange young woman, who had only just preceded him. He started. She had also seen him, and reacted, in her commencing torpor. Always marmoreal previously, she allowed a slight gesture of annoyance to escape her. However, no sign was exchanged between the two of them. They seemed to be ignoring one another.

I had noticed all that. Ourantcheff devoted himself to his pipes; but the unknown woman, who habitually remained until dawn, went away this time after two hours.

Ourantcheff and I had neighboring mats; I made him party to my intimate questions on the subject of the young woman. The Slav prince, informed of the secret, consented to tell the story briefly and curtly—as the discourses of opium-smokers, to whom speech is hostile, usually are.

"Yes, I know that woman," he said. "Her name is Natacha Woroff. She is a duchess, the last offspring of an illustrious Caucasian family. She is an orphan, and possesses immense domains out there contiguous with mine. Three years ago, she was madly in love with an adolescent worthy of her in every respect, her cousin Count Serge. He adored her. Their marriage was arranged for an imminent date . . .

"A catastrophe burst forth. Serge was arrested one night, in the name of the Tsar. A Petersburgian commissar, a vile policeman, sent into the region for an investigation, had discovered a formidable conspiracy of nihilists. Papers seized specified the involvement of Serge. For him, it was death.

"Maddened, Natacha ran to the commissar, humiliated herself and begged. If he deigned to destroy the few letters that implicated Serge—he could still do so, the evidence, seized the previous evening, not having been communicated to anyone else—that would be salvation, Serge would leave the country and never enter into another conspiracy; she swore it.

"The magistrate was a fat, ugly, sensual old man. His vulgar and libertine senility was stirred by the spectacle of that magnificent youth prostrate before him. The pig was desirous of that prettiness. Perfidiously, he showed the ineluctable danger that menaced Serge. Yes, it would be death, and what a death after what tortures! It would also be infamy. Of course, he could, as he indicated, avert that end. He could. And with abject grunts, he proposed to return that compromising papers at a price: that Natacha would give herself to him.

"She was revolted, protested, begged again. The monstrous desire of the old man was excited by that lamentable crisis. The scene was extended. The pitiless scoundrel announced that in an hour he would send the file to the Tsar and Serge would immediately be sent to prison in Saint Petersburg with his affiliates. If she wished, that would not happen.

"Before the vision of her tortured and executed soul—so young, so beautiful, so frail—Natacha was terrified, her nerves weakened, and, dying in a paroxysm of horror, cowardice and rage, she submitted to the filthy violation. It was an hour of unspeakable Hell. Sated, the tyrannical satyr returned the letters and gave orders for Serge to be released.

"Having emerged from the ignoble chamber, the awakening from the nightmare was even more frightful for Natacha than the odious act had been. She saw the truth: she had saved Serge's life, but by killing all amour. The abominable wound from which she was bleeding condemned their love. Henceforth, she could no longer belong to her beloved. Even if she confided her sacrifice to him and he declared her innocent, she could no longer be his wife. She was too nobly loyal, she loved their amour too much. The caress, now, was forbidden to them. What would their first kiss as spouses, so radiantly aspired to, be after the memory of that execrable initiation? No, that, never! Would that repugnant spoliation not weigh upon all their embraces? Would not the tenderness of their souls be poisoned, at length, by the noxious malediction of their kiss? It was over; they could no longer love one another.

"The tragedy unfolded in precipitate and fatal episodes. That same evening Natacha fled, quit Russia, leaving Serge a simple note to signify to him, without explanation, their irrevocable rupture. Liberated without knowing at what price, he supposed that he had lost the adoration of the adored because of his Nihilism. He was in despair; he could not implore her, move her to pity. Where was she? He did not know. He would never see her again! Deranged, he blew his brains out within twenty-four hours. Three weeks later, the old commissar was found dead, stabbed in his apartment in Saint Petersburg. It was thought at first to be a Nihilist vengeance, but, chance having caused the author of the murder to be caught, it was discovered that it was one of Natacha's domestics, who had received the order for the execution before her departure. And it was in that way, thanks also to secret notes discovered among the magistrate's papers, that the exactitude of the scandalous adventure was reconstituted.

"In a panic, Natacha traveled a long way. In Cairo she learned about Serge's death. She wanted to die too, and took poison. Physicians saved her, miraculously. It was then that she began smoking opium. She could not recover the courage to commit suicide. She went from one country to another, dragging her amorous mourning and disgust for her body miserably.

"Everywhere, she seeks out temples of the Good Smoke, trying no longer to remember. Has she succeeded? Just now, the fixity of those eyes was so unhappy."

Ourantcheff fell silent, enveloped by a cloud.

Had Princess Natacha been discomfited by her encounter with the prince? At any rate, she departed once again in her dolorous vagabondage. We never saw her again in the smoking den.

She was very beautiful!

May the subtle god of poppies, who is the master of our minds, be merciful to her and grant her mild forgetfulness.

Telepathy

by Théo Varlet

HASHISH—I never take it.

Not that I affect a naïve magnanimity of a Balzacian stripe and refuse to "think involuntarily". On the contrary, I envisage such poisonings as a kind of sport, and I find the new glimpses that they offer into the world of the mind seductive, in the same fashion as a trip in an automobile, a voyage in a balloon or a submarine dive.

I discovered my path too soon. It was only at the beginning of my research that I could have hesitated, eclectically, between various "artificial paradises". I certainly had a passing curiosity with regard to hashish then, but that oriental drug seemed so difficult to obtain that I kept putting the matter off, and eventually no longer thought about it. An old initiate of the good Poison, I acquired a touch of the exclusivism that makes toxicomanes like us as sectarian as priests of different religions. The morphinist treats the opium smoker like a Moorish Turk and brutes drunk on alcohol have only insults for drinkers of ether like us—and we give them as good as we get. For myself, without going so far as to suspect Baudelaire, I've always held his hashish in very scant regard.

Now, I know; it's worse than I suspected, and I won't be taking it again.

With ether, at least one knows what to expect. One can establish the formula of one's folly, the percentage of its dreams. Given a particular dosage in decigrams, I know in advance the result of each etherization.

Taking opium is still possible, in spite of the sinful sophistication of apothecaries and the tiresome lacunae of its efficacy, but if you have a mind with a somewhat mathematical bent, if you want to conserve in dementia that lucidity of analysis which produces the finest sensuality for aestheticians—to observe one's own intoxication—if you delight in launching your dream like an obedient airplane into the sky of pure madness, beware of hashish, tenebrous and perfidious hashish.

When you've absorbed hashish, that's it—nothing more to be done. You've embarked, with your hands and feet bound, on an uncontrollable machine, which has taken off for an unknown flight.

I had no suspicion of that when, one afternoon, I accepted Albert Chaylas' offer. He was astonished to find out that I, fervent for artificial paradises as I am, was unfamiliar with it. How to obtain it? Quite simple: any druggist will furnish anyone with indeterminate quantities of *Cannabis indica*. Pharmacists use it themselves, albeit for rather grotesque purposes, such as soothing corns and calluses.

Having, like many an habitué of a single poison, an enthusiasm to recruit acolytes, Chaylas was happy to initiate me in the use of his favorite drug, perhaps cherishing the hope of making me abjure ether.

According to his scrupulous rites, he made some very strong and very hot coffee, took two unequal measures of hashish from a little Delft pot, dissolved the larger in his own cup and offered me the other on a spoon. It was a sort of dark green glue, with a penetrating odor of marsh-grass and a bitter taste like that of excessively-concentrated *souchong* tea. Mixed with coffee, the stuff was drinkable, and a second cup took the taste away temporarily.

To pass the preliminary hour of waiting, when no effect is manifest, I proposed that we re-read *Les paradis artificiels*, as a tourist guide to the marvelous land in which I was about to venture. Chaylas dissuaded me. To suggest impressions thus was contrary to spontaneity; one ought to let the effects emerge as they will. And, well used to hashish, he began to talk about trivial things, without the slightest allusion to the drug.

In spite of my efforts, I was distracted. The enigmatic result disturbed me. That provisional inefficacy, the poison's silence, threw my experiment off course. What would happen next? Would there be, as with ether, an ineffable beatitude leading up to the sequence of dreams? Or opium's ocean of images, iridescent and agile ideas?

Sprawling in an armchair, next to the fire, I examined the large room, lit from above by a single electric lamp, attentively. I peered into the dark corners that the phantoms of hashish must haunt every evening . . . in vain. Chaylas, stretched out on the other side of the table—where I could only see his head, among the books and knick-knacks—nonchalantly smoked his long Dutch pipe and chatted with a placidity that redoubled my impatience.

In the intervals of the conversation I held my breath to assure myself that the clock was still ticking.

I observed myself minutely. The annoying taste of marsh-grass was prowling under my palate again. My throat was dry, but I had no desire to stretch out my arm towards my coffee-cup to drain the last remaining drops. The heat of the coke fire filled me with an irresistible somnolence that was not at all disagreeable. My legs became heavy, as at the commencement of opium's effect . . . but nothing else. It was very little, forty-five minutes after the absorption!

The high bookshelves stuffed with volumes, the paintings with gilded frames, a panoply of daggers and arrows, rifles and revolvers mounted on the walls—all loaded, in accordance with Chalyas' eccentricity—remained close at hand and stable, quite real and tangible, without the slightest appearance of the fluctuation that, after a few sips of ether, transfigures the external world into a décor devoid of relief or perspective, slack and vacillating.

"Are you sure," I asked, point-blank, "that your hashish isn't a huge hoax?"

"A huge hoax?" Chaylas riposted, slowly, in a bizarre nasal tone. "A huge hoax?" And he began to laugh—soft, dry, jerky laughter. He deposited his long pipe on the table in order to laugh more comfortably, and more wholeheartedly, his head thrown back behind the cushions of his divan. He was literally writhing with laughter. "A hoax! Hashish a hoax! I'm sure of it! A huge hoax! Fernand, old chap, you'll be the death of me!"

I found this overly familiar hilarity incongruous and disproportionate. I was offended. I let him see it.

"You're laughing? My supposition isn't so stupid, though—since I don't feel anything."

"You don't feel anything? That's true, my poor friend! You can't, any more—but you shall see, you shall see!"

That sort-of-apology softened me up. I didn't want to upset him. My question might, indeed, have seemed absurd to him. And I smiled myself.

I resumed my observations. The walls retreated, as if the room had visibly expanded. My torpor increased. It seemed that a subtle emanation was rising up from the carpet, soon bathing me up neck-deep: an emanation from which only my head emerged, in which I was about to be drowned—and I experienced a bizarre sensation of inhabiting a foreign body, of never having noticed how alien my body was.

I examined Chaylas' head. I had never looked at him either! The brass-bound edge of the table was presently adjacent to a shelf unit whose upper part was filled with books. In the glass-fronted lower part, amid the scattered knick-knacks, that strange Chaylas was a radiantly beaming Japanese mask! He made me laugh: an inconvenient dry and jerky laugh, then an outburst of broad laughter; and an absurd exclamation sprang from my lips: "An ape! My dear Albert, you have the head of an ape!"

The head formed a grotesque grimace of hilarity, the eyes squinting, the mouth twisted.

"An ape! Yes, Fernand an ape! You too! You've got one too, haven't you?"

Indeed, I had. Everything—my own words, Chaylas' head, that Japanese showcase, the entire room, including the caricaturish hands of the clock, had taken on an irresistibly clownish appearance. I stood up, and stood on the divan in order to take a panoramic view of things, and I improvised a burlesque performance of a particularly humorous character.

The jokes were flowing through me with such abundance that I had no time to develop them. I could only mark their passage by quintessential allusions—but Chaylas half-understood, even seeming to divine with an extraordinary perspicacity what I was about to say, and replying to my gibes before I had enunciated them with sparkling, and no less elliptical, pleasantries.

For those ten minutes, we held the most extravagant synod of laughter that it is possible to imagine.

Little by little, the topic was exhausted. The last volleys faded away. I sat down again.

"It's nothing," Chaylas affirmed. "It's starting."

And I realized—it was a parenthetical thought—that we were now fully under the influence of hashish.

How does one describe the inexpressible? That room seemed to me to be isolated in space, a hundred thousand leagues from the Earth; we had transmigrated to another planet; my body harbored an exceedingly agile and subtle soul; and brief flashes of consciousness were the only memory of my previous self . . .

An exquisite and disturbing prodigy, to have transgressed the fastidious bounds of my individuality, to have rejected the old envelope of quotidian appearances, to see things with new senses, and perhaps—who knows?—*in depth*, in their essential aspect!

Yes, breaking through the membrane of reality, here is the fullness of hashish. No hallucination, to tell the truth. My ideas, prompt and jerky, pass by sequentially, unrolling cinematographically, as voluble as the mechanism of a watch whose escapement has just broken . . .

At the same time, deep inside me, in the utmost depths, an indiscernible thought, as enigmatic as a beam of light rising from a mine-shaft, rises gradually towards consciousness.

Chaylas was smiling. What was he dreaming? Why, was he looking at me with that smile of complicity? Why was I, too, smiling with a secret disquiet?

We look at one another, motionless.

He would have liked to speak too, but he dared not, any more than I did. That is so embarrassing today, so dubious still! Which of us would give voice to the idea, the suspicion of which was oppressing me, setting a chill in my heart?

He has said "All right?" and I've replied "Yes, fine"— to gain time, obviously. He gets up, inspects the walls, goes to lie down on another divan on the other side of the fire, facing me . . . that's normal. No, there's no mystery there.

Another heavy silence. Again that ambiguous and constrained smile. More and more embarrassed, that ominous smile. For the secret, the terrible secret, will get out; it seethes in our brains like vapor under pressure; it expands around us, saturating the room with an atmosphere more revelatory than explicit speech. The mystery reveals itself, communicates itself without anyone having said a word. He knows too! We both know! And yet—for it is necessary at all costs that the other does not know that the other knows—we each persist in smiling, smiling with a fixed and cataleptic grimace.

And I remember. Intermittently, I recollect the series of my previous meetings with Chaylas. I analyze successively his somber character, his bouts of pessimism, his perverse taste for flirting with death. One day, he mixed with his opium pills a pill of the same appearance containing a lethal dose of strychnine, and, inviting me to imitate him, swallowed one selected at random. He was mad when, having put a live cartridge in his revolver, he made me spin the magazine blindly, then cried: "Three!" Three times, with the barrel of the gun in his mouth, he pressed the trigger, without releasing the bullet—which came fourth. And that other day when he said to me, with a strange expression, as he pointed to his mistress: "If she pleases you . . ."

I had my eyes open, though, and when these images vanished—as a face reflected in an unsilvered glass melts into things placed behind it as they become clearer—I saw Chaylas in front of me, on the divan on the other side of the fire, studying me curiously.

We were young then—it was two years ago! The poison's premature old age had not yet injected such scorn for life into our veins—but me, me! I am not so detached, am I?

"Evidently."

He has replied, aloud, to my psychic interrogation. It's clear. He knows. He is penetrating my thoughts as I am penetrating his! Our thoughts, absolutely synchronous, are progressing as one, within two brains.

Absolutely synchronous?

I see by the character of his smile, in which I read *our* ideas, that the coincidence is not complete. There is, here and there, a *temporal displacement* in the transmission.

But he must know whether it is really true, whether this prodigy of telepathy, by a mysterious effect of the Drug, effectively links our cerebral cells, whether our psychic dynamisms have really entered into communication, whether the thought is circulating between us as if between vessels linked by a U-tube.

Is it true? And I say: "Oh—that would be wonderful!"

"Wonderful, yes, isn't it?" replies Chaylas, whose gaze never leaves me. "You too?"

No more doubt.

As motionless as a statue, I do not manifest my emotion. And this is how our occult duality proceeds within me, alternating my own thoughts with others, of a somber and haggard character, which I do not recognize, undoubtedly furnished by Chaylas. An influx of comic sadness and mortal disgust—the flagrant uselessness of our life—strange ideas that I adopt, that

I *have to* adopt, as Chaylas, by virtue of the reciprocal flow, *has to* admit my thoughts into him.

Independent asides slip into the interstices of this psychic conversation: parcels of myself, protected from the contagion, reflecting in flashes on the horror of the phenomenon. An ultra-determinist, accustomed by other poisons to see my lucid consciousness as nothing but an inactive witness of fatal energies that take control of my pseudo-will, I rebel, this time, against finding myself under the direct influence of another human brain, subject to another's ideas—even with the assured revenge of the same empire over him.

And from time to time, assuming the materiality of speech, the expected replies formulate themselves at their precise moment. This is what confirms the sorcery; he replies to my mental question.

"Oh, that's right!"

"No doubt."

But I'm deceitful, at present; taking refuge in a strictly personal islet of lucidity set apart from the currents and eddies of our duplicate thought, I entrench myself there, to test whether we are indissolubly linked.

Sometimes I have the upper hand; I feel my thought running into him, like a river into the sea; sometimes, it is his that flows back into me, irresistibly, as the tide fills an estuary.

Let's go! Stronger! No? But who is in command of our psychic couple—you or me? Reply! Reply out loud, I demand it!

He says nothing. He is still looking at me. But an internal voice cries: Me! Who thought that? Him or me?

And I strive with all my might: Ah! for this, I employ free will! I stand up, bracing myself with all my strength, in order to vanquish that antagonistic will. Interlocked like wrestlers in the ideal space that separates us, seemingly indifferent witnesses, our wills engaging in a duel with wild moves. Somersaults of triumph go through me. His shoulders are about to touch! And I press down, oh, I press down! But my hold is broken without his having acknowledged defeat, and I must defend myself in my turn, terribly.

It's a duel to the death. To the death, because the oscillatory, intoxicated, whirling-dervish double thought is vertiginously interlocked in a spiral of alternate litanies descending towards suicide.

He wants to kill himself—he's mad: I should certainly have realized that—and that old obsession will be realized today. He is thinking, I know, about the weapons hanging on the wall behind him—those loaded revolvers that he sees, as I see them, without looking at them . . . ho! isn't it me who has just suggested it to him? Did he really think it?—And then you'll kill me (for he has the proselytism of suicide, he wants me to deliver myself from life, in spite of myself), you'll kill me, and then yourself; we'll kill one another, with the revolvers over there. Oh, don't come any closer! I forbid it! See, I'm staying still (to maintain him in his place too, for if I try to forestall him, he'll perceive my intention immediately, and I can't—very quiet, this, very quiet!—kill him before he can do the same to me). Enough, I forbid it! Let's think of something else for a moment, so that I can get some respite in our hand-to-hand combat, to gather strength, to tame your impulses; so that I have the time to vanquish you; let's go on to something else, let's go on! (But I don't find anything, and in the void of my suggestion, it's his mortal thought that will hold sway, filling me too . . .) Listen, I remember . . . (No, not that! I don't want to! I've said nothing! A shadow! A shadow over that!) . . . that your mistress . . . (Am I mad, then, to tell him about that? Me, I don't want to. Me? Who's me?) That day we . . . (No! Nothing! Nothing! Ah, Victory! Nothing.) Listen. I'll tell you . . .

And our black gazes, our pupils enormous, sound one another out. Our faces are terrible, oracular.

Come on! Come on! Let's go! Yes, these are our synchronous thoughts. Let's go! A mysterious communal force, overwhelming, our Destiny, springs forth from the duplicate utmost depths of our being. Come on! We're going to die!

Traitor! You lied! It's your insanity that you want to pass off as our Destiny. Me, I want to live! I will live. My strength is coming back. I will! I will!—Victory! I've taken command of the couple. (For a brief instant, perhaps? No matter, it's enough.) Stay there—I order you to stay there! Twenty seconds! Twenty seconds! I want you to stay, madman!

Ah! I've leapt up! I was able to leap up!—ahead of him—to open the door, close it from the outside, lock it, and run away, free, run away into the darkness, to my home, to shut myself in too, to lock the door . . .

The connection between us is broken. A few fragments of his thought are still floating around me.

Vanquished, he tried to turn the drama into a joke, to excuse himself prosaically . . .

After an hour on watch, revolver in hand, I sensed that he was going to sleep.

Saved! I had reconquered my individuality, my precious individuality, submissive only to the play of eternal forces, and not to an unbearable conjunction with another human brain!

I dared to go to sleep.

When I woke up from a slumber swarming with horrid dreams, the memory of the adventure disturbed me again. I had recovered my normal consciousness and my full lucidity, but, in contrast to the aftermath of the phantasmagorias of ether, I was unable to see the telepathy of the previous evening as a simple illusion. The drug's effect had ceased; I was reasoning with my everyday brain—that brain which systematically denies the possibility of supernatural force—and yet I did not believe that those stranger phenomena were purely subjective in nature.

Even if they were only an illusion due to the hashish, had they not drawn from the depths of my organism, revealed and given birth to the consciousness of a crazy inclination—latent until then—to suicide?

And what if it were true? What if it had been true?

Should I interrogate Chaylas? But today, returned to a civilized lucidity, would he not deny those savage impulses, that wild scene in which he had conducted himself like a caveman? And what about me? Had not my own role been grotesque and odious?

So I avoided him. I had him sent away from my door—after all, he might have come to ask me why I had locked him in his room!

It was necessary, however, to bite the bullet when we bumped into one another a week later on the boulevard. He was, as always, taciturn and closed off. He did not raise the question. Devoured by one of those fatal curiosities that demand the illumination of something that should forever remain in shadow, I wanted to know.

We were silent. A slight vertigo, like an after-effect of hashish, was communicated between us in spite of the positive atmosphere of the boulevard.

At the precise moment when I was about to speak, I saw a hesitation on his face identical to mine: a dread that I might reveal to him the reality of the adventure—and the least allusion, by him or by me, would be irrefutable proof!

Simultaneously, we turned our eyes away. Simultaneously, we voiced the same commonplace.

THE OPIUM DEN

by Louy de Lhuc[1]

PREY to a sort of mystical exaltation, her long glaucous eyes enlivened by kohl and shining with a strange fever, Angèle la Roussotte consented, after numerous supplications, to introduce us into an opium den, to which profane individuals had difficulty being admitted.

It was the hour when the imperious need for the deadly drug, which had become indispensable to her, made her entire being vibrate dolorously; the hour when her poor head began to give birth, long before the rapid intoxication, to the crazy and chimerical dreams that were soon to transport her into a marvelous world full of delectable and bizarre sensations, which she was already evoking silently with an ardent fervor, and into which, a few years later, her reason was to sink forever, forcefully shaken by abuses of all kinds.

A young aspirant, scarcely disembarked from the *Iphigénie*, I had heard my comrades of the *Charles*

---

1 This by-line—which does not seem to have been used anywhere else—is enigmatic, but might be a deliberate contortion of the name of the critic and film director Louis Delluc (1890-1924), whose first film was *Fumée noire* (1920).

213

Martel talk many a time about Angèle's smoking den, uniquely frequented by sailors and a few rare privileged individuals. Driven by curiosity and the unhealthy desire to smoke a few pipes of the prestigious narcotic, the attractive charms of which had so often been praised in my presence, I awaited with a feverish impatience the moment when that sanctuary of dreams and madness would finally be opened to me.

Clamart, initiated long ago into the troubling mysteries of the deadly drug, and who had served to introduce me to our amiable hostess, appeared nevertheless to be accompanying me without enthusiasm.

Although the presence of the young woman, with heavy ardent blonde hair, half-undressed in a rich peignoir of pink linen garnished with valenciennes, the broad gap of which uncovered a very white, marvelously modeled cleavage, should have eliminated any religious idea from my mind, I immediately had the impression of entering a minuscule temple and to have come in order to offer a sacrifice there to some unknown divinity whose worship was about to be revealed to me.

In a narrow room in which exotic, penetrating and subtle perfumes float, a Chinese lantern spreads a mysterious soft half-light.

A few weapons of Tartar warriors, disposed in panoplies, tastefully enough, garnish walls hung with red satin. At the back, on a very low camp bed, a large lacquer tray, on which a host of miscellaneous objects repose, separates two thin and narrow mattresses encumbered by cushions covered in embroidered silk.

It is a smoking-room with all its accessories: first of all the little tinplate oil lamp hooded by a truncated glass, short and stout; then the long bamboo pipe encrusted with nacre; the slender steel needles that will soon cook, in the little pots, the precious drug brought from Benares or Annam; spare pipe-bowls; a curved curette; and finally, a delicately-wrought bronze perfume-burner, surrounded by a few ivory Buddhas, who seem to be contemplating that familiar apparatus with a bleak gaze.

Alongside the tray, a silver theater, artistically sculpted, adds a cheerful note to the half-light of the room, in which a vast and profound divan composes, along with the camp bed, the summary furniture. Angèle slowly takes off her peignoir and puts on an elegant pale blue kimono, enlivened by little green dragons, with yellow gold eyes, deftly woven in the light silk, and lets herself fall heavily on to the couchette; with her right hand, laden with strange rings, she seizes one of the needles and plunges it delicately into a little pot.

A drop of brown liquid, almost consistent, forms at its extremity; with an extreme attention she exposes it to the flame of the little lamp, rotating the steel stem with a continuous movement between her expert fingers. The droplet swells and begins to cook; its color, maroon to begin with, becomes darker and darker; it soon arrives at the desired degree of baking and then forms a soft paste.

After having rolled the tip of the needle, entirely hidden by the opium, over the glass walls, now sticky, several times, in order to fix the opium over a small extent by means of that rotation, she plunges it rapidly, with a swift and precise movement, into the narrow opening of the top-shaped bowl of the long and heavy pipe. The drug, thus softened, remains inside; she presses the flat surface that surrounds the minuscule orifice lightly with her finger-tip, and it adheres immediately. When the metal stem is removed, the opening remains free and the pipe is prepared, with as much care and dexterity as an inhabitant of the Celestial Empire could have employed.

She approaches it to the flame in its turn, and while she pushes the opium with the aid of the needle, as it burns with a very gentle sizzle, into the fire; she inhales the bitter smoke of the divine narcotic with a single long breath.

Immediately afterwards, her head falls back on the cushions, and, her eyes in ecstasy, her face illuminated, she seems to be experiencing an infinite wellbeing; the dream commences. The pipes succeed one another at increasingly long intervals until the moment when a profound slumber introduces her to the marvelous paradise that she is already commencing to glimpse with an astonishing lucidity.

A moment before, Clamart, extremely agitated, had quit the divan on which we were sitting, and, his head between his clenched hands, his eyes haggard and his nostrils dilated, appeared to be trying to chase away a terrifying nightmare, without success.

Abruptly, he turned his livid face toward me, extended a trembling hand toward me with an abrupt gesture, and said, in a hoarse voice full of anguish: "I don't want to stay here any longer . . . I sense that I can't resist a desire to smoke, and it's unhinging me horribly."

He disappeared silently, his gait ill-assured, like a drunken man.

Two months later I learned with a real dolor that that excellent comrade, who had returned fatally to Angèle's, had just been interned in a sanitarium near Paris.

I never went back to the la Roussotte house, in spite of the very keen pleasure I had experienced beside that beautiful young woman, as lovable as she was demented.

THE INITIATION

by Frédéric Boutet

IT was for that evening. In the auto that was rolling toward the left bank, little Madame Delivry—
twenty-four years old, widowed, blonde, elegant and
candid—was huddled against the ribs of her lover,
Claude Civel, a poet by virtue of the solid income that
permitted him to publish luxurious booklets.

She had taken his hand, and she was gazing, by the
fugitive lights of the street-lamps, at his scintillating
aristocratic monocle. She was over-excited, and delectably afraid. She would have liked to be encouraged
slightly, but he was silent, pale and handsome, distant
and striving to be enigmatic, allowing his habitual
perverse smile to wander over his shaven lip—for perversity was his specialty.

In the Place Saint-Sulpice the auto stopped. They
got out and went on foot to an old house of conventional appearance in a little dead street.

"My dwelling," said Claude Civel, in a dead voice.
"My true dwelling. Over there, at the Étoile, I live for

218

social convention; it's the façade, the luxury of my status, from which I escape here into dreams, the beyond, mystery and what is called vice—why not say the word, since you're one of those who understand, since you're going to be our sister in folly . . . and wisdom . . ."

She listened, swooning. He opened a door on the ground floor. She went in after him, her heart beating rapidly, into a room hung with heavy curtains, scarcely illuminated by a green night-light.

"Take off your furs," he murmured. "No, keep your veil on, so that your features can't be seen . . ."

He took her into a large square room. The ruddy light of a sculpted copper lantern suspended from the ceiling fell diffusely over crimson drapes and low divans. Her feet sank into a profound carpet. A penetrating odor, in a heavy warmth, suffocated the young woman: incense, ether and another odor, slightly bitter and noxious, which she did not recognize. In the gloom she glimpsed two women on one of the divans, semi-enlaced, who seemed to be asleep, their eyes wide open. In a corner, a hairy and simian adolescent, hunched over, was sniffing the contents of a pharmaceutical phial, or perhaps drinking it. On the floor, side by side on thin mattresses, two men were lying; they were passing back and forth a long pipe, which they charged with a brown paste and from which they inhaled long draughts, lighting it with a little round lamp placed between them.

One of them, without anyone else budging, got to his feet and approached, vacillating slightly. He had strange foggy eyes, sparse hair, brushed up at the front, and a thin face of a stony whiteness.

"An initiate . . . she's going to smoke," Claude Civel murmured, indicating his trembling companion, who was dying of the desire to leave, but dared not do so.

"And . . . and you?" she whispered.

"Me?" He took out of his pocket a little silver box. "I prefer hashish," he said. "It's more powerful, more vibrant more visionary." He paused, and added: "Perhaps more dangerous . . ."

He took a cup of coffee from a nearby side-table, took a dark pill from his little box, and swallowed it.

Following the indications of the livid man, the young woman had lain down, as far as possible from the others present, on a mattress covered with painted silk. The man brought her a pipe, charged it and approached it to the lamp.

"Inhale deeply," he whispered.

She hesitated, but encountered the gaze of her lover, who was lying on cushions close by. She inhaled with all her might, nearly suffocated, and coughed. He prepared a second pipe for her, and then a third. She stretched herself out further on her mattress, and smoked again, courageously. Things moved, spun a little; the adolescent seemed to jig about . . . and she leapt up, shaken by a terrible nausea, her handkerchief over her mouth. She just had time to reach the antechamber, but not to go any further, and was frightfully ill there. The face of stone had followed her and, without saying a word, did his best to sustain her, charitably.

"I want to go, I want to go away," she stammered, plaintive and furious, as soon as she could speak.

Claude Civel took her away, dominating, he explained, his nascent intoxication. He was losing an evening of ecstasy, but he was only too happy to make that sacrifice for her.

She did not thank him for it; she held it against him slightly, but he deigned to joke about her naïve shame; what did the unfortunate event matter if it were the threshold of revealed paradises, the initiating ordeal of unalloyed bliss? He left her, calmed down, at her door.

The next day, while still weary, she was at home at about two o'clock, when a monsieur, coming for good works from the Saint-Sulpice quarter, had himself announced.

Intrigued, she received him. It was the livid man. In the daylight he was even more fleshless, haggard and poorly dressed. He seemed to be suppressing a tremor and blinking his eyes like a nocturnal animal. For a moment, he attached a vague staring gaze upon her, under which she blushed.

"What is it . . . ?" she stammered.

He interrupted her.

"It's necessary not to come again . . . not to come again . . . Yes, I know that today, you have no desire to do so, but tomorrow, he'll persuade you. You'll get used to it, you'll become like us . . . like me . . ." He raised his head and showed himself more clearly. She shivered. ". . . And I'm not at the end, you know. One goes much further; I'm only at the first vertigo, the first anguish. It's necessary not to come again . . . you're too . . ." He searched for a word. ". . . Too small . . . Yesterday I saw you, a true sick little girl, and so pretty . . . It's necessary not to come again. There are other things in life for you . . ."

His voice was hoarse and soft. She was impressed slightly. But by what right . . . ? She protested, haughtily: "Thank you for your advice, Monsieur, but those other banal things are insufficient for certain souls."

He made a weary gesture.

"I know . . . it's him . . . my God, what an idiot! You love him, and he'll lead you down there, with us—and you don't know what we are . . . and he'll make you smoke, and he'll make you vomit . . . No, no, don't be annoyed; it's necessary that I say these things to you, in order that you don't come any more. Me, I'm a wreck, a coward, no matter what . . . it's all the same to me . . . But me, it's true . . . and him . . . well, it isn't true . . . He gives me what I need . . . the drug, in sum . . . and me. I'm his . . . accomplice, if you like. I facilitate his comedy . . . yes, his comedy . . . his perversity, his vices . . . are a joke . . . he's far too fearful. His hashish— yes, more vibrant, more visionary—is pellets of bread tinted green . . . oh, with an inoffensive dye. He's only a clown, you know . . . only a clown . . ."

He paused. The young woman had gone pale.

"Are . . . are you sure?" she stammered.

He laughed mutely. He went on: "What's more, he's a swine. Just now, he refused me fifty francs that I needed in order not to be evicted . . . . . No, don't look for your purse . . . I'm not there yet. I knew that he'd refuse them to me. It was easier, after that, to speak to you. You understand? But it's necessary not to come again . . ."

He turned away.

"I'll come again once . . ." The young woman had a strange smile. "I'll come again on Friday evening . . ."

And that Friday, at about ten o'clock, coming as she had the other time with Claude Civel, particularly seductive that evening, she saw the conventional house again and the square room in which the ruddy light of the sculpted lamp was dying in the heavy scents. No one was there but the livid man, smoking on the floor in moderation, and the simian adolescent who was jigging about on his corner of the divan, with his phial under his nose, without knowing anything of exterior life, possessed by a turbulent chimera.

"Permit me to intoxicate myself," said Claude Civel, elegantly.

From a delightful enamel candy-box he chose the largest pill and swallowed it. He lay down on the cushions.

"And you?" he asked,

"Later" she said. "I'm tired."

He smiled. He picked up a guitar and drew a few chords from it, by which the hairy runt seemed delighted, gesticulating with his feet.

Time passed. The adolescent croaked a few inconsequential verses. The man on the floor lit a perfume.

Suddenly, Civel sat up.

"What's the matter with me?" His voice was fearful. "It seems to me . . . my tongue is dry . . . in the stomach . . . heat . . ."

223

"It's the hashish," said the young woman, coldly.

"The hashish . . . how . . . the hashish?"

"Yes, it's good isn't it? It's very fresh; I put it in your candy-box, which you were kind enough to accept, instead of your old pills. I went to a great deal of trouble to procure it . . ."

He was no longer listening. He had bounded to his feet in alarm. Fear prevailed over everything else.

"I have a sick aorta!" he howled. "It'll kill me . . . Water! Hot water!"

He ran to the tea urn, and two minutes later, saturated with warm water, in the kitchen of the house of dream and mystery, leaning over the sink—to the immense amusement of the livid man, who had followed him—without any more enigma or perversity, he was vomiting as much as he could.

DROPPING IN ON ANIKA

by Victor Marguerite

RETURNED to the Rue de La Boëtie, Monique attempted to work. The pencils and brushes would not stay between her fingers.

She came back from her laborious whim further demoralized. What could she do? What would absorb her? Courageous, yes, she could have devoted herself body and soul to any task. There was no lack of interesting ones, even impassioning ones, including that of taking up that of Madame Ambrat on her own account, and amplifying it . . .

So much misery to soothe, everywhere! So much to do! she said to herself. *But one can only be altruistic on condition of no longer thinking about oneself. Easy at forty, for Madame Ambrat . . .*

Monique, being young, thought of nothing but herself. The bad habits she had acquired, including the success in her métier of luxury, wound around her like a thousand soft but tenacious bonds . . .

225

She sent for the design of the incriminated back-cloth, and judged the brick shade, with its embroideries of fake encrusted gems, to be charming.

"What an idiot that Lair is!" she said to Claire. "I need to call in at the Vaudeville, to see the set in place. What if I were to go now?"

"They're not rehearsing, Mademoiselle. It's Thursday, in the morning . . ."

"*Zut!* Show me the cerise velvet, then, for Monsieur Plombino's study."

"We don't have it yet."

Monique left it there. Sufficient effort for one day . . . At the same time, the end of the afternoon extended its familiar desert before her. How could she pass the time until the evening, when she could go to smoke the interminable hours away at Anika's? There was a rendezvous with Hélène Suze at the Ritz, who was piloting a young Swedish couple susceptible of making purchases . . . but the idea of interested politeness . . . ! And the vision of the tea-room, with its little tables covered with interminable cakes, and the tiresome repetition of jazz bands, the stupidity of small talk!

An increasingly frequent savagery succeeded her promiscuities with the society in which she, along with the Hélènes, Ginettes and Michelles, whether minister's wives or Marquises, were worth little more, if nor even less, than a Carmen or an Irma.

She put on her hat and tailored jacket. She had adopted that uniform several days before, even in the evenings, having renounced the coquetry of her dresses since the last expedition. She thus had only one clasp to undo, and her skirt came off. And with Anika helping her to undo her bodice, she was immediately ready, at ease in the drapery of a kimono, for the quotidian ceremony.

I'll certainly find her in the process of smoking, she thought. *She must have received her drug. A good pipe! There's nothing like it!*

Suddenly decided, Monique calmed down. She was in one of those periods of intoxication in which opium was as necessary to her as air. She could no longer kick the habit. It was necessary for her to inhale the pacifying smoke, or she would choke. A cold sweat of anguish chilled her flesh.

Often, ceasing after weeks of being absorbed in that slight intoxication, she had had those dolorous symptoms. She had then succeeded, with a renewed effort of will, in spacing out the sessions. She sensed that by a prolonged abstinence, she would recover for action a lucidity that was in the process of applying itself entirely, in a sterile fashion, to dreams. But this time, having taken the poison in massive doses, she experienced only one desire: to take more.

Brutalization? No, annihilation: the marvelous scorn for everything that was not the bliss of which, from the first pipe, she felt the benefit, and through which, by the twentieth, she was penetrated, she was penetrated to the extent of the supreme joy: dissolution; evaporation!

As expected she found Anika prostrate on her cushions, in the dark. The minuscule lamp, half-dimmed by a silver butterfly-valve, was gleaming faintly on the tray of utensils. One might have thought it a funerary night-light.

"It's me," said Monique. "Don't move."

On emerging from the bright summer twilight, the studio with the hermetically sealed curtains, completely impregnated with the heavy odor, seemed as quiet as a great tomb. Already, however, Anika had turned the commutator. The lamp illuminated, with a ruddy glow, the recumbent smoker and the ritual apparatus. The violinist's face seemed corpse-like, the flesh plastered on the brown bone-structure.

In a hoarse voice, she declared: "You've come at a bad time. No jam."

"I thought . . ."

"No. The fellow who was to bring it to me—good stuff, direct from London!—got himself pinched yesterday at the Saphir. Can you imagine? Not because of the opium—they didn't know he had it—but because of the coke! They confiscated the lot."

She sniggered. Loquaciously, with the mechanical volubility that the white powder produces, she uttered, in a single breath:

"They're annoying, all those morons in Parliament, with their laws! They make me laugh! Narcotics! They've got them. Père Hutier, merchant of virtue! You see that? So what if I want to intoxicate myself? To begin with, if they want to talk about poison, let them start with alcohol! But that, they don't dare. It's the bistro that nominates them . . ."

She lowered her voice, and continued, confidentially: "I've still got some snow, fortunately. Souillarde, who looks after the toilets at the Pelican, sold it to me. Look, that boxful! You see?"

Laughing, she pointed at a little enamel candy box.

"And then, I know where to find some. There's a pharmacist at Javel! You see? But for jam, nothing doing. Do you have any left?"

"Yes, the dregs of a pot . . ."

"Fish it out. You have a light? It makes no difference, go, stay. We'll smoke the drops. I've scraped out all the old pipes. Hold on, there's still the bowl of the big one—the ivory one . . . it's full of it. The drops are good too. I don't know if I like them as much . . ."

She coughed, in spite of her armored throat, and repeated, hoarsely: "The drops are stronger. They intoxicate better . . ."

Like a drunkard, she needed stiffening.

She sighed: "All the same, if one didn't have that, in life . . . come on! Lie down . . ."

"Wait until I put my robe on."

Monique, accustomed to it, got undressed in the gloom. Draped in a Chinese mantle, she took her place alongside the tray. As she rotated the butterfly-valve of the lamp mechanically, the flame of which was inconveniencing her, Anika, who had taken advantage of the interval to stuff her nose, complained with an angry vivacity: "When you've quite finished shining the light in my eye!"

What has she taken? Monique thought. To the loquacious overexcitement of the cocaine, to which the violinist had been trying to convert her for several days, she preferred the silent vertigo of the opium.

Refusing the pinch that Anika, having calmed down, was holding out to her, she agglomerated into a ball a little of the black residue that would constitute her entire feast that evening. Once more, she would be dining by heart! But the drops, being too hard, did not roll up well, melting at the tip of the needle. That one fell back, sizzling, into the flame. She succeeded, however, in rounding out the heavy drop sufficiently, and, seizing her pipe, almost garnishing the bowl.

Then, putting the bamboo to her lips, she inhaled avidly, with a long aspiration. The smoke was so bitter that she spat it out, the ball consumed. Usually, when the opium was fresh, she swallowed the heady poison, savoring the delight of feeling it enter into her, liquefying her entire being almost instantaneously.

She set down the pipe and let herself relax on the cushions, dazed. The reek with which the studio was saturated, the insipid and powerful perfume of the black balm, had gripped her, and was carrying her away, under the violent breath of the first effluvium.

With a satisfied snigger, Anika exclaimed: "Well, my old lady!"

"Don't shout," Monika pleaded. "One would think it were a train going by!"

The noise reverberated within her, multiplied. But the sonorous wave soon faded away. The walls recoiled. Everything became distant—very distant—and simultaneously muffled, to the point that Anika's staccato verbosity was no longer anything but a whispered confidence. Time ceased to exist. Space was filled with a fluid softness. Ecstatic, Monique experienced a double impression of emptiness and plenitude.

"Say, then," jeered the voice, transposed as if it were coming from another world, "that it's having its effect! And if you'd taken a little coke . . . ! Me, it's my third gram since yesterday. You see . . . There's nothing to say . . . they invented these drugs, you know, to cure you of seasickness. Existence, that makes me vomit! A good pipe, a good pinch! That puts the guts back in place. Suppress opium and coke, can you see that? They must be stupid! It's like a doctor who refuses you morphine when you're in pain! There are some who do that, on the pretext that people get a taste for it! One can't even kick the bucket in peace, then? What right do the filthy swine have to condemn me to life? It's my wreck, not theirs. In order that they can put on airs, in their boutique! You see that? Oh la la! Love, for a start, doesn't exist. It's just rumors that are put around. There are idiots who tear themselves apart when they don't get kissed. Pleasure? Yes, the ass! A cul-de-sac that you soon get to the bottom of. Art? Oh, my dear, where's my violin? Talent, yes, I had it, perhaps. Yes, yet, a great artist, that's understood. A long time ago. And afterwards? Chopin had talent too. Only he was at least able to chew his notes . . . that sticks. Me, necessary to stuff myself . . . you see that? I played the music of others. Spoiled, see! Not even children. A good-for-nothing!"

Nervously, she opened her candy-box and took out a copious pinch. An in authoritarian tone, she said: "Take it, I tell you. It's the true remedy. With that, one can do without the rest!"

"No," said Monique. "I prefer your dirty drops."

The violence of the initial sensation had dissipated. Patiently, she set about fashioning her balls, and then cooking them, but she no longer succeeded in smoking them at a single draught. Then, nervous in her turn, and not finding the calm she was pursuing, she followed Anika's advice and took one pinch after another.

Far from relaxing her, though, the dangerous powder, ineptly dosed, exasperated her agitation. She suddenly thought that she had a wooden face, the nose, the forehead and the temples hardening, in an anesthesia so brutal that she felt that she was becoming a machine. In her turn, untiringly, she began to grind out words into the void. A complete insensibility stiffened her. With jerky gestures, she continued to perorate, incessantly.

All night long, separated by the tray on which the lamp went out at dawn, they conversed in that fashion, like deaf people.

When Monique woke up, chilled, it was after midday. The studio remained mysterious in its gloom. Anika was still asleep, so pale that she contemplated her anxiously. One might have thought that she was dead. She touched her hand, which was cold—but a faint breath was making the flat chest rise and fall, regularly.

Monique left without disturbing her.

THE NIGHT OF HASHISH AND OPIUM

by Maurice Magre

The Bad Omens

I lifted the blue gauze that was undulating before my window. A flock of black birds, emerging from the palm trees in the garden, striped the sky slowly, trailing above the scattered masts of the harbor and disappearing to the left in the gilded fleece of the beach.

A bad omen, I thought.

And I established a relationship between the color of the birds and the black color of the opium whose intoxication was to be revealed to me that very evening. The evening of opium was poorly announced!

For I have always believed that a sage providence informs us by a small sign, when we cast our first glance at things, whether the day is to be fortunate or unfortunate.

Scarcely had I lost sight of the birds than a Brahmin beggar that I knew went past on the avenue. He was protecting himself from the sun by extending his fan of areca palm leaves, and sometimes he agitated his rags. He stopped for a second before my door, raised his head and saw me, He squinted frightfully. He made a bizarre grimace, and I immediately drew back, for I was almost naked.

I murmured: "Another bad omen!"

And at the same moment, a tari, a kind of trumpet with a heart-rending tone, which signals mourning, resonated on the landward side, in the Hindu quarter.

I had also seen the Brahmin with the squint lift his fan and grimace in my direction, and I had heard a tari in the distance, firstly on the morning of my marriage, and afterwards on the morning of the day when I had discovered and read the letters addressed to my husband by a certain Juliette Romano—letters that legitimated my divorce.

The heart-rending trumpet evoked for me, with a gripping verity, that decisive day of my life.

I have noticed that, when one has just taken a bath and is not yet dressed, the soul has a tendency to appear naked, like the body. For our true soul only shows itself, even to ourselves, at rare intervals, and preferably in the morning.

In truth, I no longer loved my husband when I found the letters and learned that he was the lover of an adventuress recently installed in Pondicherry. He had almost ruined me. That wasn't of any great importance, but I felt that he was going to destroy my inner fortune, which is made of self-confidence and confidence in life. The fear of that invisible ruination had killed my love. I didn't hold against him a few base actions that I had discovered—one doesn't attach oneself to a man because of elevated sentiments—but I resented the fact that he had only considered me as a legitimate wife, and had not appreciated me as a lover.

I no longer loved him, to be sure, but I suffered nevertheless in knowing that he no longer loved me.

The tari announcing the death dragged on lugubriously that day, as today, and aggravated my pain. I remember the desire for certainty that animated me, my shrill voice calling for Scheik Sultan and my telingas, the fashion in which I traversed the garden and in which I fell into my palanquin, shouting an address. I remember my confrontation with the woman who had been depicted to me as a redoubtable adventuress, a whore capable of anything, expressly created by God to break homes and damn men.

Juliette Romano was a timid individual whose blue eyes had a slightly fleeting gaze, who would have had the appearance of an English schoolmistress full of innocence if a certain something in the milky hue of her neck, and in the solid roundness of her breasts beneath her corsage, had not betrayed a hidden ardor and a capacity for abandonment. After five minutes of conversation she had begged my pardon and confessed everything that I wanted to know. I quit her without having said a wounding word and during the hours that followed I cursed the tari player more ardently, who never ceased to rend my ears for an unknown mourning caused by the timid creature of prey who had just taken my husband from me.

All that was so far away now! In any case, it's only the present that counts. But the present was a flock of black birds rising from the right to the left; it was a Brahmin beggar who had just squinted at my door; it was a trumpet announcing the death of a Hindu in a wretched hut of compressed earth.

It was even more than that, I suddenly remembered. It was one of the good God's creatures that I had inadvertently crushed the day before; it was a chemise that my ayah had presented to me inside-out as I was about to put it on; it was a game of dominos that children were playing at the foot of the statue of Dupleix, each domino of which they had wrapped in paper—which is, as everyone knows, a sign auguring great calamities.

Never had there been as any contrary presages against me, never had I been informed with such certainty of the evil fate that was lying in wait for me.

In the pure light of the morning I saw clearly what it was necessary for me to do. I had to find a pretext to refuse Lord Portman's invitation, and not go to smoke opium at Chillambaram.

Nothing was easier. I only had to write two letters of apology, one to Lord Portman and the other to Comtesse Aurelia, who was to accompany us.

Was there not, in any case, something bizarre about the insistence that Comtesse Aurelia had put into begging me to accept that pleasure party? Comtesse Aurelia had excessively thin lips and an excessively narrow forehead. Her black hair was naturally curly and shone like the plumage of a crow. Were those not the characteristics of an evil influence? She hated me, I was sure of it, because I was twenty and she was thirty-five, perhaps more. Why had she suddenly praised the magnificence of the pagoda of Chillambaram, as she had never previously paid much attention to the ancient monuments of India, and seemed perfectly ignorant of the beauties of architecture—and of beauty in general? Why put on a show of being so passionately desirous to see me dance, as she had made fun of my pretention of learning the ritual dances of the bayaderes before all Pondicherry and all Madras? Why had she depicted to me with so much eloquence, the day before the voluptuousness of smoking opium in a dreamlike décor, when she had told me, a few months before, that she had a horror of the drug and all those who smoked it?

Was there not something bizarre about that gathering at Chillambaram of three men who had all been in love with me and all disappointed in their desires? On what was their so-called friendship based except their common desire to talk about me, to slander me collectively and to affirm after having drunk or smoked that one or another of them would have me sooner or later, now that I was divorced. For those three men were now inseparable. When they were not cruising along the Coromandel coast or hunting in the forests of Trivatore, they were getting drunk together. Lord Portman was an alcohol drinker, the Rajah of Tanjore was an opium smoker and Prince Vanini attained artificial paradises with the pellets of hashish that were fabricated for him by a Bengali physician in Madras.

It was by virtue of living in their company that my husband had been detached from me; it was with them that he had lost a part of my fortune in the gambling dens of Madras. I didn't hold it against them, and I even had the weakness to see them, because there is nothing insensate that one doesn't do to escape ennui.

But was there not something bizarre in the recommendation that Lord Portman had made me not to bring with me either the faithful Scheik Sultan, who always marched at the head of my palanquin-bearers, or my creole chambermaid, who would have been so useful to me for changing costume?

"You'll find all the necessary staff at Chillambaram," he had said. "I promise you a night such as you've never spent."

In saying those words he had run his tongue over his fleshy lips and had made me think of a wild beast about to make a meal of raw flesh.

He had immediately added, as if to reassure me: "You're risking absolutely nothing; Comtesse Aurelia won't quit you."

"What would I be risking?" I had said, immediately, putting an icy innocence in my expression.

"Nothing other than not having experienced hands to take off your dress and put on the costume of the bayadere Cammatatchi."[1]

And he had started to laugh, the distant laughter that is habitual to him, while his eyes were deprived of

---

1 "Cammatatchi, a Dancer," is an oft-reproduced print, still easily available. It is credited to the Orientalist Eugène Burnouf (1801-1852) because it was used as an illustration in one of his books, but he is unlikely to have been the artist. The portrait does not show its subject dancing, nor is her costume provocative; the author only seems to have borrowed the name.

all human expression, to the point of giving the impression that his spirit was no longer inhabiting his body.

For the evening at Chillambaram had been organized in order to see me dance. I had made the imprudent promise to do so at Comtesse Aurelia's house, one evening when Lucilio Vanini, pill-box in hand, had just described the architectural marvels of Chillambaram and made me ashamed of never having traveled the forty-nine miles that separate the ancient pagoda from Pondicherry. That same evening I had made known to the Rajah of Tanjore that desire to try, once, the effects of opium.

Lord Portman, always prompt to multiply opportunities to see me, had proposed organizing a dinner and a night in the pagoda. He had taken charge of bribing the Brahmins and getting them to empty the space for the entire extent of the vast enclosure of the walls. He took charge of having two or three rooms cleaned before the sacred pool and organizing a comfortable smoking-room sheltered from mosquitoes, lizards and snakes. We would have an orchestra and intermediate dancers, but on condition that I animated the artistic feast by dancing in the same costume and in the same place where the celebrated bayadere Cammatatchi had once danced.

I had accepted. Everyone had uttered cries of joy. Lord Portman had added: "We'll be tranquil. I'll bring my panther to guard us." Then, his eyes fixed, he had fallen into a meditation and profound as the void.

And now the day had come for the departure for Chillambaram, and destiny was sending me all kinds of warnings to incite me to postpone that departure.

I got dressed slowly. I took several turns around my room. I was going to write the letters of apology. I would not go to Chillambaram.

I affirmed to myself that what was guiding me was only the imperious notification of destiny, and not the ridiculous bourgeois sentiment that comes from fear of compromising oneself.

I have never been afraid of compromising myself, either in France before my marriage or since my arrival in Pondicherry. I deem that a well-established bad reputation is one of the conditions of happiness. One wears that bad reputation like an armor, the sparkle of which distances you from mediocre and tedious individuals. The darts of calumny slide off it and it permits the conquest of the most redoubtable of the enemies of our pleasure, which is our natural timidity.

I wandered in the garden under my parasol and I was about to go back upstairs to write the letters when I heard the prolonged cry that palanquin-bearers utter when they stop.

Behind the gate I perceived the exceedingly wrinkled face of Comtesse Aurelia.

"Well, are you ready? They've just fired the cannon of the yacht to alert us."

I ran toward the door to declare my resolution.

"No, no, I'm not stopping," said the Comtesse, with a determined volubility. "You know that I don't like to be late. Lord Portman has sent you this little golden box that you must put around your neck. It's a surprise, but it's necessary not to open it until this evening. And some news—perhaps bad news, or good, I don't know. Mir, the Rajah's son, will be with us. His father is bringing him because he asked to see you dance, it seems. But I'm afraid that one spectator more might be too much for your timidity."

She started to laugh, and before I could reply she made a sign to her telingas to start walking.

I remained motionless, considering the Chinese flowers of the silk parasol, which I had lowered. In my left hand I was holding a little gilded box suspended from an antique chain, which Comtesse Aurelia had handed to me through the bars of the gate and which I passed mechanically around my neck. How singular the flowers on the parasol were! In the calyx of each one there was the face of a student at the University of Madras: the face of Mir, the Rajah's son; Mir with the impenetrable eyes—twenty years old, like me, perhaps nineteen—whom I identified mentally with the Rama of the Hindu poems, and to whom I gave that name when I thought about him.

I started running through the garden. "Scheik Sultan!" I shouted.

Then I reflected that there was to need to run, and that the yacht would not leave without me.

The bayadere's robe had been packed the previous evening, just in case.

I threw a shawl over my shoulders and put rouge on my lips. Already I could hear the sound of the gate opening and the footsteps of the palanquin-bearers on the gravel of the path.

And at the exact moment when, sitting in the midst of cushions, I raised my hand to order the departure, a sweating Hindu child who had no garments save a loincloth and a red turban, showed his head at the window. The porters began to run. He threw on to my knees a piece of paper folded in four. I opened it. There were words traced in French in topsy-turvy handwriting that seemed deliberately disguised:

You must not go to Chillambaram.

I looked back through the window of the palanquin. Far away, on the avenue, there was a little Hindu running as far as he could in the opposite direction to that of the palanquin. As my porters had set forth very rapidly, a few seconds had sufficed for the red turban no longer to be anything more than an almost imperceptible dot.

I thought that it was too late to go back and attempt to catch up with the messenger. His flight indicated, in any case, that he had been instructed to give me the enigmatic letter and disappear without explanation.

I crumpled up the note with a hint of irritation, because I had no idea who could have sent it, and for me, unsatisfied curiosity is analogous to a mental burn.

But what a desire I had now for that night of opium at Chillambaram! All the gods of India emerging from the mystery of their pagoda and extending their innumerable arms toward me would have stopped me when I launched myself forth along the interminable landing-stage of Pondicherry. The enigma of an unknown danger summoned me with as much force as the enigma of Mir's dark eyes. Oh, the beauty of that which one does not know, and that which might be revealed to you, whether it be good or evil!

The wind made my dress flap. An odor of rotten plants alternated with the intoxicating breath of the open sea. And on the launch that took me to the yacht, to the regular beat of the oars, amid the tedious and limited faces of English sailors, I imagined that I was sailing toward dangerous pirates, who had captured me by means of an incomprehensible ruse and whose prey I was about to be.

The Bayadere Cammatatchi

I believe that all events can always be deduced in advance, read in the atmosphere, by a clairvoyant person who knows how to cast her intuition artfully around her.

I ought to have understood and foreseen. Everything was irrevocably settled in the minds of the three men tormented by desire and the woman with the face as wrinkled as an apple burned by the sun.

First of all there was the unusual insistence they put into making me drink during the lunch on deck; then the fashion in which they all repeated that Mir had preferred to make the journey on horseback in spite of the heat of the day and that he would join us at Porto Novo, where we were to disembark. There was Comtesse Aurelia's laughter, as sharp as a rapier—laughter that she rapidly veiled when she remembered that it was necessary to disguise her perfidy. She then put on an expression of bonhomie and strove to become similar to a smiling apple, devoid of all acidity.

There were words whose meaning I didn't understand and which caused a great deal of laughter. There was a question of a game of cards, a stake, a fortune won or lost, but I couldn't understand what the prize was or even whether the game had already taken place.

Prince Vanini told Comtesse Aurelia and me, in fragments, stories about the antiquity of Chillabaram, its fabulous riches, its thousands of priests and its vanished splendors. He spoke with a certain mystery in his voice, as if everything he said had the character of a secret. Everything he knew he had from the Rajah, who nodded his head in approval from time to time. For the Rajah almost never spoke when several people were gathered together, and said himself that it was only possible for him to express himself before a single interlocutor. Prince Vanini, on the contrary, was only loquacious before a numerous audience.

And there was also the story of the bayadere Cammatatchi, which should have alerted me. The Prince's voice, when he spoke about her, became even lower, and Lord Portman, who was walking back and forth smoking a cigar, stopped, and I saw his fleshy lips agitating nervously in a fashion so repulsive that I was obliged to look away.

The bayadere Cammatatchi was a priestess of Siva the destroyer, the third god of the Hindu trinity. She was so beautiful that her renown extended throughout India and pilgrims came from the most distant parts of the Deccan to contemplate her. But she had an expression in her face that drove men to despair. An incitement to death was in the lines of her body. Many pilgrims who had seen her offered their lives to Siva.

The Rajah of Tanjore, an ancestor of the one who was smoking a cigar beside me and never took his eyes off me, fell in love with the bayadere. By caprice, the marvelous Cammatatchi, who, by virtue of her profession as a sacred bayadere, gave herself to all those who brought important offerings to the pagoda, refused herself to the Rajah of Tanjore.

"The ancestor of our excellent friend," said the Prince, designating the Rajah, who lowered his eyes, "was a singularly cruel man. He resolved to have the bayadere in spite of her refusal and to punish her for it. It was the day of the feast of Sidambara . . . I'm not mistaken?" the Prince asked, turning to the Rajah, who made a negative sign with his cigar. "On the day of that feast, Sidambara, who is an incarnation of Siva, appears to his initiates."

"And then?" I said, for the Prince had stopped.

The yacht had just rounded the rocky banks of Cooleroon, and we were in sight of Porto Novo.

Lord Portman, who was leaning over the side, shouted: "I think I can see Mir on the jetty. He's arrived before us."

Everyone got up. I looked in the direction of the coast. I distinguished the torsos of a few Hindus sitting on the sand. I saw a man with a staff in his hand pushing three zebus before him, but there was no trace of a horseman.

Prince Vanini, having looked in my direction and exchanged a glance of complicity with the Rajah and the Comtesse, murmured in a low voice: "Yes, I believe that Mir has arrived first." And he started to laugh in a servile fashion, turning to Lord Portman: the excessive laughter that is not commanded by merriment but the desire to flatter someone for a mediocre joke whose value one wants to heighten by approval.

He added: "I'll conclude the story of Cammattachi this evening."

Lord Portman had indeed been joking, or mistaken. Mir was not waiting for us at Porto Novo. No one was astonished by that, and his father declared lightly that he would doubtless join us at Chillambaram.

The afternoon was not yet approaching its end, but we still had eight kilometers to cover overland in order to reach the first gopuram of the pagoda, built some distance from the village on the edge of the jungle.

Palanquins, horses and an escort were waiting for us. Comtesse Aurelia and I were to make the journey in a palanquin. I offered, out of politeness, to climb into the same magnificent palanquin as her, in which, in the midst of a stream of cushions, four people could easily have been accommodated. To my great surprise, she refused. She protested the great heat, a slight headache that she felt around her temples, and that she thought she might cure by sleeping a little. Then, there were two palanquins, and she preferred to have one to herself. And when I persisted she turned her back on me, installed herself in the first palanquin and closed the door rather abruptly.

What a disagreeable woman! I thought, privately, unable to understand that manner of acting, which was not habitual to her.

We left.

There was still time to go back. Had I not been warned? Without being very perspicacious, it required no more to see things clearly. But it is noticeable that, when we fall into a trap, it is by virtue of a faculty of blindness that is of our own making, and which blindfolds our eyes for a while.

Palanquin-bearers intone a rhythmic chant, full of vague poetry, which initially invites melancholy, and afterwards slumber. My blindness and my quietude combined so well with the changing voice of the telingas and the sway they imparted to the palanquin, that I fell asleep.

When I woke up the palanquin had stopped. I had been asleep for nearly an hour. Prince Vanini and the Rajah were in the process of dismounting and Lord Portman, standing beside the window, was considering me with his empty eyes. His lips were trembling slightly, and they appeared to me so red, so thick and sensual that I felt my stomach rise in disgust.

"It's said that a good sleep is the sign of a tranquil conscience," he said. And as I opened the door to get down he added, in a low voice: "You who are the cause of all my nights of insomnia."

I was confused and surprised. I looked around. We were at the bottom of a steep slope. I distinguished at the summit an enormous red wall, towers, successions of gopurams covered with sculptures whose ensemble formed the pagoda of Chillambaram, as vast as a city . . .

To my right, quite some distance away, was the village, with a single two-story house dominating the palm-thatch roofs, which must be the travelers' bungalow. A large number of Hindus were watching us fearfully. To the left, Lord Portman's servants formed a respectful circular group. Behind us I saw the road we had followed paling between coconut palms and cacti. But I searched in vain for the second palanquin, the one bearing Comtesse Aurelia.

I interrogated the Prince, who was beside me.

"How well you must have slept," he said, laughing. "We'd only covered a few hundred meters when the Comtesse felt her headache worsen. An hour's sleep always cures her in such cases. Lord Portman went to install her in a cabin in the yacht, and he rejoined us before we had arrived. Comtesse Aurelia will arrive for dinner, doubtless at the same time as Mir, who can't be much longer now."

Could I now refuse, without being absolutely ridiculous, to visit the pagoda, take part in a dinner long prepared and accepted by me, under the pretext that I was the only woman in the company of three men? I should have done. A false shame prevented me from doing so.

We climbed the hill on foot. A few Hindus clad in yellow and black robes conversed with Lord Portman. I assumed that they were the Brahmin guardians of the temple. I distinguished in their attitude the deference and the scorn that one has for those one believes one has duped by an excellent bargain.

The sun was about to set and projected a red wave over the great stone wall, more than ten meters high, mute and inalterable, as eternal as the religion whose

248

mysteries it encloses. We were at the foot of one of four fabulous portals formed by a truncated rectangular pyramid with seven steps. Sculpted on that portal were divinities of all sorts, maleficent Boutas, elephantine Ganeshas, Vishnus with nine arms, and faces and animal limbs that were superimposed and interlaced, and made a kind of animal forest of stone.

Prince Vanini drew closer to me and I felt his warm breath on my cheek.

"The antiquity of the monument renders the intoxication of opium or hashish more profound. You'll see."

I turned away, but the Rajah took my arm lightly while walking and said to me: "It's here that my ancestor made love to the bayadere Cammatatchi, who must have resembled you. Scarcely will I have crossed the threshold than I shall imagine that I'm my ancestor and that you are Cammatatchi."

Servants passed at a run, carrying carpets, boxes and torches: the final preparations for the dinner and the evening.

Lord Portman, who had remained in the rear, advanced toward us joyfully.

"Even the Brahmins won't be sleeping in the enclosure," he said. "They'll spend the night in the village. Chillambaram belongs to us until tomorrow, and I'll have the door locked behind us."

He made us a sign to follow him.

I would have sworn that at that moment, in the monsters and gods sculpted on the mass of the gopuram and covered with a vegetation of cryptogams, there was a sort of living stir, with facial grimaces, the quivering of horns and rumps, the advancement of snouts and elongations of claws. At the same time I was traversed by a mad, desperate, panic terror. The immensity of my folly appeared to me clearly. Mir had not been invited and would not arrive on horseback. Comtesse Aurelia was in the pay of the rich Lord. She had long been the procuress and accomplice of his pleasures. It had been agreed between them that she would spend the night on the yacht. I was delivered without defense to three men who nurtured against me the same wounded self-esteem and unslaked desire. I had fallen into a trap. I was about to be at their mercy in the confines of that redoubtable and unknown place, where I could neither call for help nor flee.

While reflecting, and almost involuntarily, I had passed through the shadow of a vault alongside Lord Portman. I was in a second enclosure, bathed by twilight. I turned round. There was a noise behind me. It was the iron-bound wooden door that had just closed.

The Pagoda of Chillambaram

As if in a dream, the ruined magnificence of Chillambaram extended before my eyes.

We crossed an enclosure strewn with isolated statues and pavilions. We passed under porticos, went along galleries, descended staircases. We sometimes encountered a marble elephant of natural size, a white bull under a mandapam with four columns, or a solitary cross-legged idol. We traversed uncultivated walled gardens, more enclosures, further rooms surrounded by colonnades, courtyards paved with stone slabs worn away by time and ordered with bas-reliefs representing mysterious scenes. Deformed statues gazed at us from niches or emerged from an upper floor of stone. We were suddenly in the presence of a hideous figure with an enormous mouth, sharp teeth curved back like tusks, pointed ears, and two long horns on the head.

We had just traversed a kind of quincunx strewn with monoliths under the dense shadow of an enormous tower with pyramidal steps when, having come through an obscure portico, I saw a wide staircase extend at my feet and I was inundated by green light.

It came from a reflection of the sky in the waters of the sacred pool. The pool was in front of us, in a square of sculpted colonnades, hexagonal towers and silent temples. It sparkled like an emerald; it was alive, like an immobile body.

But I did not have the possibility of admiring the harmony of the monuments, those looming up around me and their doubles reflected in the depths of the waters. I was listing in my mind all the reasons for rancor that the three men walking beside me had.

I saw once again the earthen color that the Rajah's face had taken on, the day when he had seized me by the waist and tried to approach his lips to mine. That was in the drawing room of my villa one evening when my husband had invited him to dinner. I had detached myself from his grip without difficulty and as he looked at me, simultaneously surprised by his own audacity and my resistance. I had contented myself with showing him the mirror that was beside him. He had looked at it without understanding, and had looked at me with astonishment. Then I had said to him:

"It's a French mirror of special fabrication. If you care to examine it with a little attention, you'll see therein that the number of years that separate us would permit you to be my grandfather."

The Rajah had remained silent, looking at the tips of his feet, and he had murmured: "I've been deceived. I thought you were a true Frenchwoman."

I could not tell whether that was an insolence directed at all the women of my country or the natural expression of his disappointment.

I saw was again the episodes of the struggle that I had had to sustain with Prince Vanini—for it is the destiny of every slightly attractive woman who has a certain gleam in her eye; she cannot be alone with a man without the latter resuscitating the primitive beast dormant within him and attempting to tip her over, like a male animal blinded by desire in the presence of a female.

In the depths of the governor's garden, under palm trees where there were no longer any lanterns, at a party one night, I had made the error of going with him. The orchestra was playing a languorous waltz, my dress was too low-cut and perhaps he had extracted from his pillbox the frenzy by which he was suddenly possessed.

He had grabbed me by the hips and lifted me off the ground, simultaneously plunging his head into the hair over my neck. In resisting, I had clung on to the plastron of his shirt, which I pulled with all my might. The plastron tore in two, causing the button holding his collar to fly off, so that the collar fell on to the pathway, with the cravat and the pearls of the plastron. He understood immediately the extent of the catastrophe, the difficulty of finding the pearls in the dark, the ridicule of traversing the illuminated part of the garden with his shirt in tatters. He had released me so abruptly that I fell.

"That's not sporting," he said. "You're a . . ."

He stopped abruptly. His voice had changed, and taken on a crapulous tone that I did not know; I divined a gross insult that he retained. I thought for a few seconds that his fist was about to strike me in the dark. Nothing happened. I had taken pity on him, however; I helped him find the pearls and readjust his collar. And as we walked back in silence toward the light I noticed for the first time that the hand posed on the rip in the plastron, the hand of the aristocratic Prince, was a hand with square fingers, singularly hairy: the hand of a murderer.

And I also saw again the scene in Madras, in a dance-hall for the usage of foreigners to which Lord Portman had taken Comtesse Aurelia and me, on an evening of idleness, after my divorce.

In the midst of the smoke, among the cries of drunken sailors, to the sounds of a deafening tom-tom, a fake bayadere had danced a synthetic nautch on a little stage. As dancing is my passion, I was following the dancer with my eyes in order to discern the element of traditional art that there was in her movements, and the extent to which she was dancing a veritable nautch.

The place where we were was so cluttered with sailors of all nationalities that we were narrowly crowded together and I felt with an invincible repugnance the warmth of Lord Portman's shoulder against mine.

When the dancer had finished her dance, she scarcely bowed two or three times, descended the steps of the stage with an extreme rapidity and went to fall on the floor at the feet of a sinister hirsute individual who was sitting cross-legged and had watched her dance with a distant indifference, smoking a cigarette. With a delectably amorous gesture, the dancer placed her arms around his neck, murmuring in a sigh; "Oh, Miguel!"

Then the man, placing his hand on the nape of the woman's neck, plastered his lips to hers brutally, by way of recompense.

That little scene in the drunken sailors' tavern was gripping. I turned to Lord Portman. His eyes were almost bulging out of his head; his lips were fatter; he looked by turns at Miguel and me, with an envious expression in his features. He leaned toward me and I nearly fainted because of the impression his proximity gave me, while he said to me: "I envy that man. I'd like you to dance before me, and put your arm around my neck afterwards. Tell me that that will happen one day."

"Never," I said, trying to laugh and consider it as a joke.

"I always succeed in getting what I want," he said. "I swear that you'll dance for me, that you'll come to put your head on my shoulder as that dancer did, calling me by my first name, and that with my hand on the nape of your neck, I'll kiss your lips as forcefully."

I started to laugh more loudly, and furthermore, as he often joked with great seriousness, I thought that perhaps he did not attach any importance to those words. But he had reminded me of them a little later, and they returned to my memory now.

"That tower you can see over there is the most ancient of all," said Prince Vanini, and he embarked on archeological explanations, to which I only listened distractedly.

"That's the place, on the edge of the pool, where we're going to dine," said Lord Portman. "I hope that you'll be satisfied by my installation."

His face, turned toward me, expressed such a puerile fear of displeasing me, a solicitude so affectionate, that it suddenly changed the orders of my thoughts.

I perceived servants clad in white; some were in the process of extending mosquito nets, others were running around a laden table. They were numerous and would doubtless remain close by. Were not my three companions, in any case, showing the most respectful courtesy in my regard? How could three men belonging to the highest aristocracy, having a name and a rank in Madras society, infringe the laws of gallantry with regard to a woman who was their guest? Would not their number paralyze their evil intention, in the hypothetical case that they had one?

It was true that they had some rancor to satisfy. I might have inspired their spite. But I ought not to exaggerate the importance of my refusals. All three were seekers of amorous adventures who made attempts on all the women they met and were accustomed to refusals as well as victories. They had classified me in the category of women one has for a friend and not a mistress, that was all. I had, on the contrary, acquired an absolute authority over them. Comtesse Aurelia had a veritable headache and, supposing that they had not invited Mir and they had deceived me on that subject, that was only a petty jealousy of aging men with regard to a very young man.

Night gradually fell and my apprehensions dissipated as I saw torches illuminated alongside the pool, on the side where the dinner was prepared. Their flames made large red circles in the green tints of the dead waters. They danced and flared up before dying down, and reappeared as if with the insouciance of the twentieth year and the love of pleasure.

Several connected rooms that preceded the sanctuary of an abandoned temple had been entirely covered with carpets, striped fabrics and Bengal veils. Champaca and jasmine flowers spread an insipid and relaxing odor.

"This will be the smoking room," said Lord Portman. "There's the stage for the dances. This room is the one where the musicians are and this is the room where I've had the chest placed that contains your robes, and where you can dress without being disturbed."

I saw at a glance that the door of that room had been recently fitted and that there was a brand new bolt that would permit me to lock myself in. I was sensible of the delicacy of that attention and that took away my final fears.

I also noticed that there were six places set at the table and I heard Lord Portman, after having looked at his watch, give the order to remove two of them. He added, in the most natural tone in the world: "There'll be time to reset them if they arrive."

My fears changed into remorse. Was I not naturally inclined only to see the bad side of things? How many times had I spoiled my existence with futile suspicions? That flock of birds, those dominos, and the Brahmin with the squint were the cause of it all. What ridiculous superstitions!

"It's time for cocktails," said the Prince, holding out a glass to me in which the colors of the inflamed sky and the emerald pool between the porticoes were condensed.

The Prince's hand was much less angular than I had thought. It was an honest hand, only a little too hairy. The Rajah was gazing silently into space with an expression of immense mildness. Lord Portman seemed timid and embarrassed, like someone afraid of not having done enough things to receive his guests.

How foolish I am! I thought.

But I almost dropped the glass that I had just emptied. A howl, or rather a low, heart-rending, terrible mewl had resounded, and its echo reverberated under the profound vaults and in the sonority of the stone temples.

My eyes must have expressed fear.

"It's nothing," said Lord Portman, laughing. "It's my panther, who needs to be given his dinner."

The Smoking Room

My security increased during the meal, where the frankest camaraderie reigned. Lord Portman drank enormously, but his gaze did not have the impressive emptiness that was customary to him and caused me such a disagreeable sensation. Only for a few moments did his large eyes recover that expression.

There was talk about amour, naturally, and women. The three men found that they had the same tastes. They could not tolerate the resistance that women thought themselves obliged to put up at a first encounter. They were in accord in thinking that what was delectable was consent, and in unanimously criticizing brutes who took women by force.

"Do you remember," Lord Portman said to me, "that dance-hall for the use of sailors to which we went together one evening in Madras?"

I made a vague gesture that signified that I scarcely remembered it.

"Well, I don't know anything more mysteriously troubling than the gesture of abandonment with which the woman who danced offered her lips to a frightful Portuguese named Miguel. I can't imagine any greater joy in the world than that of seeing the woman I love come to sit at my feet as that dancer did that evening."

It was then that his eyes reflected the infinity of the void. Scarcely had he spoken those words than the Rajah and Prince Vanini burst out laughing and pronounced two or three phrases in English, in spite of the fact that I did not understand that language and it had been agreed that they would only express themselves in French in my presence.

They apologized immediately for those involuntary exclamations. I had almost understood their meaning, or thought I understood.

The Rajah had said something that signified: "You have one chance in three, no more."

And the Prince had added a phrase in which there was mention of the Atharva Veda and a magical operation. I knew the name of the Atharva Veda from my husband, who had told me once the Prince Vanini amused himself studying magic with a Bengali physician in that ancient Hindu book.

But I did not attach any importance at the time to those incomprehensible allusions. I was penetrated by a physical wellbeing that went from the tips of my toes to the roots of my hair, and to that wellbeing was added a sentiment of amity and perfect mental tranquility.

Dinner concluded and we went into the smoking room. Mats and leather cushions were disposed in a circular fashion around a little silver lamp with a red-painted glass set on a tray. Curiously, I handled the ivory pipes, needles and little metal pots containing a dark paste that I sniffed, but was disappointed by the absence of perfume.

"Opium is a hidden genius," the Rajah told me, "which needs fire to reveal the infinite powers that it contains. It is similar to our soul, which is almost always dormant and silent; but if one warms it up with the magical warmth of amour, it spreads perfumes and allows treasures of dream to flow that one did not suspect that one possessed."

Lord Portman had just emptied a large glass of fine champagne in a single draught, and he was holding the bottle in his right hand in order to pour himself a second glass.

"I don't like this wine," he said, "although it's the best one can find in all India. The whisky is far superior." He turned in my direction with his most fearful smile and, as if he were addressing a prayer to me, he said: "It's better if you put on your bayadere's robe right away. Then you won't have to disturb yourself again and we can admire you in the costume for longer. You can dance whenever you wish, either before or after the intoxications to which our friends will initiate you; for myself, I'll remain faithful to the only intoxication that doesn't deceive."

He emptied his glass of champagne, made a grimace and went to exchange the bottle he was holding for a bottle of whisky.

I found that program very wise and I headed for the door. Lord Portman called to my attention with a gesture the fact that I could lock myself in, in order to be tranquil while I dressed, and I was surprised to hear him say: "We'll take advantage of your absence to play a hand of cards."

"I won't be very long," I said.

"A single hand will suffice," said Vanini.

He had taken a pack of cards out of his pocket and my surprise increased when I saw Lord Portman and the Rajah move closer to Vanini eagerly, and prepare to play. I even remarked an unusual gleam of passion in their eyes. I thought that they were keener gamblers than I had supposed, and I left them. I thought there was no need to bolt the door.

My costume was the classic costume of the bayadere of southern India. It was composed of a short, tight corselet around the bosom, with a colored veil over the shoulders, and bright transparent silk trousers embroidered with silver, with a bright silk skirt above them, also transparent, embroidered with gold. As the corselet was high and the trousers low, a part of the body below the breasts was bare, but the ensemble of the costume remained modest nevertheless. I rolled up my hair and enclosed it beneath a broad headband of gold and diamonds which descended over my temples. I put the rings around my ankles whose metallic clink is indispensable to the rhythm of the dance, and light golden rings on my toes.

When I had finished I darted a satisfied glance into the large mirror that formed the back of the narrow room, which was illuminated by a high lamp, and I admired the ingenuity and the comfort that had presided over the organization of the improvised dressing-room, where nothing was lacking.

These Englishmen are extraordinary, I thought.

And I rummaged through the rouges, the creams and the perfumes.

Suddenly, I heard a cry of triumph from the next room. It was Prince Vanini who had uttered it. "It's me! It's me!" he repeated. "I've won!"

His voice was followed by a kind of dull groan uttered by Lord Portman.

I was amazed and slightly annoyed to think that my companions, who had come to Chillambaram to smoke opium in my company, were putting such ardor into a game of cards commenced a few minutes before.

I opened the door slightly, and it made no sound as it swung.

I perceived the Rajah at the extremity of the smoking room, lying on a mat. He had just picked up a pipe and was dipping a needle into a little pot. In the slope of his massive shoulder and the inclination of his wooly head there was something suggestive of ill luck and resignation to destiny.

Lord Portman and the Prince had their backs to me. Lord Portman had taken the Prince by the arm and was speaking to him in a low voice. He was insisting on something that seemed to impassion his heart. The Prince shook his head to say no.

"Well, ten thousand pounds!" said Lord Portman.

"Well, if you put that price on it . . ." Vanini replied. "But it's much more than it's worth."

"You accept?" said Lord Portman, feverishly.

"I accept," said the Prince, "but I don't guarantee the efficacy of the Atharva Veda."

An extraordinary grunt of satisfaction was the Lord's response.

"I'll take charge of that," he said.

I was confounded by astonishment. They turned round and I put on a semblance of making my entrance without having heard anything.

There was a concert of exclamations regarding my beauty and my costume.

"What can you have been playing for," I said, "to bring so much passion to your game?"

"A diamond—that was our stake."

"A marvelous diamond!"

"It's the Prince who won," said the Rajah.

"No," said Lord Portman, in a peremptory tone, "I've bought the diamond. It belongs to me."

And everyone installed themselves on the mats around the little silver lamp.

I had hardly touched the cocktails and had drunk very little during the meal, sensing the necessity of maintaining all my presence of mind. How is it that I accepted one pipe, and then another, and gazed with an infinite satisfaction at the swirls of smoke that I launched at the ceiling? Perhaps it was because of the words that the Rajah pronounced, perhaps because one is impelled ineluctably to certain acts, and because the events that were about to be accomplished were written in the book of my destiny.

"I smoke every day, just as I gaze at the sunlight every day," said the Rajah slowly, punctuating his words with the little gestures that the confection of a pipe requires, "because opium, which is the spirit of plants, brings us the wisdom of the vegetal realm, the wisdom of nature, the sentiment of fraternity, and impels us to conform, with neither revolt nor sadness, to the laws of the world. Opium lifts us above ourselves and I deem that one can only comprehend amour by means of it. The most sublime sensation that one can know on earth is that of smoking in the arms of a woman one loves. Life is so complicated, and everyone strives so hard to complicate it, people are so separated from one another by their stupidity, their passions or their prejudices what I've never been able to realize that ideal. I have, however, searched for it ardently and I've come so close to the realization once or twice that, when I think about it, I can't help trembling with emotion."

I noticed then that the bronzed hand of the Rajah, which was suspending a droplet of opium above the flame of the lamp on the tip of a needle, was agitated by a slight tremor, with the consequence that it bumped into the glass regularly, so as to make a music as light and sad as a regret.

"Those who believe in God can say that opium brings us closer to God, in the sense that it enables us to communicate by means of a more subtle comprehension with the soul of things. Those who believe in amour find, with reason, that opium is the sole path that permits two human creatures avid for closeness to embrace one another intimately and veritably, for the embrace of bodies only gives an incomplete possession that leaves us unsatisfied. With opium we awaken an unknown faculty, we provide an aliment that our invisible double animates, and there is then above the caress of the lips another caress, that of our subtle bodies, which is the last word and the highest state of amour."

I watched him while he was speaking, examining the wrinkles of his face, the thickness of his neck, and the vastness of his torso, and I imagined in his place the regular oval, the sloping shoulders and the slim waist of his son Mir. The mental creation that I made was so vivid that, driven by an irresistible sympathy, I made a movement of the hand in order to take the hand of the absent young man.

The Rajah must have read my thought, for he had a melancholy smile and I heard him murmur, while he handed me the pipe that he had just finished: "Yes, I'm old and I've lost my last chance."

"We only know some of the resources of nature," said Prince Vanini, "that permit us to rise above ourselves and attain unknown joys. Opium and hashish are all very well, but Panya, my Bengali physician, claims that there are many other plants, charged with secret powers, the knowledge of which might perhaps make us equal to gods. What does the Soma used by the Brahmins in their secret rites contain? What is the peyote plant of the priests of the ancient Mexican religion? What did the knights of the Holy Grail drink from the sacred cup? There are herbal juices that contain mental virtues and we can, by absorbing them, acquire courage, clairvoyance, and even the science of the laws of the universe."

The Rajah lowered his eyelids in approval, and handed me another pipe. I smoked it in a single draught. I was possessed by an extraordinary sentiment of light wellbeing, and had the sensation that my blood was pulsing more rapidly in my veins. My imagination was more rapid. I was surrounded by charming friends of an intelligence greater than I had known thus far. The world was filled with harmony. And a time that it is impossible for me to evaluate went by in that softness.

"Personally," said Vanini, again, "I take the Gurago that Panya prepares for me. It's a complex mixture into which a little hashish also enters and a little pulverized tobacco, for there are in simple tobacco, in addition to the poisons it contains, many fecund forces of which people do not know how to make good use. Gurago transforms dreams into reality. When one has taken a sufficient dose, the light imaginary tableau of thought becomes the veritable life: the illusion of life, but an illusion so clear, accompanied by so many sensations, and embellished with such magnificence, that I find that illusion more real than reality. Gurago will be useful to me this evening."

Lord Portman uttered a burst of disdainful laughter and shrugged his shoulders. He lifted a full glass and said: "Even if I were offered Soma or the cup of the Holy Grail, I'd trade it for a glass of whisky with as much pleasure as I've traded ten thousand pounds for . . ."

He stopped suddenly, and then continued, raising his empty glass again.

"I have a particular horror for your Gurago. Personally, I'm in favor of the real reality, not the illusion. The only pleasures that exist are material pleasures, those one perceives with one's nostrils or one's palate, those one touches with one's hands. My philosophy is that there is no spirit, nothing but material forms, avid with the desire for enjoyment. What I love in a woman is the diversity of splendid matter, the ivory of the teeth, the tissue of the hair, the velvet of the skin, sanguine warmth, and the movement of the form. Outside of the possession of that physical wealth, everything else is lies."

While he was speaking his eyes were bulging from his head and his mouth was almost making the motions of eating. At that moment he appeared to me more repulsive than ever

"I only desire," he said again, "one single manifestation of spirit in a woman: her consent."

He suddenly started laughing, and cried as he fell backwards: "And one can even substitute for that, thanks to the Atharva Veda."

I was about to ask why there was such frequent mention of the Atharva Veda when Lord Portman, who, while drinking, had the attitude of a man waiting impatiently, remarked that the moment had come to take advantage of the orchestra that was in the next room, as well as the dancing girl from Madras that he had brought.

"You can dance when you please," he said to me, "but it seems to me that it will be better for us to contemplate that which is imperfect before that which is perfect, and that we remain for the remainder of the night under the impression of your beauty."

I nodded my head. He got up and went out, but from the doorway he darted a glance of intelligence at his two friends and addressed a remark to them in English in which I thought I understood that there was mention of an oath. But my bliss was too great and I was no longer capable of astonishment.

The Magical Dance

I almost uttered a cry of surprise when I saw the dancer from Madras climb the steps of the stage. She wore exactly the same costume as me, with the same embroideries of silver and gold, the same shade of shawl, the same rings and the same headband descending over the temples, and as she was the same height as me, with something analogous in the carriage of the head, I thought for an instant that it was me, and that I was about to watch my double dance.

Lord Portman was watching my face for the impression I experienced.

"That's the dancer we saw together in Madras," he told me. "I noticed, that evening, that she had some of your movements. So I had the costume of the bayadere Cammatatchi, which is yours, copied exactly."

"What costume can a bayadere wear here," said Vanini, closing his pill-box, "except that of the unfortunate Cammatatchi?"

"Why unfortunate?" I asked. "You didn't finish your story."

"That's true," said Vanini. "Well, the terrible ancestor of our placid friend took pleasure in making the marvelous Cammatatchi dance in the same place where we are. I told you that the capricious creature had refused the Rajah, out of pure coquetry, for experience informs us that the majority of women have neither appetite nor disgust, and if they affect to make a choice it isn't by virtue of their elective preference, as they would like to make people believe, but by virtue of interest, whimsy or, often, for no reason at all."

I protested, for form's sake, having been familiar with Vanini's paradoxes for a long time.

"So, it was the day of the festival of Sidambara—but isn't it the day of the festival of that god today?"

"Precisely," said the Rajah. "But the old customs have fallen into desuetude, and Sidambara has ceased to be honored."

"Having watched Cammatatachi dance, the Rajah made thereafter the gesture of taking her in his arms. She turned away, laughing, as was her habit. Instead of persisting, the Rajah told her to return to the habitation of the sacred dancers, which was situated on the other side of the pool. When Cammatatachi had gone out, the Rajah had a ferocious panther released behind her. The bayadere fled along the stairways that you can see over there . . ."

"And then?"

"The bayadere was eaten," said the Rajah, tranquilly, "and my ancestor watched the scene through a loophole."

"That's a frightful story."

"Such was the punishment of coquettish women in that distant epoch," said Vanini. "Impunity is unfortunately assured to them nowadays."

Lord Portman leaned toward me and murmured, as gently as a lamb: "I hope that you won't hold it against me for having revived the evening in Madras and having made that dancer a poor imitation of you?"

At any other moment I would have found that pleasantry absurd and out of place, but in spite of the story of Cammatatchi, a river of benevolence and tranquility was flowing through my soul. I made a sign that I did not hold it against him.

The Massalchi, or torch-bearer, who illuminates a bayadere while she dances, had come to take his place behind her, in accordance with custom. The musicians' talam and mahatalam resonated at a signal from Lord Portman with a muted tonality, and the bayadere commenced her dance.

From the start, she gazed with the fixity of a magnetized bird at Lord Portman, and never took her eyes off him. The dance is an amorous coming and going, and alternation of approach and retreat, accompanied by undulations of the arms and movements of the legs, miming by turns hope, regret or the pleasure of amour. Only Lord Portman existed for that bayadere.

I made the interior reflection that that was scarcely polite for the Lord's guests, and I was about to make that reflection to the Prince, who was beside me, when I experienced a singular sensation. It was of myself that I was about to make a criticism, it was me who was gazing exclusively at Lord Portman, me who was dancing for him alone. Without my knowledge, I had identified myself with the dancer dressed like me; I was her.

I smiled at the absurdity of the sensation, of which I was fortunately conscious. By virtue of a curious duplication, however, I continued to watch the bayadere dance as if I were gazing at myself in a mirror, criticizing myself for certain faults in the dance, certain movements of the body that I found unseemly, certain thrusts of the breasts accompanied by passionate gazes fixed on a single man, which I judged as eloquent as a direct invitation to amour. I would have liked, above all, to retain the sort of chant commenced in a shrill tone, which ought to have been gentle on the ear, taking exception the dance continued because the bayadere from Madras mingled with it passionate accents like appeals, as voluptuous as gasps of pleasure.

Suddenly, the dance concluded.

Then I saw the dancer descend the steps of the stage lightly, bound rather than run toward Lord Portman, and with the same spontaneous enthusiasm that she had had in Madras for a certain Miguel, she threw her arms around his neck, placed her head on his shoulder and said, sighing: "Oh, George!"

George was Lord Portman's forename, of which I never made use because it was antipathetic to me, without my knowing why.

Its resonance was as disagreeable to me as if I had pronounced it myself.

But I understood, or thought I understood, Lord Portman's intentions. In spite of my refusals he had had a dancer dress like me in order to have the illusion that it was me in his arms. And the words of the three friends that I had not understood came back to my mind, as well as the meaning of their card game. They had played for the dancer from Madras!

But how young they had remained, to be able to be impassioned for the possession of a woman that could be had so easily in the port of Madras! I was invaded by an immense disgust for men, at the same time as a little anger. So only one thing existed for them: physical possession. They could not spend a single evening in pure amity, with conversation and ideal speculations. We had convened for amicable hours of dreaming and smoking. That had not been sufficient for them. They had still required the perspective of a whore, whose paid caresses one or other of them would possess.

The fears that I had had were completely dissipated, to be sure! They had been replaced by a sharp ill humor.

I experienced the need to exteriorize that ill humor, and I spoke to Lord Portman in order to reproach him for his vulgarity and that I would renounce dancing.

But, to my amazement, he had completely changed his attitude in my regard.

He replied to me by a shake of the head and he contented himself with making a little sign with his finger, a sovereignly imperious sign, to express that the moment had come for me to dance.

I sensed a blush of shame cover my face at that inconceivable gesture. Then something even more inconceivable happened. I stood up meekly, and even rapidly; I climbed the steps of the stage and I prepared to dance. At another sign from Lord Portman, the bayadere from Madras disappeared through the door to the left, and while my thoughts reeled, and I made a futile effort to recover myself, the talam caused its metallic sound to ring out, the muted sounds of the mahatalam resonated with an irresistible power, with a magnetic rhythm such as I had never heard, and I began to dance.

I did not know whether it was me who was dancing or whether it was the bayadere from Madras. But as soon as the first step I plunged my gaze into that of Lord Portman and I fixed it there. From the very first step, the chant that I intoned was a plaint of amour, an appeal to the man at whom I was looking, a humble chanted supplication. I was begging him to love me.

I took account of the insensate character of those amorous notes, but I could not prevent them from emerging from my throat.

I saw and judged my folly in a second consciousness. I intimated to myself the order to stop, but my will had abandoned me and I was not capable of going back.

And I did even more. I danced as I had never danced. I extended my arms with a bewildered vehemence, to fold them again suddenly with tenderness as upon a beloved individual. I mimed the poem of desire with the thrust of my breasts, I caused the nude part of my body to protrude with an abandoned immodesty, I offered myself in the inclination of my torso, I delivered myself in the reversal of my hips.

An interior and distant voice cried as if through a fog: "Stop, fool!" But it seemed to come from a consciousness that was foreign to me. I was still looking into Lord Portman's eyes, bewildered and fascinated.

And suddenly, the talam and the mahatalam expired. The massalchi lowered his torch; the dance was over. The final note had not finished vibrating when I bounded with an incredible lightness, I fell at Lord Portman's feet, I enlaced his neck with my arms, and I said, with a sigh of my extended lips: "Oh, George!"

Then Lord Portman leaned toward me, I felt the palm of his hand on the nape of my neck and he stuck his mouth to mine.

The Stone Cavalier

I don't know how many seconds or how many minutes I remained against Lord Portman's shoulder. I don't know whether or not it was him who, with the hand with which he was pressing my neck, inadvertently released the little chain by which the minuscule golden box was suspended.

After the intoxication of the pipes and the fatigue of the dance I was in a state of languorous torpor. I was awakened by the sensation of the chain opening and the box sliding between my breasts, over the naked skin.

I wondered at first what it was, and then I remembered that Comtesse Aurelia had given it to me that morning.

Mechanically, I seized the box, and opened it with my fingernail. A little object, of very ancient gold, fell into the palm of my hand. By the vague light that reigned in the room, I did not distinguish at first what that fragment of gold represented. Then I threw it away in disgust. It was a lingam, a minuscule obscene symbol of Mammaden, the southern Indian goddess of amour,

I had Lord Portman's head against my breast and I perceived his even and profound respiration, which attested his delight, and a clear reckoning of things returned to me.

The three men, in collusion with Comtesse Aurelia, had set a vile trap for me. They had used against me a magical operation learned from the Atharva Veda, the ancient Hindu book filled with extraordinary and absurd recipes for bewitchment, some of which must be authentic. The little gold box had been the point of departure, the talisman. Then there had been the dancer similar to me. I had heard it said that in certain conditions, a human being cannot prevent themselves from reproducing exactly the actions that they see accomplished by an individual like them, acting in their resemblance, who succeeds thus in exercising a power of suggestion over them. I had heard it said that a king of I know not what Indian country had been thus led to hang himself by a sorcerer clad in a royal costume who had hung himself before his eyes. The requisite condition had been fulfilled, in my case, by the opium that had weakened my will, and had permitted the singular duplication of which I had been the victim.

I saw all the elements successively combined, and how I had been duped. It was me for whom they had played cards. I had been won by Vanini, who had ceded me for ten thousand pounds, finding that that price exceeded the value of the purchased object! I felt anger invade me. Fortunately, it was not over. Lord Portman had only obtained a kiss. So long as the three men were united they were not to be feared. I would tell them what they had done and demand that they take me back to Pondicherry without delay.

I stood up and took two or three steps, energetically and ostentatiously wiping my mouth with the gauze of my robe. I darted a glance around. But the room was empty, Vanini and the Rajah had disappeared, taking away the tray, the little lamp and the pipes.

"They've gone to smoke somewhere else," said Lord Portman, "in a room at the other end of the pagoda. I have their word. We're alone for the rest of the night."

He smiled triumphantly and moved his jaws, making his teeth click, doubtless with the thought that he was about to bite my flesh.

He too was standing, and as I took a step toward the door he added: "Our solitude is absolute. The servants and musicians had orders to quit the pagoda, and my panther has been released around the temple that we occupy, in order that no one will disturb us. Above all, don't take it into your head to go out. Remember the story of Cammatatchi!"

I saw that his eyes had lost all light. He was trembling with desire. My presence against him had thrown him into a kind of physical ecstasy, into which he wanted to plunge again. He did not doubt, moreover, that I was ready to obey him. With his two extended hands he made the gesture of capturing me as one captures an inoffensive moth blinded by the light.

Perhaps I might have been able to make him ashamed, to threaten to divulge his conduct. It's improbable that that would have done any good. He believed himself to be too close to the realization. He could, in any case, have replied to me that society would hold at fault a woman who had had the imprudence to render herself nearly naked, under the pretext of dancing as a baya-dere, in front of three men in a solitary pagoda.

I looked at my costume. I measured the transparency of the trousers and the skirt, the tightness of the corselet, the nudity of my arms and a part of my body, and the sentiment of the folly that I had committed in delivering myself without defense to a man who was repulsive to me caused me to lose all prudence and sacrifice the only chance that might have remained to me, which was to appeal to his good sentiments.

My anger redoubled when I saw the gesture of his arms, which he was holding out with a tranquil certainty of success and a basely lustful cynicism imprinted on his features.

With all my strength I slapped his face, and the blow that I struck was so forceful that I felt a pain in my hand and wondered whether I had not sprained the fingers or the wrist.

Lord Portman had never received such a slap in the face in his entire life. His immense fortune, the cares with which he had surrounded himself, must have set aside from an early age any possibility of combat. Something so new left him completely stupefied. He had the expression on his face of a man witnessing an action that tends to prodigy.

He remained motionless for a few seconds, gazing with his enormous eyes at the cause of the prodigy. But the prodigy was painful and humiliating. His chest swelled, the expression of stupefaction gave way to an expression of hatred terrible to behold.

It was my instinct that dictated my conduct. I was impelled, so great was my anger, to give him another slap similar to the first. A struggle would have followed of which the outcome was certain.

Almost without reflection, I launched myself toward the only candelabrum whose lighted candles were illuminating the room, I lifted it up and turned it upside-down. Then, with the same bound I ran into the dressing room and bolted the door.

But that would only give me a few seconds. He did not negotiate. I sensed that he was hurling himself toward the door in order to break it down. I darted a circular glance around me; there was no door that would permit me to flee, and no window. I had a moment of despair. Without having any fixed plan, I moved the tall mirror in which I had looked at myself before with such dangerous complaisance, and I hid behind it. Perhaps I thought about letting it fall on Lord Portman when he rushed me. But as I moved it I felt a violent current of air that refreshed me and inclined the flames of the expiring candles by which the room was illuminated. The mirror had been set up against a tunnel, the masking of which had been completed by pieces of fabric. That tunnel did not seem to be very long, and I distinguished a vague lunar light at its far end. As the fragile bolted door cracked under a new pressure, I blew out the candles rapidly and launched myself into the tunnel.

I traversed it in a few seconds. A prodigious lunar fresco appeared before me. The green pool, the sacred pool, was reflecting a luminous trail of moonlight in its immobile waters. I had before me an immense sheaf of widespread, shiny, animated gold spangles. In the midst of the enchantment of columns, domes and porticoes, the moon had negligently placed over the pool that living bouquet of magic crystals, which seemed to end at my feet at the moment when I surged forth from the interior of tenebrous stones, beneath the yellow and green light of the world.

But I stopped, open-mouthed. It was not one panther—the panther with which Lord Portman had threatened me—it was two panthers that had been set on sentry duty for me, which were watching the entrance to the tunnel, standing to the right and left of its entrance, in a frightful immobility.

I held my breath, and, through my mind, with a vertiginous rapidity, all the horrible stories ran that I had heard since my arrival in India of men surprised and devoured by wild beasts. Nothing had ever terrified me as much as the thought of dying between the paws of one of those giant cats with fetid breath, Lord Portman's kiss was better. But did I have the choice?

I heard a noise of breaking glass at the end of the corridor, which made me suppose that Lord Portman, after having broken down the door, was in the process of discovering the opening of the tunnel.

I had held my breath, but it was necessary for me to respire a little air. I remarked then that the panthers were not breathing; and I also remarked that they were much larger than panthers; they were tigers, and tigers larger than natural. They were not breathing because they were made of stone, because I only had before me one of the thousand reproductions of animals with which the Hindu religion populates its temples.

I slipped between them and, with an infinite satisfaction, I gave one of the inoffensive muzzles a little pat. At that same moment, footsteps resounded at the other end of the tunnel.

I launched myself at hazard alongside the pool. I had no idea how to direct myself within that formidable succession of goprurams, holy places, courts and porticos. On reflection I ought not to fear the panther. It had only been a threat to prevent me from fleeing. One does not leave a panther, even domesticated, at liberty in a place where there are a large number of servants. English law is rigorous on that subject, even for rich lords. We were no longer in the times of Cammatatchi. But where could I go? Ought I to try to find the place where the Rajah and the Prince were doubtless smoking peacefully? They now inspired me with a horror almost as great as Lord Portman.

"It's much more than it's worth," Vanini had said.

My arrival in my bayadere's costume, in the midst of musicians and sleeping servants, appeared to me to be the ultimate in ridicule.

My only hope was to be able to get out of the enclosure of Chillambaram, reach the village and obtain hospitality in a Hindu house, What welcome would be reserved for me there? How could I explain myself, given that I did not know the local language, or English?

All those difficulties appeared to me while I was running, and I could not see any practical way out of my situation. But I ran, because the essential thing, first of all, was to escape Lord Portman's embrace.

I had quit the edge of the pool, crossed an enclosure planted with coconut palms, and was going past the colonnades of a temple. The opium and the terrors I had been experiencing might have been acting on my imagination, but I thought I saw in passing the coconut palms begin to move and the columns running by my side, with their capitals on their thin shoulders.

A singular life took possession of things. An enormous solitary Buddha sitting under a cylindrical dome stood up ceremoniously as I passed and bowed as if to salute me. A tower performed a pirouette in front of me and I thought that it was about to deposit at my feet a bizarre ball covered with ornaments, which surmounted it. On the threshold of a doorless temple all sorts of divinities with several heads and numerous arms came to watch me pass by. I saw Brahma, I saw Vishnu, I saw Siva. I saw many others whose names I did not know.

I emerged in front of the chapel of the sacred bull and fell at the foot of one of its four pillars, unable to do any more, indifferent to the movements of the pillars and the strange coming and going of the bull's head.

I seemed to hear a voice in the distance calling me. It was the abhorred voice of Lord Portman. Was he exhorting me to come back? Was he threatening me with the panther again? The thought of his fat lips, his empty eyes and his hateful face sufficed to render me the courage necessary to flee.

I had recognized the pagoda of the sacred bull, which I had visited on my arrival. There could not be many of them. The only difference between the pagoda that I saw in the moonlight and the one I had seen at dusk was that the latter was motionless, with a stone bull solidly fixed to its pedestal, while this one was agitating feverishly and sheltering an animate bull that never ceased moving its head to the right and the left. And I was possessed by a bizarre agitation myself.

I recalled that, by going around the enormous monument that was to the right—which was the temple containing the Holy of Holies, on the altar of which the ineffable deity reposes, which is above the universe and the gods—I would find the boundary wall. I slid along the wall, plastering myself against it, making myself as small as possible. I darted a timid glance inside as I passed before the entrance to the temple. I had once gazed without dread, and had even smiled when I was told that the supreme divinity of the Hindu religion is worshiped on an empty altar. Now, scarcely a glance in passing, and I shivered on glimpsing, in the uncertain light, a great black stone on which nothing was set.

The enclosing wall was enormous. We had come through it by the western portal, but I knew from Vanini's discourse that there were four portals. I knew that in India, everything is dilapidation and ruins, and that doors that fall often remain for centuries without being replaced.

I went along the wall, and I perceived that I was not mistaken. I was at the eastern portal, the portal of serpents, framed by a tangle of sculpted serpents, coiled, suspended and intermingled—and the door was no longer anything but a few worm-eaten planks held together by lianas.

All the serpents—at least, I had the illusion of it—were stirring, advancing their flat heads and their bespectacled eyes, stretching toward me. But I was beginning to get used to that universal movement. I thought, with a good deal of reason, that there was more to fear from a tiny invisible snake living in the grass than the entire swarm of the snakes of the immense portico.

I removed one of the planks without much difficulty, slipped through the opening and, with a great sigh of relief, emerged from the enclosure of Chillambaram.

In the moonlight, I saw that all around the gate, in a large open space, disposed in a semicircle, there was an entire cavalcade of stone elephants and horses, with their riders. They were marvelously white and I would have admired their form and the harmony of their disposition if I had not been wondering anxiously in which direction the village might lie and what was going to become of me in the night.

Beyond that mute army, I thought I could see the white line of a road between the coconut palms, coming from I know not where to end at the eastern portal. I thought that the best thing for me to do was to take that road.

I took a few steps in the moonlight and behind me, the serpents of the portal, and the high and somber wall, agitated. In front of me the elephants were waddling, shifting their trunks, and the stone cavaliers leaned over in their saddles. I even heard the whinnying of a horse. But had I not seen the columns running, the sacred bull stirring between its four pillars, and astonishing idols appearing on the thresholds of temples? The effects of the opium were familiar to me now and their phantasmagoria could not stop me.

I advanced with a firm tread between the elephants and the cavaliers. There was one that was not wearing the same costume as the others and not standing in the same alignment. He leaned over to the point of falling, and I thought I was about to hear the sound that a block of marble makes when it breaks.

How surprised was I when he uttered a cry of joy with a human throat, when he enlaced me in his warm arms and deposited me, palpitating, in his saddle, against his young man's breast!

The Return to Pondicherry

Having lifted me from the ground, Mir did not replace me on the ground for explanations. It was only afterwards that I told him about my adventure in the pagoda of Chillambaram, and how he had been able to find me in the threshold of the eastern portal in that unexpected costume. I took care, in any case, to transform the truth slightly in order not to make his father play the odious role that I left exclusively to Lord Portman.

It was only afterwards that he explained his providential appearance to me. The day before, he had received a laconic note enjoining him depart without delay for Chillambaram, where I was in danger. He had only found the note in the afternoon and had spent the night *en route*.

For the moment, I did not seek to discover who had written that letter, as well as the one that I had received, who the protector was who had watched over me and was endowed with sufficient penetration to judge Mir capable of crossing forty-nine miles at a single stretch solely on the indication of a danger threatening me.

In fact, I never knew for certain. But when I learned that a liaison of sorts had been created between Vanini and Juliette Romano, I supposed that the latter had received from Vanini the confidence of the Chillambaram project.

Vanini must have believed that Juliette Romano hated me and that he would give her pleasure by describing the trap that had been set for me, and my imminent humiliation. Vanini knew the admiration that Mir had for me and the latter, in spite of his reserved nature, might perhaps have confessed his sentiments to him. Juliette Romano must have experienced to a high degree—at least, I supposed so—the patriotism of the weaker sex that sometimes urges women to unreflective revolts and impels them to aid one another against the egotism and bestiality of men.

She had only warned me by means of an anonymous note, not wanting to quarrel with anyone, but she had also warned Mir, whom she must have supposed to be my lover. In formulating the last hypotheses she was, in any case, only mistaken by a matter of hours.

But while Mir carried me away along the road to Pondcherry, there was certainly no question of all that. There was only a question of the thirst that was devouring both of us—or even all three, for the forty-nine miles crossed by night had exhausted the horse on which Mir was hugging me with more timidity than desire.

The night ended and a light pallor spread over the spread over the landscape, outlining the clumps of palmtrees, the bare hills and the monotonous alignment of rice-fields. Mir remembered that after Gondelour he had passed over a bridge and had had the sensation that the bridge was extended over a flowing stream and not a dried-up bed, as is often the case.

We traveled a long distance in the hope of that bridge. One of Mir's hands maintained me in the saddle, wrapped around my midriff, which was the part of my body not covered by any garment.

We finally reached the promised stream, dismounted, drank several draughts and enabled the horse to drink. When our thirst was slaked we used the pretext of the water we had spilled, he over his neck and I between my breasts, to laugh together for a long time, because of the joy we were each secretly experiencing in finding ourselves together in a solitary landscape, bathed by the delightful freshness of the morning.

The horrible danger that I had run, and the difficulty of getting back to Pondicherry without scandal, were effaced from my mind at the same time, to give way to a puerile, almost sportive pleasure, the kind one experiences when one departs early for an excursion, and the unconscious elements of which are the wealth of one's own health and an odor of damp earth.

We started walking along the river; a great insouciance was in us. We agreed that the wisest thing to do was for me not to show myself during the day in my bayadere costume, which would not have failed to pique the curiosity of anyone who saw me. The best course of action was to find a refuge for the day, and only go back by night. By going back late we had every chance of not encountering anyone. We immediately adopted that plan, which had the advantage of permitting us to remain together for quite a long time.

The day had concluded and the bad omens of the day before were no longer exerting their action. I was certain that, if I had looked into the sky, I would have seen white birds flying from right to left, that it would have been impossible for me to discover the smallest spider in the longest grass, and that if I had leaned over the pebbles of the stream, I would immediately have seen a minuscule pink stone shaped in the form of a heart by gods desirous of informing a favored creature, by means of a sign, that amour is close at hand.

But I did not have the leisure to gaze at the sky, the grass and the pebbles; I was too fully occupied with the silence that had just suddenly fallen on Mir and me, and by the thousands of words with which we were communicating silently.

Finally, a cabin was offered to our eyes. It had no door, and was composed of badly-jointed planks. It must have served as a shelter for peasants when they came to work in the nearby rice-field. We decided to rest for a while there, and go on later.

Mir tied up his horse to one side and examined the grass-covered ground of the cabin carefully, in order to get rid of the snakes if there were any.

We lay down side by side. Mir's timidity led him to leave rather a large gap between us, but the chill of the morning, further augmented by the proximity of the water, had gripped us since we had dismounted from the horse. I shivered, and instinctively put both hands over my bosom, with the movement that one gives to one's shoulders to narrow them when one is cold. I think, to be sincere, that I was deliberately exaggerating my sensation of cold. Mir was also shivering, perhaps also with exaggeration.

I do not know whether it was him that made the first gesture of drawing together. I believe that it was me, and that I legitimated it immediately by shivering again. But the sun was rising rapidly; it warmed up the planks of the cabin very quickly, and if we had needed a pretext to be close to one another that of cold would no longer have been valid. But we had no need of a pretext.

Late at night, a bayadere whom a young man was holding tight on the saddle of his horse passed through the mute streets of Pondicherry. She was very weary, half-asleep, but she was smiling at her strange adventure, especially in thinking that the most marvelous intoxication of her life she did not owe either to opium or hashish, but to a day spent fasting in a wretched cabin of planks, on the bare ground.

ACKNOWLEDGEMENTS

"Le Club de des Haschischins" by Théophile Gautier was first published in the *Revue des Deux Mondes* 1 février 1846. The translation is original to the present volume.

"Le Pipe d'opium" by Théophile Gautier was first published in *La Presse* 27 septembre 1838. The translation is original to the present volume.

"La chambre double" by Charles Baudelaire was first published in *La Presse* 26 août 1862. The translation was first published in *The Dedalus Book of Decadence (Moral Ruins)*, Dedalus, 1990.

"Le Club des Hilarants" appeared in *Nouveaux contes excentriques* by "Charles Newill" (Charles Basset), Hachette, 1859. The translation is original to the present volume.

"Les Hallucinations du docteur" by X. B. Saintine appeared in *La Second Vie*, Hachette, 1864, translated as *The Second Life*, Black Coat Press, 2018.

"Les Portes d'opium" by Marcel Schwob appeared in *Coeur double*, Ollendorff, 1891 after previously appearing in *L'Écho de Paris*. The translation first appeared in *The Second Dedalus Book of Decadence (The Black Feast)*, Dedalus, 1992.

"Le Rêve du fumeur d'opium" by "Pompon" was first published in *La Lanterne: Supplement Littéraire* 30 mai 1889. The translation is original to the present volume.

"Opium" & "Smara" by Jean Lorrain first appeared as two episodes of the story-series "Astarté" in *Le Journal* 29 decembre 1899 & 4 janvier 1900, before being reprinted as two chapters of *Monsieur de Phocas. Astarté*, Ollendorff, 1901.

"Parisian Orgies" by Jane de La Vaudère first appeared as three chapters in the novel *Les Androgynes, roman passionel*, Méricant 1903; translated in *The Demi-Sexes and The Androgynes*, Snuggly Books, 2018.

"Le Malais" by Jean Richepin was first published in *Gil Blas* 29 juillet 1890; the translation first appeared in the Richepin collection *The Crazy Corner: Horrible Stories*, Black Coat Press 2013.

"Le Dieu vert" by Gabriel de Lautrec first appeared in *L'Initiation*, février 1904 as the second episode of the quasi-autobiographical novella "Le Feu sacré"; the translation first appeared in Lautrec collection *The Sacred Fire*, Black Coat Press, 2019.

"Fantôme d'Opium" by Louis Latourrette was first published in *La Lanterne* 24 janvier 1905; the translation is original to the present volume.

"Télépathie" by Théo Varlet was reprinted in *La Bella Venere*, Malfère, 1920, having reportedly first appeared in 1910. The translation first appeared in *The Germans on Venus and Other French Scientific Romances*, Black Coat Press, 2009.

"Fumerie d'Opium," signed Louy de Lhuc, was first published in *Le Supplement* (of *La Lanterne*) 18 juin 1914; the translation is original to this volume.

"L'Initiation" by Frédéric Boutet was first published in *Le Journal* 22 mars 1913; the translation is original to the present volume.

"Dropping in on Anika" is a translation of part of a chapter of *La Garçonne* by Victor Margueritte, first published by Flammarion in 1922, translated as *The Bacheloress*, Black Coat Press 2015.

La Nuit de haschich et d'Opium by Maurice Magre was originally published by Flammmarion in 1929; the translation first appeared in the Magre collection *Lucifer*, Black Coat Press 2017.

A PARTIAL LIST OF SNUGGLY BOOKS

Ingram Content Group UK Ltd.
Milton Keynes UK
UKHW042153250423
420698UK00052B/1023